Bestselling author Merryn Allingham was born into an army family and spent her childhood on the move. Unsurprisingly, it gave her itchy feet, and in her twenties she escaped an unloved secretarial career to work as cabin crew and see the world. The arrival of marriage, children and cats meant a more settled life in the south of England, where she's lived ever since. Having gained a PhD, she taught university literature for many years and loved every minute of it. What could be better than spending one's life reading and talking about books? Well, writing them perhaps.

Six Regency period romances followed, then those itchy feet kicked in. The Regency was abandoned and *Daisy's War*, a wartime trilogy, found its way to the top of the Amazon charts, followed by the Summerhayes books—a saga of romance and intrigue set in the Sussex countryside during the summers of 1914 and 1944.

But itchy feet never rest and in 2020 she finally went over to the dark side! The crime series, the Tremayne Mysteries, is set in locations around the world and features Nancy, a feisty 1950s heroine, turned amateur sleuth.

Keep in touch with Merryn via the web:
Website: **https://www.merrynallingham.com**
Facebook: **http://www.facebook.com/MerrynWrites**
Twitter: **http://www.twitter.com/merrynwrites**

Other Books in this Series

The Dangerous Promise (2020)
Venetian Vendetta (2020)
Caribbean Evil (2020)

CORNISH REQUIEM

Merryn Allingham

CORNISH REQUIEM

This novel is entirely a work of fiction. The names, characters and incidents portrayed in it are the work of the author's imagination. Any resemblance to actual persons, living or dead, events or localities is entirely coincidental.

First published in Great Britain 2021 by The Verrall Press

Cover art: Berni Stevens Book Cover Design

ISBN 978-1-8382742-5-2

Chapter One

The call came in the middle of the night. Unusual. Disturbing. But not so disturbing that Nancy, warm and sleepy, was stopped from burrowing more deeply into her pillow, even as she felt her husband slide from the bed.

But Leo was gone too long and, concerned at his absence, she shook herself awake and switched on the bedside light. She was feeling for her slippers when a soft footfall sounded on the polished floorboards and her husband appeared in the doorway. Harsh lines scored his face and his skin seemed to sag into greyness. For once, he looked every day of his forty-seven years. He stood motionless for a moment, his shoulders slumped, his eyes blank.

Nancy forgot the slippers and rushed over to him. 'What's happened? Who was that on the phone?'

'Perry,' he said in a voice that had lost all expression.

'Your brother? Is he in trouble?'

'No, not Perry. It's Dad. A massive heart attack.'

Nancy wrapped her slender arms tightly around him. 'I'm so sorry, Leo,' she murmured. 'But is …?' She didn't like to go on.

'He's alive still,' Leo said, answering her unspoken

1

question and stroking the dark waves of her hair. 'In the cardiac ward of the Royal Cornwall. But the prognosis isn't good.'

'I'm so sorry,' she said again.

'We have to go—straightaway.' Leo seemed suddenly to come to himself, breaking free from her embrace and holding her at arms' length. 'To Cornwall. This morning. Early.'

She glanced at the bedside clock. The hands showed half past three. 'We'll need to get some sleep first. I'll set the alarm for six.'

'Yes, do that. You'll come with me, Nancy?'

'Of course I'll come.'

She didn't fit at Penleven, the Tremayne family house, and she had never felt comfortable with her father-in-law. Leo knew that. But this was an emergency and being there for her husband was important.

Leo turned back towards the bedroom door. 'I'm going to wake Archie. I need him to sort out travel.'

'Do you have to wake him now? He can buy train tickets first thing in the morning.'

'He's my assistant, Nancy. It's his job. It's why I have him living on the top floor. In any case, we won't need train tickets. Archie can fly us down, but he'll have to get on the phone pretty sharp to book an aircraft.'

'Fly?'

She must have sounded incredulous because Leo's response verged on the tetchy, the lines on his face more deeply etched. 'Why ever not? The chap has a pilot's licence. It's the reason I paid for his flying lessons—so that I can travel quickly, if I need to. We can fly to St Mawgan and hire a car from there. We'll be at Penleven within a few hours.'

So Archie was to accompany them to Cornwall. Nancy hadn't expected that, and it wasn't good news. Since they'd

2

returned from the Caribbean, she had hardly seen Leo's assistant—or for that matter, Leo. Her husband was in huge demand for his expertise as a valuer of Renaissance art works and over the last six months the two men had travelled halfway around the world together: the Far East, Australia, Chile, as well as several trips to Amsterdam and Milan.

Archie's frequent absence had helped her a little to forget the strain of having him live so close and, over the last few months, she'd come to enjoy being the sole occupant of Cavendish Street. At first, she'd felt vulnerable, left alone in the large townhouse—Mrs Brindley, Leo's severe housekeeper, went home at night—but Nancy's worries that Philip March, her erstwhile stalker, might track her down had soon evaporated. Marriage to Leo appeared to have put paid to the man's vendetta; she could say goodbye at last to that terrible episode in her life when she'd been driven almost insane by her former fiancé.

She was immersed now in her apprenticeship. Art restoration had become a passion and, coming home from a hard day's work, she had begun to welcome the peacefulness of an empty house. It wasn't that she didn't miss Leo, more that she revelled in this new freedom to come and go as she wished, no longer feeling the need to account for her movements.

Her husband, though, had made sure that he was home for Christmas, and they'd had fun decorating the house together. It was the first time number ten Cavendish Street had known holly and baubles—even Mrs Brindley had managed a smile. It had been fun, too, choosing gifts for each other in the London stores.

Best of all, they'd had Christmas alone. Archie had travelled down to Cornwall to spend several weeks with his family. The longer he was away, the easier it was for Nancy to forget. Not that she would ever forget what had happened in Malfuego, the way Archie's kiss had made her feel. In her heart, she hoped he wouldn't either. But it was forbidden fruit and, since then, they had been scrupulous in avoiding further temptation.

Waiting for Leo to return, Nancy climbed back into bed, tucking her silk nightdress tightly around her. Despite a week of bright sunshine, the April nights were still chilly. She hadn't long to wait and, when her husband reappeared, she patted the embroidered quilt, a wedding present from one of his clients, and gestured for him to sit down. But he ignored the invitation and instead crossed to the bank of wardrobes that lined one wall, pulling from it several pairs of slacks, some freshly ironed shirts and two pairs of highly polished handmade shoes.

'Archie will make the call to the airport as soon as he can.' Leo was sounding more composed now. 'And we'd best get packing.'

When Nancy said nothing, he turned round to face her. 'You're not scared of Archie flying us, are you? You went up with him in Malfuego when he'd only just started to learn. I'd have thought that far more frightening.'

She wasn't scared of flying. It was Archie she was scared of, or at least her feelings for him, but she made her excuses and hoped she did it well.

'I'm not worried at all,' she said confidently. 'I know Archie is brilliant. He showed how good a pilot he was in Malfuego before he'd even gained his licence. I assumed we'd go by train, that's all. That you'd want to leave him here. After all, you're both extremely busy and someone has to keep the office working.'

Nancy wondered if that might change her husband's mind, but she was disappointed.

4

'The office can wait,' he said. 'I want Archie with me.'

His tone of voice puzzled her. He sounded so emphatic, as though his assistant might be needed for something more than keeping the files in order.

'Do you think your father has been unwell for some time?' she ventured to ask. 'Perry might have known but not wanted to worry you?'

Leo shook his head and turned back to the wardrobe, reaching up to the top shelf for two suitcases. The shrill of the alarm would be sounding in less than two hours' time, but she could see that he was too tense to sleep again.

He heaved one of the cases onto the bed. 'The attack came completely out of the blue. Perry was stunned and I can see he's finding it difficult to cope. I need to be at Penleven as much for him as for Dad.'

The brothers were not exactly intimate—they were such different people and their paths through life could not have been more dissimilar—but it was clear they held a deep love for each other. Perry had been the 'big' brother, looking after Leo at boarding school, comforting him when their mother died, trying to bridge the gap she'd left. And shielding him, Nancy had no doubt, from his father's irascibility. Leo was the 'cuckoo' in the Tremayne nest, his interests a million miles from those of his family. It was something with which she could sympathise.

'Does Perry have any idea why it happened?'

'He's completely at sea and, as you'd expect, the hospital aren't saying much until they've run their tests.'

'Your father still works at the mine, doesn't he? Perhaps worries over the business got too much for him.'

'It's Perry who runs Wheal Agnes, in fact. Has done for ten years or so, though Dad still maintains a keen interest. He's at the mine most mornings, so you could be right. Perry says the place is losing money badly and at the moment he can't see an obvious solution. Still …'

To Nancy that seemed as good an explanation as any to why a seventy-five year-old had succumbed to such a devastating heart attack. The mine was Ned Tremayne's life and always had been. To see it struggling to survive without any evident way out would be hugely stressful. So why did Leo seem uncertain? And he *was* uncertain. He'd abandoned the cases and begun to pace the floor, back and forth between the window and the bed. His shoulders were hunched and his steps stiff and uneven.

'Is there something more?' Nancy asked.

'No. I suppose not. It's just that… that Perry sounded odd on the phone.'

She sat up in bed, hugging her knees, and trying to reassure. 'It's not surprising that Perry didn't sound himself. He must have been the one to find your father and travel with him to hospital. It would have been a distressing experience.'

In the dim light of the bedside lamp, she glimpsed Leo's expression. It was perturbed, uneasy, as though he was deciding to confide something that he'd hoped not to. He gave up his pacing and plumped himself down on the bed.

'I accept that, but Perry didn't just talk about my father's illness, Nancy... he told me that Treeve Fenton is dead.'

The name meant nothing to her, and she looked questioningly at him.

'Treeve was probably Dad's oldest friend,' Leo said. 'Certainly his closest. They've known each other since they were children. He's Perry's godfather.'

'You think his death was a factor in your father's illness?'

'It seems likely. Contributed to it at least. Treeve was found dead yesterday morning, only hours before Dad had the heart attack.'

'Was Mr Fenton the same age as your father?' If he was, it seemed strange that her father-in-law had suffered such a violent response to the news. Seventy-five wasn't exactly ancient, but most people would consider that Mr Fenton had reached a good age.

'Treeve was a year younger. When Dad inherited Wheal Agnes, he made Treeve a partner. They worked their socks off together. They had disagreements, I'm pretty sure, but never truly fell out. Treeve was Dad's mainstay, particularly after my mother died. He retired from the business five years ago. Said he was feeling his age and knew Perry was competent to run the mine on his own whenever Dad decided to call it a day, too.'

'He sold his share of the business to Perry?'

'He exchanged it for a lifetime pension paid out of the mine's profits.'

'Then that would be an additional worry for your father— if the mine is as financially shaky as Perry told you.'

'Hmm.' Leo seemed unconvinced. He swung his legs up on the bed, lying by her side on top of the richly embroidered quilt.

Nancy reached out for his hand and squeezed it hard. 'It's sad that Mr Fenton has died, but it's not unusual for a man of his age. And he may have had a medical problem your father was unaware of. It's why his death could have come as a shock.'

Leo turned on his side, looking into her face. In the lamplight, his eyes seemed a darker brown. Certainly more troubled. 'That may be true. Treeve wasn't someone who'd broadcast that anything was wrong with him. Except—he was found in his bath.'

When she looked bewildered, he said a trifle harshly, 'Drowned, Nancy.'

7

She gave a gasp. 'He slipped getting in?'

'Perhaps. No one knows.' There was a long pause before Leo continued. 'The thing is… he was a shower man. Always was. It came from working in the mine—at the end of their shift the men soap off the day's filth in the Dry—and a shower was part of a routine that Treeve carried into retirement.'

There was another long pause before Leo said, 'Perry is sure that Treeve never took a bath in his life.'

Chapter Two

Archie wasn't happy. He'd been woken in the middle of the night from the best sleep he'd had for weeks and told to find a plane. Didn't Leo know that airfields like Croydon weren't staffed through the night? It was hours before he could telephone and hope to find someone at the desk. Whether they'd be able to come up with a spare Cessna at such short notice, let alone someone to fly it back from St Mawgan, was doubtful. Leo seemed to think you could lift the phone and an aircraft would be waiting for you.

But even if he were lucky enough to bag one, his employer would be impatient, hovering around Archie's shoulders, irritated, fidgeting, not understanding it took time to plot a route. And Nancy? She'd been doing what she always did around Leo these days. Soothing, sympathising. Concealing her true feelings?

Archie went back to bed as soon as his boss left, but he couldn't get comfortable. The sheets felt hot and rumpled, tangling his legs until they seemed to burn. Frustrated, he flung himself to the other side of the bed and closed his eyes tight. But who was he kidding? He wasn't getting back to sleep. He knew it for a fact. Insomnia. He'd never suffered from it before but these days it plagued him. He had a fair notion why, though he'd tried to erase it from his mind. Tried to erase Nancy from his mind. Whatever was between them shouldn't be. Of that, Archie was clear. But the feeling had been there from the very first day he'd met her, and ever since he'd been unable to break free.

Two years ago, he'd returned from his family in Cornwall to find Leo married and the new wife established in Cavendish Street. It had been a shock, and even more of a shock when he'd looked into Nancy's eyes, shaken her hand, and felt a visceral connection. At first, he'd adopted indifference, then escalated it to belligerence, making sure that on the few occasions they spoke his remarks hurt or at least annoyed her. But his antagonism had been manufactured and proved short-lived. It hadn't been long before he'd been drawn into helping her, involving himself in the crazy investigation she'd decided to pursue in Venice when she and Leo were supposedly on their honeymoon. And after Venice? He'd decided that simple friendship was the key. He had wanted to believe it was possible, but friendship hadn't worked any better than hostility. Nothing, in fact, worked. And after that kiss last summer, he knew that nothing would.

He threw back the bedcovers in a furious movement and lay on his back, glaring at the ceiling, his limbs stretched into a taut star-shape. Nancy had married out of fear, Archie understood that. She'd been stalked by some nutter—Philip March—and Leo had been her saviour. But she'd been wrong to do it. She might admire his boss, respect him for his expertise, feel gratitude to him, even love him in a low-key fashion, but she wasn't *in* love. The way she had kissed him last summer told Archie everything. Okay, it had happened when they'd been in danger—when they'd escaped with their lives and hadn't expected to—and people did strange things in those circumstances. But the way she had felt in his arms, the way she had felt beneath his lips, went way beyond the moment. That was the problem.

He swung his legs out of bed and shuffled to the window, pulling back the curtains a few inches to expose a chink of light. It was going to be another cool, bright day. Dawn had arrived and a hazy glow spread across the horizon. Or what he could see of the horizon. The view from the top of a Marylebone townhouse was roofs, hundreds of grey roofs, with a solitary splodge of green—Regent's Park—just visible to the left.

Archie closed the curtains and found his dressing gown. It was still too cold in the morning to walk around naked. Switching on the light, he made for the kitchenette. He might as well drink tea until it was properly light, maybe read a book if his eyes would stay open. He liked his apartment and, over the years he'd been with Leo, had grown to feel it home, choosing paintings he particularly liked—copies, not the real thing. Leo didn't pay him enough for that. And gradually furnishing the rooms to his taste: a Chesterfield, a rocking chair, a solid oak desk for the living room. Ma had made him a neat pair of curtains in bright blue cotton and one Christmas his sister-in-law had presented him with cushions she'd made from a dark blue velvet. Why did women have this thing about cushions?

But since Nancy's arrival, the apartment had lost its lustre. Living with the two of them had become a bad dream. Nancy was everywhere: every room of the house held the trace of her. It wasn't just the house either. On every trip abroad with Leo, she was in Archie's head, in every dream she was in his heart. There was no escape, except to find another job. And that was easier said than done.

Now apparently the three of them were to travel to Cornwall together, a happy or not- so-happy band of comrades. Ned Tremayne had had a heart attack. A massive one, according to Leo. His boss had looked pretty ill when he'd woken him and that was understandable. A sick father was a big blow. Not that Archie had ever liked Tremayne himself. Curmudgeonly old bugger. But it came as a shock when you realised your parent wasn't going to live for ever. Still they didn't have to be in such a rush. The old bloke was safe and sound in the best hospital in the area and they'd see him all right. Leo could have gone down by train almost as quickly, taken his wife and left Archie in London to work his way through the piles of paperwork spread across his desk.

He put the kettle on to boil and slumped down onto a wooden stool. He should try to think positively. At least he'd get to see Ma, stay with her for a while until Leo had had enough of Penleven. Her health had improved since the scares of the last few years, but he still worried about her. Especially now that Lowen had moved to Plymouth and she was on her own in the Port Madron cottage. It was true that his eldest brother, Rich, lived nearby, but he had a wife and children and a business to run. A business that like all Cornish fishing was struggling.

The kettle's piercing whistle jerked him from his reverie, and he stumbled over to the gas ring, his movements slow and clumsy. He desperately needed to sleep, but that wasn't going to happen. Leo would be back in an hour or so to see what progress he'd made. The man had been extremely agitated. Now Archie thought about it, perhaps more agitated than the situation demanded. There was something making Leo uneasy, something more than his father's illness, but whatever was going on in Cornwall, his boss wasn't saying.

Archie would work it out soon enough once he was back home in Port Madron. And if he didn't, Nancy would. He'd never known a woman with such determination to get to the bottom of things, with such a passion for justice. But he

12

liked that in her, as he liked so many things. He'd make sure, though, that he kept his distance from the Tremayne family. Stayed clear of Penleven and whatever trouble was going on there. Stayed clear of Nancy.

Chapter Three

A round two o'clock that afternoon, the hire car swept up the gravelled drive of Penleven, Archie at the wheel. The journey had gone more smoothly than Nancy had expected. A last minute cancellation had freed up a light aircraft, and the flight itself had been straightforward—except for the small matter of returning the Cessna to Croydon. But the stakes were too high at the moment, with Ned Tremayne struggling to survive, for any of them to worry too much about it. What worried Nancy more was Leo's uneasiness about the death of his father's friend. Her husband was not a man to find problems where none existed, and she felt a prickling in her skin that she might be about to step into a situation where once again she'd feel compelled to investigate.

Archie had barely brought the car to a halt, when a tall, lanky figure rushed out of the house to greet them. Perran Tremayne had obviously been on the watch.

'Leo! Nancy!' He pulled open the rear door. 'Here already. How wonderful!'

Their small amount of luggage was quickly unloaded and Nancy found herself hustled into the hall by a relieved Perry. 'Here, let me take your coat.' The bright red raincoat was found a place among a line of tweed caps and ancient waxed jackets.

'You must come and eat,' her brother-in-law said eagerly. The smell of warm soup— pumpkin, she thought— came from somewhere close by. 'I'm sure you must be hungry.'

'I will, but just one moment, Perry.' She was without her handbag, Nancy had suddenly realised. She must have left it behind in the car.

Hurrying back to the vehicle, she found Archie propped against the bonnet and Leo issuing instructions. 'Drive down to the village,' he was saying. 'We'll use my brother's car to get to the hospital. And take the rest of the day off. You deserve it—for getting us here so quickly.'

She saw Archie give a nod and a half smile, before he drove away. The relationship between the two men was complex, she'd come to understand. During the war, they had served together in the Duke of Cornwall's Light Infantry, Leo as an officer and Archie a corporal. Leo had told her that he owed his life to the younger man and had tried to repay the debt, at least partially, by taking Archie on as an assistant when work in Cornwall was scarce. Archie had more than justified his employment: he was willing and efficient, doing whatever was needed with the minimum of fuss. Organising their journey today was just another task to him.

It was right, though, that Leo showed his appreciation. At times Archie could be chippy and awkward—that had been Nancy's first impression—and always conscious of the gulf between himself and his boss. Not just differences in wealth but an immense social divide. Archie had grown up a fisherman's boy in a family struggling to make a living, while Leo had known the best of everything: prep school, public school, Cambridge University. And now there was his marriage, she thought guiltily. Something else to divide them, though mercifully Leo seemed to have no notion of the feelings that swirled just below the surface.

'Do you mind if we eat in the kitchen?' Perry asked them, when she and Leo returned to the house. 'Kitty has some soup on the go. We weren't sure when you'd get here so nothing elaborate, I'm afraid.'

'The kitchen is always cosy,' Nancy said, making her way there, 'and whatever Kitty has made smells delicious.'

'Thank you, kind lady.' A sturdy woman with a handsome face stepped forward and bobbed a mock curtsy.

'This is Kitty,' Perry said, somewhat unnecessarily.

Nancy held out her hand. 'It's good to meet you.' And it was. She liked the woman's open face and the tight blonde curls that clustered around a ruddy complexion. She was young, Nancy noticed. It would be good to have an acquaintance of her own age in a place where she felt a stranger.

'Do you cook professionally?' she asked, taking a seat alongside the brothers at the scrubbed wooden table.

'No, my luvver. I help out, that's all.' Kitty began to ladle pumpkin soup into three china bowls.

'She helps out a lot,' Perry put in. 'The ancients around here wouldn't be without her. She runs the village shop, too.'

Nancy's eyebrows rose. 'You must be very busy then.'

'Needs must.' Kitty gave a cheerful smile. 'Now, I've cut some bread, but you must cut more if you need it. It's a fresh loaf, baked this morning, and there's fruit to follow.' She gestured to a plate of neatly sliced melon, orange and apple. 'You can make the tea, Perry? When you're ready.'

He nodded and said between mouthfuls of soup, 'So will we see you tomorrow?'

'I'll bring some stuff up from the shop at lunchtime. Will pasties do?'

'Perfect. It will give Nancy a chance to try our Cornish speciality.'

'Hasn't she tried them before then?' Kitty seemed

surprised.

'I've only been here once,' Nancy said a little awkwardly. 'It was Christmas time, so I think the pasties got forgotten.'

'You've got a treat coming. You'll love them,' Kitty assured her, picking up her basket and jacket and waving them a cheery goodbye.

'She must be a good find,' Leo said, after the front door had shut behind her.

'Kitty Anson is worth her weight, as they say. She's kept us well fed for months. Mrs Cheffers still 'does' for us, but her cooking isn't up to much and half the time she doesn't remember if she's left any supper or not. I've become quite a dab hand myself in the kitchen, would you believe?' Perry grinned at them across the table.

'It's more than Nancy has,' Leo said.

'Nancy doesn't get much of a chance,' she retorted. 'Mrs Brindley rules the roost in Cavendish Street and her kitchen is forbidden territory.'

'Just as well. My wife wouldn't have the time to cook, now that she's launched on this apprenticeship I told you about, Perry. Doesn't have a minute to breathe.'

The apprenticeship had been a bone of contention between them for a long time. Leo didn't want his wife working; he'd made that plain. He wanted her at home—as a decoration, Nancy thought, when she was feeling particularly angry— but she was surprised at how annoyed Leo had sounded just now.

Ever since she'd lost the baby last year, when she'd accompanied him to the Caribbean, he appeared to have accepted her daily departure to the studio with good grace. It was evident now that her assumption had been false, and Leo's views had remained unchanged—he'd simply decided to say nothing.

17

Perry shifted uneasily in his chair. 'I thought we'd go to the hospital this afternoon,' he said to his brother. 'If that's okay with you?' Nancy could see he was trying to smooth over the awkwardness filling the room.

'That would be good.' Leo put down his soup spoon and pushed aside the empty bowl.

'If you want to get off, you can leave the washing up to me,' Nancy said brightly before anyone could suggest she go with them. She would see her father-in-law eventually, but it wasn't the right time. While the man was lying so desperately ill, it was better that his sons visited alone.

For a fleeting moment, Leo looked vexed, but then his face cleared. 'That sounds sensible, darling. And when we've seen how things are with Dad, you can come, too—maybe the next time I visit.'

'Of course I will.' Nancy gave a tight little smile. She was glad to have escaped so easily.

Once the brothers had piled into Perry's car and driven away at top speed, she was quick to clear the few bowls and plates they'd left behind. Her hands were busy, but her mind was drifting. Where it often did—to Archie, by now ensconced in his family's cottage by the harbour. No doubt he'd been greeted as the wanderer returned and made a huge fuss of. He'd have plenty to talk about to his mother. Not about Nancy, though. He wouldn't mention her.

She hung up the tea towel and looked around, thinking how to spend the next few hours. She would make a tour of the house, she decided. The Christmas that she'd visited, she'd never dared to explore thoroughly and now was a chance to do it unobserved.

Penleven was a large building, a solid square of Cornish stone, with high ceilings and heavy oak doors. It was a no-nonsense kind of house: four rooms on the ground floor, four bedrooms and two bathrooms on the first. And that was it.

Perry had carried her suitcase up to what he called the guest bedroom. Her husband's old room, so Leo had told her, the one he'd occupied all his childhood except for absences at boarding school. Perhaps it had been the bedroom in which he'd been born.

The thought prompted an image in Nancy's mind of Rachel Tremayne. What had she been like, Leo's mother? There was little trace of her in the house, except for her paintings. They were mainly Cornish landscapes and hung from nearly every wall. Leo had told her that his mother had been a brilliant artist, had been studying at the Royal Academy, but a holiday in Cornwall and falling in love with a Cornishman, had meant the end of that particular dream. Once married, she had only ever painted for friends and family, never exhibited, never gone public. Nancy wondered why. Had it really been Rachel's wish, or had it been Edward Tremayne's? He was a formidable man and Nancy was sure that he'd exert maximum pressure against anything he didn't like. Rather like his son.

The afternoon was chilly but calm and, after her tour of the house, she grabbed her raincoat and wandered out into the garden. It was neatly kept but a little dull. Where there should have been greenery, there was gravel, and where there should have been flowers, dark shrubs still dripped from a morning shower. She took the path of stepping stones that wound its way over the close-cut lawn. The stones were of grey slate and by far the most attractive feature of the garden. Perhaps an artist-inspired pathway?

Following it as it bent around a corner, Nancy found herself facing a summerhouse that she had never seen before. But then when she'd visited, the weather had been cold and miserable, and she'd ventured no further than the narrow terrace outside the kitchen door.

The summerhouse was delightful. Airy and delicate, originally Victorian, she decided, surrounded by a towering circle of silver birch, their thick fronds seeming a barricade against the world. The doors opened to her touch and, stepping inside, she was immediately bathed in warm air. On good days it must be a veritable sun trap. From here, Penleven was invisible and any occupant of the summerhouse would be equally invisible from the house. A true haven, but one that appeared unused. Several wicker chairs, badly in need of repair, occupied the interior space, along with a circular mosaic-topped table. A beautiful Moroccan rug, a little gnawed at the edges, was spread across the wooden floor.

One corner was filled by a tall cupboard and, interested as always—nosy, Archie would have said—Nancy opened it. A stack of canvases greeted her, several rusting tubes of paint, and a large glass jar full of brushes, stiff from disuse. This had been Rachel's studio, she realised, and for some reason felt excited. The woman she had never known, the woman that Leo had loved with all his heart and lost at such a tender age, had spent her days in this beautiful building, surrounded by the natural world, alone and peaceful. While they remained at Penleven, Nancy determined she would spend as much time as she could in this beautiful setting.

Right now, though, she should probably return to the kitchen. If Mrs Cheffers had forgotten supper as Perry suggested was likely and Kitty Anson only brought lunch, she should at least make the attempt at an evening meal. Dab hand at cooking or not, poor Perry looked exhausted and should be spared the additional chore of feeding two extra mouths.

***

Perry's car arrived at the house as Nancy put potatoes in the oven to roast. There had been no sign of Mrs Cheffers, but she'd found vegetables in the scullery and chops in the refrigerator and was hoping they would be sufficient. Kitty had left a splendid looking Victoria sandwich and that would have to do for dessert.

'How did it go?' she asked, as her husband came into the kitchen, Perry a few steps behind.

'Dad is pretty poorly, but the nurses say he's rallied quite a bit overnight.'

'He looks better, I think.' Perry threw his car keys down onto the kitchen table. 'Better than when he was admitted, at least. Yesterday was shocking, what with Treeve being found dead and then Dad keeling over.'

'Will he be well enough to attend Treeve's funeral, do you think?' Leo asked.

Perry looked uncomfortable. 'He could be, but I doubt the funeral will be just yet. The police are still poking about.'

Nancy stopped chopping carrots, her knife in the air. 'Why are the police involved?'

'Hopefully they won't be. At least not for long. But I guess with Treeve living on his own, they want to be sure.'

'So it may not have been an accident?'

Her husband gave her a warning look.

'Leo said your father's friend never took baths so I can see why the police, faced with a drowning, would be concerned.'

'Well, there's always a first time for everything,' Perry said weakly. 'An accident is what I've told Dad, and it's best to keep to the same story—now that he seems to be recovering.'

'Did he know you when you walked in?' she asked.

'It took him a while to realise *I* was there,' Leo said wryly, 'but he knew Perry instantly. We only stayed for half an hour. He can't talk much, and he gets very tired.'

'And the nursing staff were keen to dish out an early supper,' Perry added. 'So we made for the door.'

'You've been a while getting back.' There was a questioning note to Nancy's voice.

'We came back via Wheal Agnes,' Leo said. 'Perry wanted me to see the mine again—it's a while since I was last there. He's been filling me in on his plans for the future.'

'Maybe,' his brother said diffidently. 'You've started supper, Nancy.'

'It will be basic, I'm afraid, but it should fill our stomachs. Go and sit down the pair of you, you look utterly weary. I'll call you when it's ready.'

Chapter Four

Morwenna Jago threw up her hands in surprise, then rushed over to her son standing in the doorway and gave him an enormous hug.

'Archie! What on earth are you doin' here? Oh, but it's some good to see you!'

'Hallo, Ma.' He hugged her back, kissing her on both cheeks. 'I brought Leo down— he needed to get home. Old Tremayne has had a heart attack. You must have heard.'

'Yes, of course, poor man. The village is talkin' of nothin' else. Come and sit yourself down, son, and I'll get some tea on the go.'

Morwenna put the kettle to boil, then gathered the books she'd been consulting into a pile on one side of the table and laid out cups and saucers in their stead.

'I thought mebbe Ned Tremayne's boy would come down from London, but I didn't expect you as well.'

'We all had to come,' Archie said wearily. 'I was needed to fly the plane to St Mawgan, then drive the hire car to the house.'

'Fly the plane! You said you'd got this pilot's licence. Fancy that, I've a son who's an airman as well as a soldier.'

'Flying a Cessna isn't exactly Battle of Britain stuff, Ma.' Archie settled himself down into one of the much-loved easy chairs Morwenna kept in her kitchen. The faded cushions sunk beneath his weight.

'No, but still... have you heard how Mr Tremayne is?'

'Pretty bad, I think. Leo is going to the hospital this afternoon, so we'll know more after that.'

'His brother will be glad to see him, that's for sure. It's a lonely life Perran Tremayne lives. At least your boss has got himself a wife now. After all these years, too. I did wonder if either of them would ever marry.'

'So did I.' He couldn't stop himself sounding sour.

'What's the matter? Don't you like his wife?'

'She's okay,' he said grudgingly, not trusting himself to say more. 'So, how's Rich and the girls?' If he could turn the conversation to family, his mother would soon forget Nancy.

Morwenna pulled up a wooden chair beside her son and handed him a flower-patterned cup. 'Rich is strugglin', poor lad. But you know that from my letters. Since the pilchards decided to pass Cornwall without stoppin', it's been hard.'

Archie nodded and took a drink of tea.

'When you think that when you were a babe I'd go out and help bring the pilchards in,' his mother went on. 'They weren't so plentiful even then, but the water would be sizzlin' and we'd be haulin' in the nets from shore and the fish leapin' and writhin', trying to escape. My grandma told me that in her day the shoals could be so great that even before the nets were shot, the fish would be driven up on to the beach and lie there gaspin'. Now Rich has to venture further and further out to get a decent catch and even then he can come back with nothin'. But it's the same for all the men. Some of them have taken to pottin'—crab and lobster. Crawfish, too. It's closer to shore and less dangerous. Clem Hoskins is one of 'em, but Rich refuses. Somehow, for him, it's not proper fishin'.'

'Hoskins was always a timid one.'

'If you can make a livin' and keep yourself safe, what's wrong with that?' his mother asked a trifle tartly.

Archie grinned. Same old Ma—warm and welcoming, but not afraid to speak her mind. 'And Lowen?' he asked of the brother next in age to him. 'How's Plymouth going?'

Morwenna beamed. 'He's some happy, and I'm glad. Though ...' Her face fell a little. 'I do miss the boy. But your brother has got him a job at the same department store—I told you, didn't I? Not such a special post as Steve's, naturally. Lowen is only just starting out, but it's a wage and he's managed to rent a decent flat for him and that new wife of his. Looks like life is workin' out for them both.'

'And how's it working out for you?' His mother was a dab hand at effacing herself and her problems.

'What do you mean?'

'Don't play the innocent. Never mind Ned Tremayne's heart, what about yours?'

'I still suffer a bit from the arrhyth, the arrhyth... you know the thing.'

'Arrhythmia.'

'Yes, that's it. But the pills they've given me have done a power of good.'

'Are you still working, though? You say next to nothing of yourself in your letters.'

'Why wouldn't I be?'

Archie got up from his chair and walked over to his mother, putting his hands on her shoulders and speaking into her ear. 'Do you have to work? Really? You shouldn't be gutting fish at your time of life.'

Single-handedly, his mother had raised four sons—he couldn't remember his father's face even, the man having slipped and drowned in an alcoholic haze when Archie was still a young boy—and surely it was time now for Morwenna to put her feet up. She'd had a hard life and deserved a rest.

'At my time of life. Listen to him! I'm still capable of puttin' in a few hours at Milford's. And it's only part-time now. Gives me plenty of time for the garden, and for botany.' She gestured to the sturdy pile of books on the table. 'The one your boss gave me—what a wonderful book that is. Where did he find it?'

Archie wandered back to his seat. 'Venice,' he said, remembering the day Leo had bought the book. The day he'd rescued Leo's new wife.

'That's right. Venice. It was their honeymoon, wasn't it?'

'Sort of. Leo was attending a conference there.'

'Funny kind of honeymoon. But then work is needful, and your boss is a very important man, so I understand.' Morwenna lifted the teapot and waved it in front of her son. 'Another cup, my love?' When Archie shook his head, she went on, 'Who would have thought little Leo would become an expert on pictures and be travellin' the world?'

'Who would have thought,' Archie said drily.

'Still, a honeymoon's important, too. But that postcard you sent me last year—that was the Caribbean, wasn't it? That would have been more of a honeymoon.'

Archie said nothing but looked down at his hands still clasping the cup.

'What's the matter, Archie? Don't you like the job anymore? Or is it the maid? Do you find her difficult?'

Trust his mother to land full square on the problem. 'No,' he said abruptly. 'It was a surprise when Leo married, that's all.'

'But he's been wed these two years now.'

Archie could feel his mother's eyes on him and scrambled to find an excuse. 'It's changed the way we work, but I'm getting acclimatised,' he lied.

'So you should after two years. And he's a good boss. Thank the lord he saw you on one of his visits down here. Otherwise you'd still be guttin' fish with me.'

They were silent for a moment, but it seemed his mother's fascination with Leo and his marriage couldn't be put aside just yet. 'Two years is a long time,' she mused, 'and no babe. Leo would be an old father, 'tis true, but there's plenty older.'

'His wife had a miscarriage,' Archie muttered.

He could see that his mother wanted to ask more, but his expression must have deterred her. Not for long, he thought. She'll be keeping it for later.

Aloud he said, 'How about I take my case upstairs?'

'You're stayin' with me then? Not at Penleven?'

'Why would I stay there?'

'Your boss might need you.'

Archie stood up. 'If Leo needs me, he knows where I am,' he said truculently. 'Don't you want me here, Ma?'

She bustled over to him and gave him another immense hug. 'Want you here? Just you try leavin'!'

Chapter Five

When Nancy walked into the sitting room later that evening, she knew something was wrong. Or at least more wrong than when they'd sat around the table at dinner. Perry had lit a log fire to ward off the April chill in the stone-built house and the brothers were sitting close to the hearth, their chairs drawn together, heads almost touching, intent on an object Nancy couldn't see.

'Something interesting?' she asked.

Leo's head came up immediately. He was trying to smile, but Nancy wasn't fooled. Perry had tucked what looked like a sheet of paper into his pocket and had tried to do it surreptitiously.

'Please tell me.' She walked across to them and saw the two men exchange a reluctant glance.

'It's rubbish, Nancy,' Perry said harshly. 'Absolute rubbish.'

'Perry found a letter, a message, that Dad received a day or so ago,' Leo said in explanation.

'May I see it?'

Unwillingly, Perry pulled the sheet of paper from his pocket and handed it to her. 'Rubbish,' he repeated once more.

Nancy sat down a little way from the blazing fire and unfolded the sheet. The paper was lined and jagged down one side. It seemed to be a page torn from an exercise book and a string of bold letters marched across the middle. Letters that had been cut from a newspaper. Reading the single line of text several times over, she felt her stomach give a twist.

YOU ARE MURDERERS. YOU DESERVE TO DIE.

When Nancy felt she could speak without her voice wobbling, she asked, 'Who do you think the "you" is?'

'Who knows?' Leo spread his hands. 'Some unhinged individual must have sent the message. We can't hope to make sense of it.'

Did Leo believe what he was saying? He sounded dismissive now, yet after Perry's phone call in the night, she'd known he was deeply uneasy. His father's ill health was obviously a huge concern, but it hadn't only been that, Nancy was sure. He'd said at the time that Perry sounded strange on the telephone. It was no wonder if his brother had found this note.

'It was sent to your father?' She looked across at them. Neither man answered, but Nancy assumed she was right. 'Could the "you" include Treeve Fenton?' she asked tentatively.

'No!' This time Perry spoke and the harsh note was back in his voice. 'Treeve's death was an accident.'

She wasn't convinced. Perry might be adamant there was no question of foul play, but Mr Fenton might well have received a similar note. It was certainly worth finding out.

'But if his death wasn't accidental?' she pursued.

'The police consider it an accident and that's good enough for me.'

'And me,' Leo put in.

It seemed her husband had decided to put whatever concerns he'd had about Treeve's death to one side. Or perhaps it was to prevent her getting involved. Nancy's need to discover the truth, the desire to pursue justice no matter what, had caused conflict between them in the past.

But she couldn't stay completely silent. 'Have you shown the police this note?' she asked.

'Good grief, no,' Perry said. 'They've enough to do without chasing after a local idiot.'

Their minds were made up, and she understood why: if Mr Fenton's death wasn't the accident they insisted on, if the "you" was meant for Ned Tremayne, then further 'accidents' were more than possible. Something neither brother could contemplate.

Sent by an unhinged person, Leo had said. Maybe. But the sender had deliberately singled out Penleven and the message itself suggested sanity and intent. Was it the threat, as much as his friend's sudden death, that had been responsible for Ned's heart attack? If so, the sender must be feeling pleased with his or her work.

The missive should be taken seriously, Nancy thought, but who might be responsible? The exercise book, the lined paper, the letters cut from what looked like a popular newspaper, suggested a working man. Someone perhaps from the village. Unless that was what the writer wanted them to think. A case of misdirection. It could be somebody quite other.

For a while all three of them sat gazing into the flames, absorbed in their own thoughts. Only the hiss and crackle of apple wood broke the silence.

'That was good,' Perry said at last. 'The meal, I mean. Thank you, Nancy.'

She blinked at the complete change of subject, then saw that the piece of paper in Perry's hand had disappeared— back into his pocket, she imagined. For him, the matter was closed.

'You're a guest,' he went on. 'You shouldn't be cooking.

Mrs Cheffers and I will have to have words!'

'Nancy isn't a guest,' Leo objected. 'She's a Tremayne, remember. And it *was* good.' He sounded surprised. 'When we get back to London, you can take over the kitchen more often — if Mrs B permits.'

'I doubt she will.' Nancy smiled. 'But she might make an exception for you.'

'Me?'

'Men cook, too, don't they, Perry?'

'Only when they have to.' He sounded fatigued and turned to his brother. 'So, what do you think of the Silva offer?'

Nancy's ears pricked up.

'As against your plans for an under-sea extension?'

Perry nodded.

'I'd go for selling.'

'You're planning to sell the mine?' She was astonished.

'No. At least, there's no definite decision. It's not something I thought I'd ever consider,' Perry said quickly. 'But we've had an offer and now Dad has this heart problem …'

'What does Dad think?' Leo asked. 'I presume you've told him?'

'I had to, though I knew it would worry him even more. That's why he went round to Treeve's the other night. The night the poor old chap died. He wanted to talk over the offer.'

'Who better?' Leo said. 'He'd get good advice from Treeve.'

The snap and crackle of logs had quietened and, as the fire burnt lower, Nancy could feel the chill creeping around her shoulders.

'Does Mr Fenton … did Mr Fenton,' she corrected herself, 'have a say in whether or not Wheal Agnes was sold?'

'Not since we bought him out,' Perry answered. 'It's my father and I who are sole partners. We're the ones to make the decision. But Treeve was Dad's best friend. Had been since they were at school together. They formed a strong bond there, two working class boys in a private school. Then all those years working together. It was natural for Dad to go to Treeve for advice.'

'I can imagine,' she said.

'Can you think how badly it hit Dad, when he learned the man he'd been talking to only hours before, the man he'd known intimately for sixty-odd years, was suddenly no more?'

A new silence filled the room until Perry got up and poked at the burning logs, encouraging the flames to leap again.

'But why did this Silva chap make an offer?' Leo asked. He sounded puzzled and Nancy couldn't blame him. An offer for a tin mine whose finances were known to be shaky was something of a mystery.

'Apparently Mr Silva has mining interests around the world—in Europe as well as South America. He comes from Brazil.'

Nancy's eyes widened.

'I know,' Perry said. 'It sounds strange. But he's a businessman through and through. He's into logging as well—in Canada. I think this is just another opportunity for him, with tin mines going cheap since the slump after the war. Most mines have already been sold. Wheal Agnes is only one of two left in Cornwall and he thinks he can make a go of it. He's certainly got the finance behind him. And he'll need it. We've made all the savings we can think of and we still can't turn a profit. Add in the fact there's a large loan outstanding and the bank is getting restless, and Silva's offer is one I can't ignore. It's a generous offer, too,' he said thoughtfully.

'If you sold, what would happen to the men who work at Wheal Agnes?' Nancy asked.

'Ah, there's the rub. I can't be sure how many of them

Silva would keep on. He wants to bring at least of some of his own chaps over—from his business in Minas Gerais. It's the biggest mine in south-east Brazil, in the same region as Rio de Janeiro. He mines iron ore there and I'm pretty sure he'd bring engineers with him. But the miners themselves? I've met his representative a couple of times, but he's never offered a firm commitment on how many of our men they'd employ.'

'If his expertise is mining iron, he'll want people who know tin, surely?' Leo yawned, stretching his legs towards the fire and toasting his feet.

Perry gave a shrug. 'Maybe. But we mine iron, too, though in small quantities.'

'You spoke of meeting his representative. Mr Silva isn't here then?'

'He has a sidekick. A chap he obviously trusts. It's him I've been dealing with. I haven't found it easy, though. Apart from the language problem, he's not exactly a character you could warm to.'

'If you did sell,' Nancy ventured, 'What would happen to Penleven? Would you stay here?'

'The price Silva is offering would keep Penleven going for the rest of my life, I think. Certainly the rest of Dad's which is what I have to think of primarily. But Silva wouldn't want me at the mine. It never works having an old owner working for a new one. I'd have to find something else.' There was a hopelessness in Perry's voice.

'Still ...' he rallied. 'It would mean that Dad was completely free of worry – about the mine, about this house. He could live out the rest of his life in peace.'

'Silva's assistant,' Leo said. 'Where does he hang out?'

'He's staying at the local, the Tinners Arms. I must admit I don't much like him. I find him too pushy—and maybe that's influencing me when it shouldn't.'

Nancy didn't think a pushy negotiator was likely to sway Perry's decision, not when his own future and those of his men were in the balance, but he'd said nothing of what he'd do if he didn't accept the offer. Leo had mentioned something about an under-sea extension, but she'd no idea what that involved and didn't like to ask.

Perry must have been contemplating this sale for months, but it was Ned Tremayne's illness that was pushing his son towards the drastic move. Listening to her brother-in-law talk, Nancy had been taken aback at how bad things must be. Leo had said the mine had a few financial problems, but he couldn't have guessed how serious they were.

'You've got to like the man you do business with,' Leo put in. 'You have to trust him. Are you stuck with this chap? Or will you meet the chief at any time?'

'That's another worry. Silva is flying into London from Rio tomorrow and travelling down here the next day or so. He seems impatient to get serious negotiations going, even though I'm still undecided. I'll have to invite him to dinner on Saturday—I can't see how I can get out of it. I've been wondering if Kitty would oblige and cook for us that evening.'

'If you like, I'll go and see her tomorrow,' Nancy offered. 'I'm sure she'll help out.'

She crossed her fingers that Kitty would 'oblige'. Lamb chops were one thing, but a dinner party for a Brazilian millionaire quite another.

Chapter Six

Nancy found the silence of a Penleven night troubling. Its intense darkness, too. No rumble of traffic, no passing footsteps, no street lamps. On her last and only visit she had been wakeful most nights and it seemed that she was destined to sleep as badly this time. Beside her, Leo slumbered heavily as though cocooned in a warm web. For him, that's how it must feel. Despite the elegant London townhouse and travels around the world, she sensed that home for him would always be Cornwall. And this room.

She had hoped to talk to him as they'd made ready for bed, but Treeve Fenton's death, the anonymous letter, the surprise offer for Wheal Agnes, remained undiscussed. Was Leo deliberately pushing away the problems his family faced, or did he genuinely believe they didn't exist?

Turning to lie on her back, Nancy gazed blindly at a ceiling she couldn't see. She would have liked to make a hot drink but was worried she would wake her husband or Perry if she ventured to the kitchen. In Venice, she had been wakeful, too, slipping from the bed while Leo slept heavily beside her. But even at night the palazzo had been filled with light, enough for her to find her way easily to the kitchen. She'd sat drinking tea with Archie, who'd returned late from an evening at one of his favourite bars. It was then they'd begun to know each other. From that moment in the small hours, Nancy had known him for a friend. If only it were that simple now. Irritated, she flung herself to the far side of the bed, her eyes tight shut.

***

When she tumbled downstairs the next morning, the brothers were already in the kitchen, eating their way through slices of toast.

'No cereal, I'm afraid, Nancy,' Perry said apologetically.

'I'm due to call at the village shop to see Kitty,' she reminded him. 'I can buy it then.'

He looked relieved. 'Thanks. I need to be off soon—to see the men before the next shift begins—and it would really help if you could do some shopping.'

'Are you going with Perry?' she asked her husband, as he was spooning marmalade onto a second piece of toast.

Leo shook his head. 'I'm off to the hospital this morning. Perry needs to work but I'd like to check how Dad is doing. I'll walk down to the village and find Archie. He can drive me over to Truro. If I find Dad a little better, we can arrange to visit together. Tomorrow or the next day?'

'Good idea.' Nancy smiled brightly. 'Maybe then, *I* could go with Perry this morning? I'd need to change my dress for slacks, but it won't take me a minute.' Perry looked slightly startled and she added, 'If I won't be in the way, that is. I can do the shopping later, and I'm interested in the mine.'

Her interest was sparked not so much by tin but by her growing conviction that Wheal Agnes lay at the bottom of whatever was going on in Port Madron: Treeve Fenton's unexplained death, Ned Tremayne's heart attack, the generous offer from a Brazilian businessman to buy a failing mine. There was a link between them and, despite her tiredness, she felt the old excitement rising. Hoping Leo would clear the kitchen, she ran up the stairs to change into the one pair of slacks she'd packed and, within minutes, had rejoined Perry outside. This morning, the chilly mist that had hung over Penleven since they'd arrived had dissolved, leaving the air clear and luminescent.

'I can drive us there, if you'd prefer,' Perry offered, 'but it's only a twenty minute walk and the weather looks good.'

It did. The sun was shining and the sky almost cloudless, and Nancy was eager to see something of the Cornish landscape Leo so loved. On her first visit, it had been too cold to venture far.

'Let's walk,' she agreed.

For a short while, they took the same road as yesterday, but then turned into a lane that wound its way downhill, seemingly towards the headland, tall hedgerows of bramble and briar masking the view ahead. A sprinkling of slate-roofed, granite-stone cottages bordered the lane, but this early in the morning there was little sign of life, except for an old man bent double, planting a straggling line of what Nancy thought were onion sets. Her father had always planted them at this time of the year. The man straightened up as he heard them approach.

'Mornin', Mr Tremayne,' he said. ''ansome day, innit?'

'It certainly is. Nancy, this is Mr Enys.' Perry was head and shoulders taller than the old man and had to bend low in order to be heard. 'Mr Enys was a miner at Wheal Agnes for most of his life. Denzel, this is my sister-in-law.'

The old man nodded at her without offering his soil-begrimed hand. 'You off to the mine then? I 'eard trouble was brewin'.'

Perry's brown eyes held a tense expression. 'I've a meeting this morning.'

'Don't you let that Pascoe fella make trouble. "e's a bad'un if I ever I saw 'un.'

'I'm hoping to keep it civilised. But it's good to see you looking so well.'

'I am that. But look after yersel, Mr Tremayne.' Denzel bent down to continue his planting.

'The meeting,' Nancy said as they walked away, 'is it to do with the offer you've received?'

Perry stopped walking. 'No one knows about that, Nancy. It's strictly confidential.' He looked as severe as Perry ever could.

'I'll say nothing,' she promised, and they continued to walk swiftly along the lane. But it didn't stop her from speculating. If the meeting wasn't about a possible sale, what was it about?

As though he'd heard her thoughts, her brother-in-law said, 'If I don't accept Silva's offer, I'm thinking of extending the mine—it will help us access new lodes. I already have detailed plans in the drawer, prepared years ago when my grandfather was running the mine and Dad was his assistant. The first part of the extension was completed, but then the work came to a stop.'

'The meeting is to talk about the plans?'

'The men know about them already.' Perry's voice was strained. 'That's the problem. Jory Pascoe has managed to convince them that extending will be a dangerous business. At the moment, the galleries run only a short way beneath the sea, and it's true that we'll be digging a half a mile beyond, but I wouldn't do it if I thought it was dangerous.'

'This Jory obviously disagrees.'

'Pascoe is a trouble maker. He was a fisherman for a few years but couldn't get on with any skipper he sailed with. Then he took up mining—about five years ago. Fishing and mining are traditional for Cornishmen, and Pascoe is Cornish born and bred, though from a different village.'

'Is that important? That he doesn't belong to the village?'

'It's taken him a while to get the men on his side,' Perry said grimly. 'Port Madron tends to be suspicious of outsiders. But Pascoe married a woman from the village, mainly I suspect to get himself a comfortable berth. She owns a cottage on the far side of the harbour.'

For several minutes they walked on in silence, until her brother-in-law burst out, 'That man has a talent for stirring up conflict.'

'What does he do exactly?'

Nancy was intrigued. She felt considerable sympathy for Perry but interest, too, in what this rogue miner was up to and how it might play into events at Port Madron.

'When he was on the boats, he tried to whip up hostility to the skipper on the basis that the crew weren't given a fair share of the catch. He was sacked twice and after that, no other skipper would take him on.'

'If he's such a troublemaker, why was he employed at Wheal Agnes?'

Perry's voice was bitter. 'My fault entirely. He told me some hard luck tale—I didn't get the real story till later—and I felt sorry for him. For a few years he towed the line and looked as though he'd make a good worker. But when I was forced to ask the men to take a modest pay cut... that's when he started his nonsense.'

It seemed quite reasonable to Nancy that the men's loss of income had created trouble. 'Why the cut in pay?' she asked.

'It was the last thing I wanted, but I had no option. The mine did extremely well during the war—you can imagine how much tin was needed then— but afterwards the price started to dip badly. Eventually we were selling at a loss. I had to ask the men to share the burden.'

Perry picked up a stick and swished at a bramble curling its way out of the hedgerow and into the lane. 'I took a bigger loss, of course. But Pascoe started complaining that while the miners had to take a pay cut, the Tremaynes lived in a big house with a big garden and servants— that, by the way, is our part-time housekeeper and very part-time gardener. I should sell Penleven, he said, instead of reducing the men's wages. And on and on in the same vein.' Perry sounded thoroughly miserable.

'And people listened to him?'

'Not at first. The men were very loyal, and I know they defended my decision, but when it looked likely that a second pay cut was on the way, they started to listen to Pascoe. Now he's attacking my plans to develop below the sea.'

As they emerged from the end of the lane, Nancy found herself on open downland, the sound of the ocean close by and growing gradually louder. Cresting the slight rise of the cliff, she saw the sea laid out below them, a ruffled sheet of cobalt blue, glinting in the sheen of the sun's rays.

Perry walked her to the cliff edge and Nancy stood entranced. On her last visit, she had barely left the house, yet all this beauty had been within a hand's reach. She peered cautiously down, seeing wave after wave of towering water crash headlong into the jutting rocks, spumes of white spray leaping feet into the air.

'It's quite beautiful,' she said. The dramatic fall of slate grey rocks, the rolling green headland, the indigo blue of the sea, was an artist's dream.

'It's why I could never leave,' Perry said simply, 'no matter what happens to the mine.'

They turned away from the cliff, taking the narrow path a few feet inland that led directly to the mine. Ahead, Nancy saw what she took to be the chimney stack of Wheal Agnes, naked against the sky and belching smoke. Then the ivy-covered engine house, the heavy chug of its machinery sounding loud against the roar of the sea below. As they approached the gates to the site, the men who had been on the last shift came into view. They were gathered immediately in front of a line of what Nancy took to be offices, their clothes stained with mud and clay.

'I'll keep it short,' Perry said to her. 'The men haven't had the chance to get to the Dry and they'll be wanting to get cleaned up.'

He kept it short as promised but, from where Nancy was standing, it seemed it would not have mattered if he'd uttered only a single word. The miners varied in age from barely out of school to near pensionable, but their expressions were universally sullen.

'Extending the mine is a way for us to keep the place going,' Perry insisted, a desperate note entering his voice. 'As I've said before, the tin should be higher quality than the stuff we've been mining lately, which means we can sell it for more and make a profit at last.'

'So who gets that profit then?' Jory Pascoe's Cornish accent was strong. And loud, Nancy thought, sounding above the shuffling of several dozen boots.

'We all get it,' Perry explained patiently. 'But if we don't do something, Wheal Agnes will continue to lose money and I can't be sure of its future.'

It was evidently the first time he'd mentioned the possibility of closure and the men began muttering among themselves, several beginning to look uncertain. But it was evident Pascoe intended to keep feelings running high. He stepped forward, his chin jutting aggressively.

'You keep tellin' us the tin'll be better, but 'ow do we even know there's more tin to get?'

'I have a detailed survey in my office and you're very welcome to consult it. All of you. The survey suggests there are several rich seams if we push out to sea a little more.'

'A little more.' Pascoe sneered. 'It's 'alf a mile, if it's a yard. That's some pushin' out. And 'ow safe will it be? You've never answered that.'

Nancy looked down and saw the man's fists were clenched.

'All mining has its dangers.' Perry tried to reason. 'We all know that, but I wouldn't suggest extending if I thought it unsafe.'

'You're bound to say that, aren't you? It's not your life you're riskin'. You'll be tucked up nice and cosy-like in there.' The man pointed to a low brick building that had to be Perry's office.

Her brother-in-law said nothing and Jory Pascoe, obviously emboldened, took a step closer until he was glowering into Perry's face. 'We're the ones riskin' our lives. We should be paid more, not less.'

There was a murmur of approval from the gathered men, and immediately Nancy thought of the fearful message she'd read last night. These were unhappy workers and any one of them could be its author.

'I can't pay more,' Perry said, his hands pulling down the pockets of the battered corduroy jacket he wore. 'Not at the moment. The price of tin on the world market—'

'The price of tin? What about the price of a man's life?'

The murmur got louder, then a number of the miners turned away making, Nancy imagined, for the Dry where they would shower and change out of their overalls. One by one, the other men peeled off with only a few stalwarts left facing Perry.

'Sorry, boss, but 'e's got a point,' one of them said. Then they, too, drifted away.

'That went well,' Perry said brightly, turning to face her.

'I'm sorry.' Nancy reached for his hand. 'You did your best, but they didn't want to hear. That man, Jory Pascoe, what's his motive? Is it really to increase wages or is there something else?'

'Something else?' Perry blinked. 'He's a natural agitator, I guess, and this gives him the perfect opportunity to practise.'

Nancy nodded as though she agreed. Pascoe was certainly an agitator, but was there more to it than that?

Chapter Seven

Nancy left her brother-in-law walking towards his office, shoulders stooped. She tried hard to shake off the feeling of mounting trouble—it was such a beautiful morning—but it was difficult. Jory Pascoe was an angry man, a possibly violent one. She recalled the clenched fists. It wouldn't have taken much for him to have lashed out at Perry.

Thoughtfully, she retraced her steps along the coast path in the direction of the village, the smell of the sea pervasive and the thud of waves a rhythmic accompaniment to her walk. The sun shone from a sky filled only with cotton wool clouds, warming her body, loosening her limbs, bringing a smile to her lips. Despite her concern for Perry, she felt invigorated and filled with a sense of freedom.

She had walked nearly half a mile before the uneasy sense that she was not alone crept up on her. She swung around, convinced there was someone following. But the path behind was empty and the headland dozed peacefully in the bright sun. It was the worries at Penleven, she thought, and the unpleasant scene she had just witnessed, prompting old fears to rise. With a determined effort, she fought to free herself of the feeling that someone had been watching her.

Nevertheless, she increased her pace, knowing that at some point she must turn inland, and hoping the footpath to the village would soon appear. Several minutes later, she saw a narrow track to the left that seemed to wind its way back across the headland and into fields of pasture, broken only by the high hedgerows. Port Madron had to be very close.

As soon as Nancy walked past the first cottages, she remembered the village. She and Leo had sometimes walked down to the harbour the Christmas he'd introduced her to his family. It had been a welcome break from the tensions of Penleven. Ned Tremayne had barely spoken to her that holiday and both Leo and Perry had tried too hard to smooth things over, only succeeding in drawing attention to their father's irritation with a daughter-in-law he evidently thought unworthy of the Tremayne name. Tomorrow or the next day she was likely to meet him again and, though he was a sick man and she felt sorry for him, it was not something she welcomed.

The village shop was halfway down the main street, combining a post office as well as a grocery and hardware store. Port Madron boasted only two other shops, a baker's and a butcher's, but with fresh fish sold from the quayside and homegrown fruit and vegetables, the fishing village was almost entirely self-sufficient.

It was nearly midday before Nancy walked through the shop door. She'd been concerned that Kitty Anson might have left for lunch, but the young woman with the blonde curls and bright face was crouched behind the counter, seeming to be stocktaking. She jumped up as the bell clanged noisily overhead and, seeing Nancy, gave a wide smile.

'Hello, my luvver. How are you?' Kitty wasn't a native of the village, maybe not even of Cornwall, but she seemed to have adopted the locals' greeting.

'I'm well, thank you. I need a few items for the larder, but to be honest, Kitty, it's a favour I'm after.'

'Then ask away.'

'Perry is planning a dinner party on Saturday evening—just the family and one, maybe two, others.' Nancy wasn't sure if Mr Silva's assistant was to be invited. 'I'm afraid that cooking a three or four course meal is beyond me. Though I'll help, of course,' she added quickly.

'So, you're after the Anson magic for your kitchen?' Kitty joked.

'We'd be very grateful. I would especially. If you let Perry know a fee, I'm sure he'll be happy with whatever you suggest.'

'I'll do it,' she said. 'As it happens, I've nothing planned this weekend, so why not cook my little heart out?'

'Thank you a hundred times. You can't know what a relief that is!'

'So what can I get you today?'

'If you could slice me some bacon—maybe half a pound. And a dozen eggs.'

'Help yourself. They're new laid today.' Kitty gestured to a rack of eggs.

'And if you could cut me some butter. Oh, and I'd better take some cheese.'

'Cheddar's all we've got. Not exactly high society here.'

'Cheddar will be fine.'

'Do you know what you want to eat at this dinner party?'

Nancy looked crestfallen. 'I haven't a clue. Soup maybe to start— that was delicious pumpkin you made—and maybe fish as a main course. I guess there'll have to be fish.'

'And a posh pudding?'

'If you can manage it.'

'Leave it to me. I'll enjoy getting stuck in and it's extra cash, now I've lost one of my best customers. Treeve,' she said when she saw Nancy's puzzlement. 'Treeve Fenton. Grace

Jago cleans for him, but I was there most days delivering his food. The house is only a few minutes' walk down Roscannon Lane.'

'Did you see him the day he died?'

It sounded a ghoulish question, but Nancy was keen to find out who had seen Treeve that day, apart from Ned Tremayne.

'I took up his supper as usual. He seemed fine. Better than fine. He was expecting old Mr Tremayne for the evening. They were great buddies, you know.'

'So I understand. The accident must have come as a shock to you.'

'It did. Poor old Treeve. What a way to go.'

'Do you have any idea what could have happened?'

Kitty pulled a face. 'The old boys probably had a drink or two that night, and Treeve was getting on. Maybe he was a bit on the go, if you know what I mean, and when he climbed into the bath, he wasn't too steady on his feet. He must have slipped and hit his head. Probably knocked himself out.'

'My husband told me that Mr Fenton never took baths.'

'Well, he did that night.' She laughed. 'Accidents happen, my dear. No good taking it too much to heart. Here, I'll put this stuff in a basket for you. You can bring it back when you come again. Anything else?'

Nancy thought. 'Marmalade perhaps... and a box of cornflakes. That's about all I can carry.'

'Send that husband of yours down for anything extra,' Kitty advised, and rang up the bill.

'You've made this shop very attractive.' Nancy looked around her. 'I remember when Leo brought me in here—the Christmas before last—everything seemed a bit haphazard. But it's so clean and neat now.'

'That's me. Can't resist tidying. I like a sense of order!'

'The Bolithos—they're the owners, aren't they?—must be delighted to have found you.'

'I was delighted to have found them. I fetched up in Port Madron quite by chance. I'm down from London, as they say here, but my husband loved Cornwall and, when I lost him, I knew it was the place I should go. Not to settle, mind. Just for a holiday, a long break. I rented a cottage over at Zennor and travelled around, just mooching really and thinking of Trevor. It was kind of therapeutic.'

Nancy gave a sympathetic nod.

'Anyways, the bus dropped me off at Port Madron one day and I wandered round the village, then saw the advert for help in the shop. It was an impulse really. I'd done shop work before—very different. A high-class jeweller's in Bond Street. But a till is a till, and the Bolithos were thrilled to have someone live in as well as manage the shop.'

'You live here, too?'

'Up there.' Kitty pointed to the ceiling. 'It's a sweet little flat and rent free.' She gave a throaty laugh. 'Even better, don't you think?'

Chapter Eight

By the time Nancy had called at the baker's, it was nearly one o'clock before she arrived back at Penleven, only to find the front door locked and no sign of Leo. She had expected him to be back from the hospital by now and felt stupid that she hadn't thought to ask for a spare key. She need not have worried, though. Walking round to the rear of the house, she found the kitchen door opened at a touch. Did everybody in the village leave their back doors open? If so, anyone could have visited Treeve Fenton late at night, after Ned had left for home. Nancy wondered if the police had considered that.

She unpacked her purchases and, when there was still no sign of Leo, spread some of the crusty bread with butter, cut a hunk of cheese and took several spoonfuls of a chutney she'd found in one of the cupboards. The sun was still shining and the air even more mellow than when she'd walked to the mine, so with tea in one hand and a plate of ploughman's in the other, she sauntered out into the garden and made her way to the summerhouse. It was delightfully warm, and she was quick to discard the lambswool cardigan she'd worn all morning, luxuriating in the feel of bare arms beneath her short-sleeved blouse. The last time she'd enjoyed that sensation, it had been August in the Caribbean.

Her modest lunch over, Nancy was tempted to look

through the canvases stored away in the summerhouse cupboard. Having worked for years in one of the best auction houses in London and now an apprenticed restorer, she knew something of art, and could see immediately that Leo's mother had had real talent. True, Rachel Tremayne hadn't ventured further than landscapes and one or two portraits, but that might simply be an illustration of the narrow life she'd led. Been forced to lead perhaps?

There were portraits of each of the boys, singly and together. Nancy smoothed down her grey cotton slacks and balanced one of the pictures on her knees. Leo hadn't changed much. Still the same wide brown eyes, the same thick, dark hair, though today turning silver. Now in his forties, he was still a handsome man. She loved him, Nancy told herself, giving a gentle sigh—if only she could love as a wife should.

She looked again at the portrait. Those eyes were intelligent, sharply alert. They said clearly that this young boy wouldn't be content with the life his father had planned for him. He was going to do things differently. And he had. The youngest professor of art history and a man who was wanted throughout the world for his Renaissance expertise. Nancy sighed again. Sometimes she wished her husband wasn't quite so well-known. It might mean more time spent together and, possibly, the deeper relationship that had eluded them from the very beginning.

Stacking the canvases carefully to one side, she walked back through the garden and into the kitchen, then washed and dried the dishes as she waited for Leo. By the time she'd hung the tea towel to dry, there was still no sign of her husband. What should she do? Instinct was urging her to investigate the crime she suspected had been committed. But this wasn't Venice or a Caribbean island. This was Port Madron and Leo's home, and her desire to probe was tempered by that fact. Yet Treeve Fenton's death niggled at her. Could she turn her back on it? Could she dismiss Ned's shocking heart attack as bad luck and ignore the menacing letter he'd received? Then there was the angry miner, Jory Pascoe, and Perry's muttering workforce.

She would go to Mr Fenton's house, Nancy decided suddenly. Why, she wasn't sure, only that it seemed the right thing to do. Kitty Anson had mentioned it was nearby. Roscannon Lane, that was the name of the road. It would be easy enough to find in a village consisting of a mere three streets.

***

If the police had ever taped off the house as a crime scene, the tape had disappeared—Treeve Fenton's death must officially have been declared an accident. Nancy walked up the neat front drive, unsure of her next move. She'd had the wild idea of trying to view the bathroom, trying to work out how Treeve could have slipped so badly that he'd knocked himself out and fallen into a bath full of water. The police must already have done that, she scolded herself, and yet there were so many troubling things in this village, that it would be foolish to accept everything at face value. If the back door should be open...

The blank windows of the house stared back at her, seeming without life now that it was bereft of its owner. It made Nancy feel uncomfortable and she walked quickly around to the rear but, just as she was about to try the kitchen door, she was brought up sharply by a figure emerging from the house, brush in one hand and a rug in the other.

'I'm sorry,' Nancy stammered. 'I didn't realise anyone was here.'

The young woman, hair tied back with a flowered scarf,

looked bemused. 'Were you lookin' fer Mr Fenton?'

'No. That is, I… ' Nancy trailed off. How on earth was she to explain her interest in the poor man's death? Explain the constant hum in her mind that was telling her something was wrong.

'I'm Nancy Tremayne,' she said, hoping the name would save her from being judged a prowler.

The young woman's face cleared. 'Hello, Mrs Tremayne. Morwenna mentioned you. That's Archie's Ma. You know Archie, of course.'

She knew Archie. Far too well, Nancy thought, but aloud, she said, 'Yes. I'm Leo's wife.'

'And I'm Grace Jago—married to Archie's big brother, Richard. Rich, we call 'im. But won't you come in?'

'I can see you're busy. I don't want to intrude.' Even as she said this, Nancy was desperate to cross the threshold.

'Don't be daft. Beatin' a few old carpets and clearin' up after the police is all I'm doin'. I thought I owed it to Treeve to make 'is house right and tight again.'

'Did the police make much mess?' Nancy asked, following Grace into the kitchen.

'It weren't too bad, I s'ppose. Now how about a nice cup of tea?'

Nancy was already brimming with tea, but a drink would make talking easier. 'I'd love one. Thank you.'

Grace put the kettle on and reached for the tea caddy. 'They've all got size twelve boots—them police—and they didn't think to take them off before they marched all over Treeve's new carpet. Cream it is, too. I warned 'im it was a daft colour, but 'e liked it and said 'e were an old man now and 'e'd 'ave what 'e enjoyed around 'im.'

'He sounds nice.'

'He were a lovely chap. I were that shocked to hear what

'appened. Rich, too. And when Lowen knows, 'e'll be some upset. The two of 'em used to go fishin' together before Lowen went to Plymouth. Lowen's another brother,' she said in explanation.

'There's a lot of them.'

'Four last time I counted.' Grace smiled. 'Steve and Lowen are in Plymouth now—Steve's been there years. Got a really good job, so we hear, and now 'e's found work fer Lowen. And Archie—'e's the baby—travellin' round the world. Well, you know that. It's only Rich left. And 'is Ma, of course.'

Nancy nodded, enjoying Grace's recital. It was clear Archie came from the kind of close family she could only dream of.

She sipped her tea slowly before saying, 'I suppose Treeve wasn't infirm in any way?'

'Infirm? Gracious, no. The man walked a good five mile a day. He were a miner, you know, before 'e went into management. As tough as boots.'

'You must have been surprised when you heard he'd fallen?'

'Shocked. I said to Rich, what were 'e doin' in the bath? He never used it. If I cleaned that bath once in three months, I'd be surprised. It were the shower always. A brisk shower, Treeve would say, a five mile walk and two pints of beer at the Tinners, that's the way to keep healthy.'

'It does sound strange,' Nancy agreed, 'but perhaps that night he had a fancy for a bath?'

'More than strange.' Grace's face darkened. 'I've a hunch somethin' odd went on. I dunno why everyone thinks it's natural for a healthy man to fall into a bath. He's seventy, they say, what d'you expect? But 'e had the body of a fifty-year-old.'

'I spoke to Kitty Anson at the village shop. I believe she came here most days with food for Treeve. She didn't seem to think anything was too amiss.'

'I wouldn't take too much notice of what Mrs Anson tells you.'

'Why is that? I liked her,' Nancy said candidly.

'Well, you would. That's what she's good at. Gettin' folks to like 'er.'

'But you don't?'

Grace put her cup down on the kitchen counter with a thud. 'I don't trust 'er.'

'Is there a reason?'

She tipped her head back. 'I can't name one specially. I just don't trust 'er. She tells all these tales of what she used to do in London. Mebbe they're true, mebbe not. But why come 'ere if she 'ad such a good life up north?'

'Up north?'

'Anything past Plymouth is north, Mrs Tremayne. For some 'ere, anything past Truro.'

'Mrs Anson mentioned a husband,' Nancy remarked mildly.

'That's another thing. This husband she 'ad. S'pposed to love Port Madron, 'e did, but no one in the village remembers 'im.'

'I think maybe it was Cornwall in general that he loved.' Having found Kitty amenable and very willing, Nancy had no wish to discredit her. In all likelihood, Grace's hostility sprang from nothing more than a dislike of someone new in the village, someone who had obviously found her feet and was well-liked locally. It wouldn't be wise to set too much store by this young woman's feelings.

'If you've finished ...' Grace said, and when Nancy nodded, collected up teapot and cups and emptied them into the sink. Nancy sat watching her swift, decisive movements as the washing-up bowl was filled and various pieces of china plunged in and out of hot water.

'I've just to pick up the rubbish,' the young woman said over her shoulder. 'Then I'll walk into the village with you.'

'Can I help?'

From where she sat, Nancy could see through an open door to the study beyond. A wicker basket bursting with paper stood to one side of the desk. 'I can empty the wastepaper bin at least.'

She slipped off her stool and walked into the adjoining room, picking up the basket and at the same time trailing her hands through its contents.

The bin slid from her fingers. Nestling beneath several torn invoices and an empty chocolate wrapper was a page that looked familiar. Staring up at her, a sheet of lined paper. Torn edges and big black letters cut from newsprint. Treeve had received the same message as Ned. Quickly, Nancy squirrelled the page away in her handbag.

At that moment, Grace appeared in the doorway. 'Alright?'

Nancy tried to breathe normally and fixed a glassy smile at the young woman. 'Fine. Here's the basket.'

While Grace was shovelling the rubbish into the dustbin she'd brought inside, Nancy took a decision. She would say nothing of the anonymous letter, but she would see that bathroom.

'Before we leave, do you think we could go upstairs?' she asked.

Grace's eyebrows rose sharply, and Nancy murmured an explanation. 'You said you thought there was something odd about Mr Fenton's death—and I'm quite good at investigations.'

'You're a detective?' Grace's mouth opened in surprise.

'Nothing like that. I work in art, at a restorers' actually, but twice when I've been abroad with Leo,' she was careful not to mention Archie, 'I've discovered bad things when nobody else wanted to know. Maybe that's the case here.'

Grace nodded. 'It's just my hunch, mind. But come on up, Mrs Tremayne and I'll show you.'

'Nancy, please.'

'It's lovely to meet you, Nancy.' Grace stopped on the stairs and turned to offer her hand. 'You're quite different from what I imagined.'

'How is that?'

'Much younger fer one thing! And very pretty. Mr Leo chose well fer 'imself.'

Nancy coloured but gave a gentle laugh. 'I hope he thinks so.'

Grace pushed the bathroom door open. 'It's only a small room—the shower is over the bath, with a curtain to protect the floor.'

It was possible, Nancy supposed, that Treeve had climbed into the bath to have a shower and then slipped. But why then was the bath full of water? And why a shower late at night? Grace had said plainly that he liked a morning shower before a good walk.

'Was there a bathmat on the floor?'

Grace shook her head. 'He wouldn't 'ave one. I 'ad to throw out the old 'un a year ago. He tripped on it and said it was dangerous. Then he 'ad these cork tiles fitted— they absorb water if you splash. Warm to the feet, too.'

Nothing in this bathroom spelt danger. No mat, no slippery tiles. It was a cramped space, but the basin was a good distance from the bath and the toilet was housed separately. There was little chance of accidentally knocking against one of the fittings and catapulting into the bath. You'd have to be a circus performer for that to happen.

Nancy felt excitement rising again. Treeve Fenton couldn't

have had an accident, she was convinced. Someone had pushed him and, falling, he must have knocked himself unconscious. Then the taps were turned on.

'Gracie, are you there?'

Nancy knew the voice and felt her stomach tighten.

'We're up 'ere, Archie, luv.'

'We? Who are you hiding?'

Archie's footsteps sounded on the stairs and then he was filling the doorway. He gave a faint exhalation of air when he saw her. 'Nancy?'

'Yes. Me.' She smiled weakly. 'I was taking a walk.'

He looked at her long and hard. 'Taking a walk and…'

'And nothing. I thought I'd call in, that's all. Kitty Anson told me where Mr Fenton lived.'

'So you decided you'd take a look at the scene of the crime? Or what you've decided was a crime.'

'Grace was kind enough to show me.'

'That's because Grace doesn't know you.'

And you do, Nancy thought. You know me like you know yourself. She raised her head and looked into a pair of startling blue eyes, while they looked steadily back at her. The tension was palpable and Grace, uncomfortable with feelings she could sense but not understand, busied herself taking off her flowered apron and rolling it into a bundle.

'Well, I'm finished for the day. Have you come to give me a lift 'ome?'

'The car awaits,' Archie said grandly.

'Did you get to the hospital?' Nancy asked him, as they trooped down the stairs in single file. 'How is Leo's father?'

'He seems better. Not that I spent any time with him, but Leo came out looking a lot more cheerful than when he went in.'

'I expect I'll see for myself very soon.'

'I expect you will,' Archie said laconically. 'Leo has your visit planned. Come on, Gracie. I'll drop you first, then I'll take the car up to Penleven.'

'There's no need,' Nancy said quickly. 'I can walk from the village.'

'I'm sure you can but I have to see Leo about tomorrow. I don't know if he'll want me to drive—he was waiting to talk to you.'

Archie sounded indifferent, brusque even, but she wasn't fooled. He wasn't indifferent and, coming across her unexpectedly, seeing her with Grace, had definitely unsettled him. His sudden appearance had unsettled Nancy, too. But also made her happy. She missed him when he wasn't around but, when he was, she found herself tied into knots. There seemed to be no solution.

Grace lived in a granite-stone cottage behind the harbour and, having dropped her at her door, it was only a short drive back to Penleven. Archie stopped the car but made no effort to get out.

'Can you tell Leo I'm here?'

He spoke as though to a stranger. More aloof than she'd known him for a very long time. Nancy wondered if it was because he was back on home territory. Or simply that the situation between them had become too difficult to cope with. And now they were stranded for several weeks in a small village together, but at least they weren't sleeping under the same roof.

'Don't say anything about Treeve Fenton's death,' he added, as she swung her legs from the car. 'Leo doesn't need any more complications.'

'I wasn't going to mention it.'

'You were. But for once, Nancy, take my advice.'

'Why should I?' she demanded sharply, angered by his

rough manner.

'Why indeed?'

His face showed what he was thinking. Why should she consider what he had to say? He was only the man who had kissed her so passionately that she thought her heart might stop.

'If it interests you, Treeve Fenton received an anonymous letter before he died. It threatened him with murder.'

Archie stared at her. 'Are you sure?'

'It was in his wastepaper bin—torn in two.'

'And you went rooting for it? '

'Only because Ned Tremayne received the same letter. Leo has dismissed it as unimportant. Perry, too. At least, that's what they're pretending. It was almost certainly a trigger for their father's heart attack, though.'

'So what are you intending to do?'

'You know what.'

Archie sighed. 'Count me out. Port Madron's my home. I'm not getting involved.'

'Fine.' She gave a defiant flick to her hair and marched into the house.

Chapter Nine

The following day Nancy had been expecting to make the hospital visit she was dreading and was surprised when, over breakfast, Leo suggested a walk instead.

'It's a lovely day again,' he said, dropping a kiss on the top of her head. 'We should make the most of it. Get out and do some exploring.'

A different kind of exploration was itching at Nancy, but Leo's offer was tempting. 'What about the hospital?' she queried.

'I have to go to Truro on business this morning,' Perry put in. 'I can fit in a visit to Dad afterwards.'

'And I can go this afternoon,' Leo said. 'As long as Dad is up to it.'

When an hour later Nancy found herself on the coastal path once more, walking side by side with her husband, all thoughts of pursuing the perpetrator of those anonymous notes vanished. It was simply too beautiful a morning to spend in any other way. This time the walk took her in the opposite direction to Wheal Agnes, the cliff path climbing steadily upwards to the headland, the slope gradually growing steeper and the track narrower. As they reached what Nancy took to be the highest point, a huge swathe of coastline came into view.

'On a really clear day, you can see almost to the tip of Cornwall,' Leo told her.

'To Land's End?'

'That's the most westerly point. But yes, the coves and inlets leading to Land's End. There are literally hundreds of them. They were the haunts of smugglers once, but today it's tourists that do the haunting. Lamorna, for instance. It's a hidden gem — truly beautiful. *Rich*, we'd say here.'

'That's Cornish?'

He nodded. 'The language of home, though I've been absent from it for most of my life. School... university... work.'

What had it been like for a young boy to find himself so far away from a landscape he loved? Arguably, the Shropshire countryside was as beautiful in its own way, but for a child it must have felt a foreign land. An alien land perhaps. Perry had shared the experience, and it was no wonder there was such a tight bond between the brothers, even though for the most part it remained unexpressed.

Nancy's gaze moved from sea to land. Not far away the chimney of an abandoned mine came into view. Then another and, further into the distance, yet more.

'Those chimneys,' she said. 'They're such a sad sight. How many are there, do you think?'

'Too many. They're a sign of the times, I'm afraid, though it's true some have lain abandoned for a very long time. There's been mining in Cornwall for hundreds of years, though the first tinners didn't need chimneys. They worked in the open, streaming tin from ore that was exposed in the rock face. It's said the rivers ran red because of the residue.'

'And the chimneys? When did they appear?'

'With the steam engine. That's what really got underground mining going. Steam power enabled mines to be dug deep into the ground and way out to sea. When Levant was operational—it was over Penzance way—' Leo nodded his head in a westerly direction, 'the workings extended a mile from shore and a third of a mile beneath the seabed. The men must have been aware of the ocean above their heads. Constantly. Imagine hearing the roar of waves against the cliffs and feeling the saltwater seeping into the rock crannies where you're working.'

'Brave men.' She felt her skin prickle at the thought.

'It was a job, when there was little else available. Cornish mining is more or less finished now, but at one time it was a huge industry. Last century, there were two thousand mines across the county.'

'It's impossible to imagine that number.'

'Travel through Cornwall and you will. The relics of mining are everywhere, and the ruins are well-preserved— mine shafts, engine houses—probably because the industry declined at such speed. A long history, but one that's almost over. Shall we walk down to the chimney?'

Nancy nodded and they began to make their way down towards the sea, but as they drew closer to the derelict mine, the path became more difficult to negotiate, the track overgrown by brambles and, at times, almost impassable. Leo pushed a way through, holding back the briars for Nancy to squeeze past. Within a few minutes they were standing at the foot of an ivy-covered mine shaft. A battered wooded board to one side announced that this was *Wheal Harmony*.

Her gaze travelled beyond the red brick chimney, to the sea below where the surf thundered against the rocky shore line. 'It's a dramatic landscape.'

'We're on the south coast here, but the north is even more dramatic and the sea more dangerous. The Atlantic rollers have immense power.'

She stood a while, thinking of how many men had worked here—women and girls, too, she'd read, in their thousands. Bal Maidens they were called. While they didn't work below the surface, they still laboured. Brutally, before machinery was introduced. Along with young boys, they broke up the ore-bearing rocks with hammers. How many men, how many women, had been injured in this unforgiving industry? How many lost their lives?

It was a sobering thought, and for long minutes, Nancy stayed silent. Then a solitary black-backed gull rose out of the ruins, uttering its harsh cry, and she was returned to the present.

'Will Perry sell, do you think?

Leo's brow puckered. 'Truly, I've no idea. Wheal Agnes is losing fistfuls of money and that can't continue. Yet if it goes to a foreign owner, how beneficial will it be for local people? The industry used to employ thousands and now it's down to a handful. But when mining is the only way of earning a living, other than poor fishing and seasonal tourists, that handful is important.'

'When Mr Silva visits tomorrow, we must do our best.' She tried to sound cheerful. 'But if he's heard of the trouble at the mine, the problem with Jory Pascoe I mean, he might withdraw his offer.'

Leo took her hand and they began to walk together, back up the slope to the coast path. When he spoke, he seemed unsure. 'Silva might withdraw, I suppose. Or it may be that stirring trouble is a ploy on his part. A way of encouraging Perry to sell.'

Nancy stopped and looked at him, a frown on her face. 'How is that possible? Silva hasn't been in the country. He's not even here now.'

'Don't forget, he employs what Perry calls a sidekick,' Leo

said quietly. 'The man at the Tinners. The man my brother hasn't taken to. He'll be coming to dinner with his boss by the way. I don't know if Perry mentioned that, but perhaps we should warn Kitty Anson.'

'I don't think it will matter. I've given her an approximate number and there should be enough to eat for us all. But you're suggesting that this man may have deliberately fomented trouble at Wheal Agnes?'

'If he has, I wouldn't be surprised. It's not exactly a legitimate negotiating tool, but it's happened before. Perry let slip that he saw the chap talking to Pascoe a few weeks ago, which made me wonder. It might be nothing or it might be everything. Though why Silva should take so much trouble to buy a failing mine is beyond me.'

'You don't think there's more below ground than Perry knows? A valuable commodity of some kind?'

'Wheal Agnes produces copper and arsenic as well as tin, but in microscopic quantities. It can't be that. And even if there is something hidden that's worth digging for, how would Silva know? There's no way he could have commissioned a survey without Perry knowing.'

The topic seemed finished, but it had given Nancy more to think about. If Mr Silva and his henchman were indeed trying to destabilise Perry's workforce, then wouldn't a fatality do the trick better than anything else? The death of a previous partner in the mine, the possible death of a present one. It was a very long shot, but it was one she felt she couldn't ignore.

Several paces further and they'd regained the coast path, stopping to look down once more at the waves thundering below. Nancy glanced across at her husband and frowned. He was very pale and his breathing seemed shallow. She touched him gently on the arm.

'Are you okay, Leo? You've gone white.'

He gave her a wintry smile. 'I'm fine,' he said, taking a long breath. 'Let's get moving—I need to walk into the village.'

They were soon in sight of Port Madron again and Leo tucked her hand in his, bending his head towards her. 'How do you like your first real view of a Cornish landscape?'

'It's quite beautiful. Breathtaking, in fact.'

'On a day like this, certainly. You might feel differently when the white mist comes. Which it will. It drifts in from the sea and only dissolves in patches. You can be shivering in one village and basking in the next.'

'We've been lucky so far.'

'And long may that continue. The prevailing wind is a south-westerly which means a mild, damp climate and a green landscape. But it's also a wind that brings furious storms. Wait till you feel the rain lashing and hear the sea roaring.'

'It will be a different kind of beauty, that's all,' she said staunchly.

He tickled her under the chin. 'Ever the optimist. I'll be walking on to the village, but I'll show you the shortcut to Penleven when we get to the crossroads.'

So far Nancy had said nothing of her visit yesterday to Treeve Fenton's house, but she was aware of the message she'd found burning a hole in her pocket. Despite Archie's warning, she had an irresistible urge to confide what she'd discovered. Leo had seen the letter to his father, so surely he should know about this second threat.

He was preparing to say goodbye to her when she reached out and grasped his sleeve. 'Leo, I want you to know something. Treeve Fenton received a message like the one Perry showed us the night we arrived.'

Nancy waited for her husband's reaction, but he said nothing, his face immobile.

'Don't you think we should take both letters to the police?' she asked, her voice strained.

'You have this letter?'

'Yes,' she admitted. 'It's been torn in two, but the message is still clear. It's the same as the one sent to your father. The police—'

'The police have already decided that Treeve's death was an accident,' Leo said abruptly. 'No good can be served by handing in this… this rubbish. The messages are ridiculous, and we'd be the laughing stock of the village if it got around, and it will. They're probably the work of one of Perry's disaffected miners, an attempt to cause upset with no real substance to them. If the police are happy, so am I. I want nothing more to upset Dad.'

'He needn't know about it. And the village needn't know. We could pass the letters to the police quietly.'

'And have that heavy-footed mob traipsing through Penleven or crowding around Dad's hospital bed firing questions at him? And if you think it wouldn't leak out to the village, you know nothing about village life. No, Nancy. We'll do no such thing.'

A chill was in the air that hadn't been there earlier, and she was glad when Leo pointed to a pathway opposite where they stood.

'Follow that and you'll come out at the back of Penleven. I'm off to rouse Archie from whatever he's doing. He's had far too much free time lately.' Leo sounded cross, but she knew it wasn't Archie making him annoyed.

'He can drive me to the hospital this afternoon,' her husband went on, 'and ferry us both there tomorrow. I take it you'll come.'

'I said I would.'

The smile Leo managed was a poor effort. 'Fine. I'll see

you this evening then.' He gave a brief wave of his hand and Nancy felt dismissed.

Miserably, she followed the path Leo had indicated, and within minutes found herself at the rear of the house, once more letting herself in through the kitchen door. She walked across into the hall, her footsteps echoing on the stone floor. She was alone here, it seemed—Perry must have gone straight to the mine when he got back from Truro.

She walked slowly back into the kitchen. It was cold and empty, with no sign of anything that could be used for dinner that night. She had better forgo a late lunch and start a raid on the cupboards. Her cooking expertise was being tested in a way she hadn't expected.

The temperature seemed to have fallen sharply and she shivered in the dank atmosphere. Remembering that she'd left a cardigan in the summerhouse, she decided to retrieve it and maybe sit there for a while before she began work. It was a peaceful place and, after the upsetting conversation with Leo, peace was what she needed.

Once out of the house, she felt a good deal warmer and, as she rounded the hedge, saw that part of the summerhouse was still bathed in sunshine. Opening the door, she walked over to the chair she'd used. She had draped her cardigan over it, she was certain, but now there was no knitwear spread across its wicker. No knitwear adorning the other chair either. No sign of the garment anywhere. Had she taken it up to her bedroom and forgotten? She was sure that she hadn't.

Then she saw it. The door of the corner cupboard was open, and the stack of Rachel's paintings still piled inside, but one canvas had been extracted. It was the portrait of Leo as a small boy and ugly slashes had torn through the child's face. She bent to retrieve it and the painting fell to pieces.

Nancy clasped the chair for support and lowered herself

down into it, breathing in tiny gasps, her throat seeming to close up. Drops of sweat dotted her forehead. A panic attack, she thought. I'm having a panic attack. Something I believed I'd left behind.

A missing item. A loved object destroyed. This had all the hallmarks of the man who'd pursued her so relentlessly, who'd threatened her safety and her sanity. Her stalker—Philip Marsh. But how could that be?

Chapter Ten

A rchie arrived at Penleven early the next morning. Leo had been clear that he wanted their visit to the hospital over before midday, so that he could take Nancy into Helston for a quiet lunch. It would be very quiet, Archie reflected, when he saw the couple emerge from the front door, neither of them speaking. They greeted him briefly before climbing into the car.

As he drove, Archie watched Nancy in the mirror. She looked desperately unhappy. Had she quarrelled with Leo? If so, it was a rare event these days. Most often she went along with what her husband wanted. Archie wasn't above silently urging her to make a stand at times and not let gratitude define her. But he could be wrong about the quarrel. The two of them sat side by side on the back seat, shoulders touching, and no evident discord between them.

Perhaps it was this visit to Ned Tremayne that was making her miserable. Nancy had never spoken of her reception at Penleven, but Archie knew without being told that the old man would have cut up rough when presented with his new daughter-in-law, and, though he was now a very sick man, his tongue would still be tart enough to hurt.

But the pallid face and the dark smudges beneath her eyes suggested there was more keeping Nancy awake. Archie would bet his last fiver that it was Treeve Fenton's death. He had known, as soon as he saw her at Treeve's house, that she was readying herself to play detective again and he'd sent up a small prayer that she would hit a blank wall.

He wasn't in any doubt that the old bloke's death was smoky, but this was a small community and it was best not to stir too many embers. Nancy should realise that. She hailed from a village herself, albeit in Hampshire. But the rules were the same. Her village no doubt swirled with gossip, rumour, innuendo, just as Port Madron did, all very enjoyable as long as it didn't provoke serious trouble. But if there was something Nancy was good at, it was trouble.

The journey to the Royal Cornwall was made in almost complete silence, the tension dissolving only when Archie's passengers climbed out of the car and disappeared through the main doors of the hospital. He would stretch his legs, he decided, and enjoy a ciggie. There was a patch of grass opposite the main entrance that would do nicely. From there, he'd be visible when the couple reappeared, ready to take them on to Helston.

Was this to be a romantic lunch for them both? It seemed doubtful. These days the marriage appeared to have steadied, lacking any great excitement, but lacking the earlier fireworks, too. It hadn't been easy for either of them, Archie knew. Particularly when last year Leo had insisted his wife go with him to the Caribbean.

For Nancy, it had been brutal, losing the baby her husband had so much wanted. At the time, Leo hadn't reacted well, but relief at finding his wife safe from the dangers she'd faced had tempered his anger. Now he appeared to have forgotten the trip entirely.

Had Nancy forgotten Malfuego, too? The kiss Archie had shared with her? Somehow, he didn't think so, but by dint of never being in the same place together for more than a week or two—he'd travelled widely with Leo these last six months—they had contrived to stay clear of each other.

The travelling had kept them apart and apart was how they must stay. Nancy was bound to her husband, if not by passionate love, then by gratitude and loyalty. And wasn't that true of him, too? The loyalty of an ex-soldier and gratitude that Leo had rescued him from the drudgery of life in Port Madron. He loved the village, but he couldn't live there. Gratitude and loyalty. The exact same qualities, he reflected wryly, that Leo had shown him, from the day Archie had pulled the wounded man to safety on a Normandy beach, beneath a bombardment of fire.

He took a long draw on his cigarette. If they weren't with Ned Tremayne too long, he could make it back to Port Madron by lunchtime. Ma wouldn't be working, it was mornings only for her now, and this afternoon he could offer to drive her somewhere she fancied. Take her out for tea perhaps. She rarely got to ride in a comfortable car, and he wanted to treat her in some way. It seemed her heart problem had settled, but he couldn't be sure, and most of the time he lived at too great a distance to know what was going on, let alone offer help. When he met Rich at the pub tonight, it would be the chance to question his brother and get a better idea of how things really stood.

Archie had taken only a few more puffs on his cigarette when the doors opposite burst open and a nurse came rushing across to him.

'You better come. Your boss needs you.'

'What the blazes—?' He was mystified but threw his cigarette onto the grass and ground it out with his heel.

The nurse, her face strained, hurried towards the hospital entrance. 'There's trouble,' she threw over her shoulder.

Trouble. Nancy. What had happened to her? It needed no further words to galvanise Archie into a run, passing the nurse and crashing through the main doors. A noise, verging on the cacophonous, sounded from the end of the corridor and he bounded towards it. Staring wildly around, he saw Nancy and felt a surge of relief. She was leaning back against the dirty cream of the wall, her face paler even than before. Leo, his form rigid, stood beside her. Meanwhile, what seemed an army of doctors and nurses rushed to and fro, or trolleyed equipment into a ward whose doors stood open. As Archie advanced on the couple, the ward door slammed shut, a blanket of silence suddenly descending.

When Leo caught sight of his assistant, he walked rapidly towards him.

'It's my father, Archie. There's been an accident. The IV drip… it's a beta blocker to make the heart beat more slowly, but …' His hands harrowed through his hair as he tried to explain.

'The drip was faulty?' Archie suggested.

'It must have been. Somehow the wrong stuff, whatever it was, was being pumped into Dad and he's had a seizure.'

'My God! They—' Archie gestured to the closed door, 'they think it will be okay, though?'

'I've no idea.' Leo's expression was stricken. 'You must take Nancy home. She can't be here. If anything …'

'And you?'

'I have to stay. I'll let my brother know what's happened. He's at the mine, but he'll come if I need him. I can use the phone at the reception desk.'

'Then call me, too, when you know more,' Archie said. 'Ma still has the phone you set up for her. I'll come back for you when you need me.'

'Good man. Thank you. Take Nancy now. She looks

dreadful — I'm worried she might keel over.'

Leo walked back to his wife, still propped against the wall. 'I'm sorry, sweetheart, no lunch in Helston today.'

'That's the last thing you should think about, Leo.' Nancy's voice was faint. 'But shouldn't we find somewhere to sit?'

'I will, in a minute. But you must go back to Penleven. Archie will drive you.'

Her eyes clouded as she looked from one man to the other. 'I should stay. Keep you company.'

'This isn't the place for you right now. And Archie — a tot of brandy wouldn't come amiss.'

'Sure thing, boss.'

Archie put out his hand to guide her towards the entrance. With a single backward glance at her husband, Nancy allowed herself to be escorted down the corridor and out of the main doors.

When he'd settled her in the car, Archie slipped into the seat beside her. 'Are you all right to go back to Penleven? Or do you need a drink first? A stiff one.'

She gave a weak smile. 'Alcohol isn't going to sort this out, Archie.'

'What will?'

She was silent for a moment and then said in a quiet voice, 'The drip wasn't an accident. The Tremaynes are being deliberately targeted.'

'Why would you think that?'

She twisted round in her seat to face him. 'Tell me, what nurse puts up a drip that is so dangerous to a sick patient that it brings on a seizure? I heard the medical staff talking. They kept their voices low, but I heard nevertheless. They were baffled and angry. The nurse in charge of the ward was incandescent. She felt she was being blamed for something she had no idea about. When they've stabilised Ned, if they stabilise him, there'll be an investigation. Then we'll know for sure.'

Archie pressed the starter button. 'An exciting morning. A poisonous drug to add to the threatening letters.' His tone was half teasing.

'You're not convinced? Don't forget Treeve and the bath. He wasn't a Tremayne, but he was very closely associated with them.'

'Most likely he took a shower late in the evening when he'd had a few too many,' Archie said prosaically.

Nancy shook her head. 'No,' she said firmly. 'I grant you it's possible he decided to take a late shower, though it's unlikely. It's possible even that he slipped. But there's no way the bath would have accidentally been full of water. No way he could have drowned.'

Archie said nothing. Nancy had a nose for wrongdoing, but targeting the Tremayne family sounded a bit dramatic, even for her. Who would do that? Ned Tremayne wasn't particularly well-liked in the district, true enough, but his sons were a different matter. No one, as far as Archie knew, would wish them ill. And as for Treeve, he was one of life's gentlemen.

But he could feel Nancy's shock as she sat beside him. Feel her slender figure tense, her shoulders hunch defensively. He knew she believed every word she said, but what a strange combination she was. Distressingly vulnerable—the trauma of the baby she'd lost in the Caribbean was still vivid to Archie—yet, at the same time, determined and brave. A woman who would confront an adversary without another thought, if she believed it was the just thing to do. No wonder his feelings for her were so complicated.

'Would you like to come back with me?' he asked suddenly.

'Back with you?' she repeated. 'To your home?' She sounded astonished.

'My mother would like to meet you. She'll be back from work by now, and I doubt there'll be anyone at Penleven to keep you company.'

Nancy gave a tremulous smile. 'That's kind of you. Yes, please. I'd like it.'

But when he pulled up outside the cottage in Anchor Row, Nancy made no attempt to get out.

'Changed your mind?'

'No. It's something else. Something I didn't say, but I want you to know. It's not just Ned being threatened or Treeve. It's me, too.'

Just how badly this morning's drama had affected her was unclear to him. His expression, though, must have been sufficiently doubtful to make her burst out, 'Don't look like that. I'm not going mad. Not yet at least. Someone is out to get me, too.' And in a quiet voice, she told him about the missing cardigan and the slashed portrait.

Archie sat back in his seat. 'You could have mislaid the cardigan,' he said hopefully.

'And the painting? Did I slash that in a fit of absent mindedness?'

'You're sure it wasn't damaged when you stacked the canvases?'

'Quite sure. I'd had that particular picture on my lap at lunchtime, studying it—it was a portrait of Leo as a young boy. Before I left the summerhouse, I was careful to replace it at the front of the stack.'

'Anyone could have got into the place, I guess. All they needed was to walk round to the back of the house. There's no gate or fence. But think, Nancy, who would do it? Most people here don't even know you. Why would they want to frighten you?'

He thought it was a reasonable question, but she had an answer. 'It's not me particularly, don't you see? It's because I'm Leo's wife. In their eyes, I'm a Tremayne and so fair game. And if that isn't it, then it's something even worse. For me, at least.'

Archie's brow wrinkled. 'Cryptic. What do you mean?'

She looked as though she was about to spill out whatever was going on in her head but, before she could, the front door of the cottage opened and his mother walked down the path towards them, a wide smile on her face.

'So who have you brought to see me, Archie?'

Chapter Eleven

'Bring the maid in,' his mother urged, and led the way into a small square kitchen, pushing a fat bundle of a cat from one of the room's easy chairs and shaking up its cushions. 'Come and sit down, my luvver.'

'Don't fuss, Ma.'

'I'm not fussing. Mrs Tremayne is a guest. She's more important than Misty. The cat,' she explained, seeing the question in Nancy's face. 'He adopted me ten year ago and I've not got him off that cushion since. Now, Mrs Tremayne—'

'Nancy, please.'

Morwenna beamed. 'Now, Nancy, what will you have?'

'A cup of tea will be fine.'

Nancy glanced around the kitchen. It might be small and a little shabby, but it had the comfort of a place well-loved. Like the old shoes you always returned to, despite any number of newer pairs in the wardrobe.

The noise of the front door opening straight into the kitchen had Nancy look up.

'Just popped in before I collect the girls.' It was Grace Jago. 'Well, hello again, Nancy.'

Nancy greeted her warmly. She had liked the woman when they'd met yesterday and now today, after the trauma at the hospital, Grace seemed to bring with her the stability

Nancy needed. The sheer ordinariness of her coming home from work, meeting her daughters from school, calling in for a few minutes to see her mother-in-law, was comforting.

'Don't forget the sugar, Ma,' Archie intervened, as Morwenna brought a laden tray to the table.

If she wasn't getting brandy, Nancy thought wryly, sugar was Archie's antidote to shock. So far, he'd not mentioned to his mother the situation they'd left behind and by tacit agreement, she kept silent, too. It couldn't help to talk of it and might very well make things worse if rumours started circulating the village. Rumours that someone was out to get the Tremaynes.

'How's Mr Tremayne?' Morwenna asked, unloading cups and saucers and teapot and bustling back to the kitchen counter for a plate of biscuits.

'Not that good,' Nancy said, looking across at Archie who maintained a bland expression.

'I'm that sorry to hear it. A cup for you, Gracie, luv?'

'No thanks, Ma. I need to be off soon.'

Morwenna's ample figure plumped down beside her daughter-in-law on the sagging settee.

'Well, when you get the chance, my dear,' she said to Nancy, 'you tell that husband of yours how sorry I am to hear of his father's trouble. And Mr Perran, too. I haven't been up to Penleven for months—I used to be a regular there sellin' my fish, you know—but I've seen nothin' of his father or him. It's a sad day for the village. Losing Treeve Fenton as well. Gracie told me how she'd met you. Up at his place.'

Nancy fidgeted with the spoon in her saucer. It was clear that news travelled fast in the village, but she should have expected it. 'I was walking in that direction,' she said vaguely, unable to think of a more sensible explanation.

'I've just come back from there,' Grace put in. 'I finished

cleanin' up yesterday, but when I got 'ome I found I'd left my best feather duster and a tub of polish. Treeve never would buy polish. Let the house alone, 'e'd say, but 'e were always glad to see the furniture shine.'

There was a small silence before Grace suddenly leaned towards her brother-in-law, sitting at the kitchen table. 'Archie, I need advice.'

'Don't come to me then,' he joked. 'Ask Rich. He's the big brother.'

'I don't want to mention it to Rich. He's enough worries of 'is own, what with the fishin' bein' so poor.'

'What's worryin' you?' A frown dulled Morwenna's usually sunny face.

'I wasn't worried till today. But when I went to fetch my stuff from Treeve's livin' room—I knew I'd left it there— I noticed… I noticed Treeve's carriage clock were missing. I was checking the time cause I'd promised to be at Honeysuckle Cottage by ten. It weren't on the mantelshelf . I don't remember when I last saw it, but when I looked around more, that lovely porcelain bowl that Treeve inherited from his grandma—eighteenth century 'e said it was—that 'ad gone, too.'

'You're sure of that, Gracie?' her mother-in-law asked, and when Grace nodded, she said, 'Must be thieves then. No doubt from out of the village. Rascals who'd heard about Treeve's death and decided to try their luck.'

'But how did they get in? I were careful to lock up. Archie you were there and Nancy, too.'

Archie nodded agreement. 'You can't worry about it, Gracie. If necessary, I'll testify you locked the doors. In the meantime, if someone's broken in, it's hardly your fault.'

'But I'll be blamed, don't you see? I'm the one with a key. The only one.'

Nancy was about to say she believed that Kitty Anson had a key, too, but decided against.

'And there were no sign of a break-in as far as I could see,' Grace went on. 'Do you think I should go to the police?'

'You could tell Aiden, I s'pose. He's our local bobby,' Morwenna explained to Nancy. 'But I can't see him doin' much. Who's goin' to know the stuff is missin' anyways?'

'Treeve's beneficiaries,' Archie remarked laconically. 'Whoever they are.'

'I don't think he 'ad any.' Grace clasped her hands together in a tight knot.

'Well then, the whole of his estate will go to the Crown and the Queen isn't going to be too worried about a carriage clock and a porcelain bowl.'

Nancy could see that Archie was trying to make light of it. For Grace's sake, she presumed, but she knew him well enough to know that he would be concerned. Coming after the events of the last two days, it was another part of an increasingly complex puzzle. An increasingly nasty puzzle.

'I hope you're right.' Grace jumped up from the settee. 'Sorry, I gotta go. The girls will be out of school soon. I'll bring 'em for tea tomorrow, Ma, if that's okay?'

Morwenna smiled. 'I'll bake 'em a heavy cake. Your Susie loves a slice of that.'

At the door, Grace gave a smile and a wave. 'Hope to see you again soon, Nancy.'

Nancy put down her cup and saucer, making ready to follow her. There was warmth in being among such a close family, but hurt, too, emphasising as it did how alone she'd felt for so much of her life. Her parents had fed, clothed, sheltered her, tried to guide her, she supposed, but she had never felt truly loved. They had been older parents, ill-equipped to cope with a small baby, even more so a baby who, for them, had been the wrong sex. That was something the Nicholsons seemed unable to forgive.

Morwenna began to clear the tea things. 'Would you like to see the book your lovely husband gave me?' she asked.

'Nancy has seen the book, Ma. She was with Leo when he bought it.'

'Of course she was. Silly of me. How did you like Venice, my luv?'

This was perilous territory and Nancy was aware of a stiffening in Archie's figure. 'It's a beautiful city,' she said. A dangerous one, too, as both of them could testify.

'Nancy has to get going,' Archie said firmly, taking his cup and saucer to the sink. 'Leo will be back from the hospital by now and he'll have news of his father.'

'You'd better go then. But come and see me again. Promise now!'

Nancy allowed herself to be enfolded in Morwenna's ample bosom. The woman was so full of kindliness, of goodwill. How lucky Archie was to have such a mother.

They had neared the front door when it was pushed violently open and a dishevelled figure fell over the threshold, almost cannoning into them.

'They're goin' to do it,' the man spluttered.

'Come in, Clem. Don't stand there loiterin',' Morwenna said. 'Goin' to do what?'

'The mine. Extend it fer miles. I 'eard it today. They'll be ruinin' me. My pots'll be disturbed. That'll be the end of crab n' lobster.'

'Never say that.'

'I do say it. It's rotten. Port Madron's rotten. I warned Perran Tremayne if 'e goes ahead with drillin' any further, 'e'll be sorry. Somethin' bad'll 'appen, mark my word.'

The man pushed roughly past them and slumped into one

of the easy chairs. 'A cuppa wouldn't go amiss, Morwenna.'

'Where's your manners, Clem?' Morwenna scolded. 'This is Clem Hoskins, Nancy. He fishes round the shore—crab and lobster mainly.'

'Clem—' Morwenna said. Reluctantly, the man got to his feet. 'This is Mrs Tremayne, Mr Leo's new wife. Well, nearly new wife.'

Hoskins lumbered over to Nancy, still standing by the door, with Archie a few paces behind her. 'Well, we were talkin' of somethin' rotten and 'ere it is right in front of me.' He towered over her, an ugly sneer on his face, and Nancy felt herself blench. She didn't even know this man, yet evidently he hated her.

She sensed Archie move up beside her. 'Watch your mouth, Clem,' he said in an even voice.

'Watch me mouth, must I? You're just as bad, Jago. Cosyin' up to the Tremaynes. Goin' on fancy trips with your man and his fancy woman.'

It was the spark that lit Archie's anger. Stepping forward abruptly, he grabbed the man by the collar, pulling him upwards until Hoskins' face was level with his own. 'Button your lip, you tuss, or I'll button it for you.'

'Hush, Archie.' Morwenna sounded distressed. 'There's no need for that. I'm sure Clem meant no real harm.'

'He meant harm all right, Ma.' Then turning to the unfortunate Hoskins, still held in a vicious grip, he spat out, 'Mrs Tremayne has nothing to do with you, Hoskins. Got it? Nothing whatsoever.' He let the man go, Clem subsiding into a heap on the settee.

Nancy's heart was beating too fast. It had been a bewildering scene as well as an ugly one and all she wanted to do was walk through the front door and breathe fresh air again. But she was concerned for Archie's mother. Then she caught sight of Morwenna's face and saw sudden illumination in the woman's eyes. Nancy's stomach gave an uncomfortable flip. She knows how Archie feels. What mother doesn't know her son?

'Come on,' Archie said sharply. 'I'll drive you up to Penleven.'

Chapter Twelve

'Alright?' Archie asked when they were outside and walking to the car. He was sounding more Cornish by the minute.

Nancy took a deep breath. 'I think so,' she lied.

She wasn't right at all. The dreadful panic at the hospital was still vivid in a mind already haunted by thoughts of a missing cardigan and a portrait torn into pieces. Now to add to her fears, she had been verbally attacked by a man she'd never even seen before.

But she must pretend and, at the car door, she stopped and looked across at Archie. 'Could we call at the village stores before we make for Penleven? Kitty Anson is cooking dinner tonight and I thought I'd check to see if I can help take anything up to the house. That's if Perry hasn't already rung and cancelled. I guess it will depend on Leo's news from the hospital.'

'Fine.' Archie gave one of his expressive shrugs. 'We'll stop there.'

She slipped into the seat beside him, comforted by his warmth, his solidity. The encounter with Clem Hoskins had been a frightening incident, coming out of nowhere. For a small place, Port Madron appeared to be seething with discontent, most of it centred on the Tremayne family.

'That man, Hoskins—' she began.

'You don't want to worry about him.' Archie's voice was rough. 'He's a bad-tempered bugger. Teasy as 'n adder, we'd say. But weak, too.'

'He didn't sound too weak,' she ventured.

'That's because he thought he had a soft target.' There was a pause before Archie added, 'If he really knew you, he'd have scarpered so quickly, we'd have seen only dust.'

Nancy gave a sad smile. 'People here don't seem too happy.'

'Do you blame them? The mine is under threat and everyone knows it. And the fishing is piss poor.'

'Hoskins seems to blame the Tremaynes for his woes.'

'It's a good cop-out, isn't it? The mine is extended—if it is—and his pots don't bring in as much income as he wants. So, he puts the two together and blames the family, when the reality is that he's not a great fisherman.'

'Could Hoskins be behind what happened to Treeve, do you think? Mr Fenton wasn't a Tremayne, but he was closely associated with the family.'

Then there was what had happened today, to Ned himself. The hospital was still investigating—it could have been an accident—but Nancy's heart told her it was almost certainly an act of deliberate harm.

'Clem is too limp for that. He's not a man of action. Whining is more his forte.'

Archie sounded contemptuous, so sure that Clem Hoskins could never be a threat. Nancy was unconvinced. Had the man been too limp to creep into the Penleven summerhouse, she wondered, steal her cardigan and reduce Leo's portrait to pieces? Had he been too limp to send threatening messages to Ned and Treeve? None of it had required too much bravado.

'Would Mr Hoskins be more likely to write anonymous

letters?' she asked.

'I doubt Clem can even write,' was her companion's laconic answer.

He might scoff at the idea of Hoskins as a villain, but Nancy wouldn't easily forget the man's anger, or his evident hatred of the Tremaynes.

In a few minutes, Archie had brought the car to a halt outside the village shop. Nancy went to climb out, but with a light touch, he detained her. 'No point in going.' He nodded towards the shuttered window. 'The shop's closed.'

She was surprised, but then reasoned that Kitty could be busy cooking for tonight and had shut up the store to spare herself interruptions.

'I'll try the bell—in case she's upstairs in the kitchen. I'd like to be some help, if I can.'

But when Nancy rang, she heard the bell clanging through empty space. She tried several times with the same result and returned to the car, puzzled. 'I hope nothing bad has happened.'

'Kitty will be somewhere around,' Archie said. 'Penleven then?'

She hesitated. 'Yes, I suppose so.'

'What's the matter?'

As so often, Archie had tuned into her discomfort. 'I don't like being there alone,' she confessed. 'Not after yesterday.'

'Think sensibly, Nancy.' He twisted in his seat and took her by the shoulders. She felt his warmth coursing through her body. 'I know you're wondering if this Philip March character has shown up again, but how could he? He doesn't even know you're married, let alone who your husband is, or where Leo lives. Not to mention where you might be at the moment. It's a coincidence that the same kind of things are happening to you here as happened before. Someone is clearly playing games. Maybe the same someone who lifted those items from Treeve Fenton's living room. But someone from this area, not your stalker.'

Nancy wished she could believe him. She would rather the perpetrator be Clem Hoskins than have her old nightmare return. 'You better drive me back,' she said, trying to sound confident.

'Perry should be home by now.' He was trying to reassure her, she knew. 'Leo will have rung him at the mine, and he won't have stayed working if he knows his father is in danger.'

'He might have gone to Truro. Joined Leo at the hospital,' she suggested.

'If he has, I'll stick around until one or other of them gets back.'

Nancy took his hand and squeezed it. She shouldn't touch him, shouldn't get this close. But it was hard to keep her distance from a man with whom, for all his faults, she felt so completely at ease.

To cover the awkward moment, she said, 'Do you think Ned will be okay?'

'I've no idea. None of us have. It's in the lap of the gods.'

'There's this dinner party tonight to worry about as well. What on earth am I to do about it? Mr Silva will be here in two hours. I don't know if Perry will want to go ahead and I can't get in touch with Kitty to warn her that all her hard work might be for nothing.'

'Then you'll just have to wait and see.'

When she climbed out of the car at Penleven, though, Perry appeared almost instantly, leaving the front door ajar and rushing towards her, his arms outstretched.

'Nancy! Good news! Dad is going to be okay. Leo has just phoned to say the docs are satisfied that he's stable again. It's put his recovery back a little but he's in no immediate danger.'

'Thank goodness.' Nancy kissed her brother-in-law on the cheek. 'You must be so relieved.'

Archie had followed her out of the car, but at Perry's news he got back into the driving seat. 'I'll be off then,' he said, through the open window. 'Leo can let me know when he wants me tomorrow.'

'I'll tell him,' Perry said, waving a goodbye as the car sped down the driveway on its way back to the village.

'That call was a huge relief, Nancy.' He took her arm and walked with her into the house. 'Such a terrible shock when Leo phoned to tell me Dad had had a seizure! I was at Wheal Agnes, trying to sort out tomorrow's rota but came straight home. I've been waiting for another call ever since. It seems like hours. I'd almost given up and was about to set off for the hospital.'

He closed the front door behind them. 'I thought I'd find you here when I got back,' he added.

'How were things at the mine?' She was reluctant to tell Perry where she'd been. Her visit to Archie's home was something she wanted to keep to herself.

'No major confrontation today, but Jory Pascoe's still making trouble. Not in person this time. He simply didn't turn up which left his shift short-handed. He's bought some wreck of a car, I'm told, so perhaps he's on a scenic tour of the county.' Perry tried to joke, but his face was serious. 'The man could be sick, or he's walked out of the job. The latter, I hope, but none of his mates seem to know his whereabouts, and I'm in the dark—and very short-staffed. A few of the men have called in sick and tomorrow's team is patchy, to say the least.'

Perry's words landed in Nancy's mind with a thud. Jory Pascoe had been absent from work. Was he ill in bed as Perry suggested? His wife would surely have called at the mine to report his sickness, since unexplained absence could mean Pascoe losing his job. If not ill, then where was he? At the hospital switching drips? But that wasn't yet proved. And how would he do it anyway?

You're being fanciful, she told herself, and to distract her mind from the pointless circling, she said, 'I'm presuming the dinner party will go ahead?'

Perry looked surprised. 'It has to, Nancy. But, of course, you wouldn't know. Silva rang me from Dorchester. They'd stopped to eat lunch, but his driver reckoned he'd be in Port Madron around seven o'clock this evening. I've offered the chap a room for the night. I didn't think the Tinners would be quite his taste. And thank heaven I managed to get hold of Mrs Cheffers. She was just leaving for a day out in Truro, but as a special concession—and a special price—she cancelled and came in to clean the spare room and make up the bed.'

The mention of Mrs Cheffers reminded Nancy that Kitty Anson had disappeared. On a day out, too? Not wanting to alarm her brother-in-law and add to his worries, Nancy said cautiously, 'Do we need to do anything for the meal? I haven't seen Kitty today.'

'She dropped some soup in earlier. The pot was on the doorstep when I got back from the mine. I'm hoping she'll be here very soon. I guess the main course needs starting.'

As if on cue, a small battered van turned into the driveway and together they peered hopefully through the window. Kitty! Thank the Lord, was Nancy's thought.

***

Leo had still not returned from the hospital when Nancy went upstairs to bathe and change. She had helped Kitty chop and slice vegetables and, with Perry's approval, set the table as elegantly as she could, polishing the crystal glasses and silver cutlery until they gleamed. The dining room itself was a bleak space, facing north and little used—Perry and his father, Nancy assumed, must always eat in the kitchen. She would have liked to make the room more welcoming but short of shaking the rather shabby rugs that covered the polished wood floor and dusting down the leather dining chairs, there was little she could do. A large bouquet of flowers would have helped, and she was annoyed that she hadn't thought of it, but the garden at this time of the year was bereft and where in the village would she have found flowers?

She mounted the stairs to her bedroom, already wanting the evening over and hoping that Leo's long absence didn't signify that Ned Tremayne had taken a turn for the worst. But when, some time later, she came out of the bathroom, it was to see her husband lying full length on the bed.

He smiled at her, stretching his arms above his head. 'After a day like that, the last thing I want is to be entertaining some Brazilian money man.'

'I know,' she said sympathetically, 'but we must do it for Perry.' She wrapped her dressing gown around her and plumped down on the bed. 'How did you leave your father? Perry said he was stable again.'

'Stable, but a lot weaker. He was making good progress, too. I'd like to …'

She turned to face him. It was unusual to hear Leo sound so bitter. 'Like to what?'

'There's something going on, Nancy. I wasn't going to mention it because I know you'll be like a dog after a rabbit, but some bastard tried to hurt Dad today, I'm convinced.'

It shocked her to hear Leo swear, and shocked her even more to hear him admit that something bad was happening. He always refused to accept there was darkness in the world, when to Nancy it was plain.

She moved closer to him. 'The faulty drip wasn't an accident then?'

'Did you think it was?'

Nancy shook her head. 'But then I have a suspicious mind. I like to poke around—that's what you say, isn't it?' It was how Leo described her compulsion to find the truth and it wasn't intended as a compliment.

'In this case, I think you might be right.' He gave a long sigh and sat up, putting his arm around her. 'The hospital was tight-lipped about the whole incident, but I got it out of one of the porters. He must have overheard the doctors talking. Apparently when they looked more closely, there were small puncture marks on the rubber seals—made by a syringe in all probability—where a foreign substance could have been introduced. They've told me nothing so far, but when they confirm details, I'll make sure it's referred to the police.'

She clasped his arm, stroking the soft cotton of his shirt sleeve. 'How very dreadful! Do they have any idea—'

'Who would want to hurt my father? None.' Leo's shoulders slumped. 'He could have died, Nancy. He very nearly did. Is that what this person wanted?' He sounded despairing. 'Who could hate Ned Tremayne so much they would risk arrest for attempted murder?'

She touched his cheek and felt it damp with half-shed tears.

'I've no idea, but I'm going to find out.'

Instantly, he shook himself free. 'You'll do no such thing!'

'But Leo,' she protested, 'someone is hurting your family. Your family's friends, too. We have to stop them.'

'*We* don't have to do anything, Nancy. The hospital will discover what has gone on and make a report to the police. It's their job then to investigate.'

'It won't happen,' Nancy said with conviction. 'The

hospital won't welcome a police investigation—they won't want the upheaval. It's to their benefit to decide it was an accident. They'll come out with all the stuff about making sure it never happens again, but they won't involve the police. Unless we do something.'

Leo grabbed her hand and held it so tightly it hurt. 'Listen to me! Under no circumstances are you to start the poking and prying that leads to trouble. I've had enough of that and I would have thought you had, too. If I'm right in my suspicions, the police will deal with it.'

His face was stern, his figure unbending, and Nancy felt like a chastened schoolgirl. Leo couldn't be more mistaken, she thought, but he'd never agree with her. Even after he'd judged disastrously in Venice and been wrong, too, in Malfuego, he still believed he knew best.

But Nancy knew otherwise.

Chapter Thirteen

An hour later, she was being introduced to Senhor Silva and, contrary to expectation, she found she liked him. His bright blue eyes reminded her of Archie and perhaps that was the reason she took to the man straightaway. But he had an open face and his grip, when he shook her hand, was firm. He seemed delighted to be at Penleven and to meet the family with whom he'd been negotiating, albeit from a distance.

His henchman, though, was another matter.

'Let me introduce my most trusted assistant,' Senhor Silva said in excellent English. 'Tomas Almeda. But you will already know him well, Mr Tremayne.' Francisco Silva gave Perry a clap on the shoulder.

The man he'd introduced was short and dark with a small forehead and a thick head of hair that fell so far forward that his eyes seemed in perpetual shadow. With a guarded smile, Nancy held out her hand, but Almeda's only response was a slight downwards movement of his mouth.

As soon as she could, she left the men talking business and went swiftly to the kitchen where a pink-faced Kitty was ladling soup into beautiful art deco bowls. They must have been Rachel Tremayne's choice, Nancy guessed, and still pristine from lack of use.

'Do you think this is okay?' Kitty asked. 'Serving it here?'

'I think it's brilliant,' Nancy said thankfully. 'Otherwise I'd be the one ladling and that could be disastrous.'

Kitty grinned. 'Good,' she said. 'Then let's get this show on the road. Chivvy them into the dining room and I'll load these bowls onto a tray—I found the largest one you can imagine on top of the china cupboard. I only hope I can carry it!'

Nancy looked at the woman's substantial arms and felt confident that the soup would arrive at the table in one piece.

For the next hour or so, she dashed back and forth to the kitchen, removing dirty dishes with each course, whipping out fresh plates warming in the Aga, loading and unloading serving dishes on the enormous tray, while Kitty calmly put the finishing touches to a magnificent meal of whole baked sea bream with scalloped potatoes, green beans, pea and mint relish and creamed spinach.

Meanwhile Perry assiduously filled wine glasses, the company growing louder and jollier by the minute, until once the dessert had been cleared—a towering baked Alaska— even Tomas Almeda managed a faint smile.

When Nancy returned from carrying coffee and a plate of chocolate mints to the sitting room—a far more congenial space—Kitty had already begun the washing up.

'Stop that,' she ordered. 'You've been superb, Kitty, and it's time you went home. Leo and I can tidy the kitchen once Mr Silva has gone to bed and his horrible henchman sloped back to the Tinners.'

'You don't like the little chap?'

'Let's say he doesn't appeal to me.'

Kitty untied her pinafore and tucked it into her bag. 'He reminds me of a mole,' she said, walking to the door. 'Be careful he doesn't burrow too deeply.'

Nancy blinked at the cryptic comment, but decided to ignore it. 'I'll bring the serving dishes back tomorrow,' she told her.

'There's no hurry—I won't be using them any time soon. Come when you can.'

Back in the sitting room, the chocolate mints had almost disappeared and Perry was pouring a second round of coffee.

'We have hardly seen you, Mrs Tremayne,' Francisco said. 'You have been so busy. What a magnificent meal.'

'I can't claim credit for that,' Nancy said.

'You have arranged it all and it was most delightful. Now, tell me, are you often in Cornwall? From what I have seen, it is a most beautiful county.'

'It is,' she agreed, 'but our home is in London. It's quite a distance to travel and Leo works abroad a great deal, so we don't get to visit that often.'

Nancy always felt awkward when asked how much time she spent in Cornwall. She was a reluctant visitor, dragging her feet whenever the possibility of travelling to Penleven was mentioned.

'And such a wonderful drive,' Francisco Silva went on. 'From Dorset—it is Dorset?—the sun shone on us. Tomas tells me that you that you have sun for some days now, but I am hoping for more. Tomorrow I make a visit to the mine. It's true that we will be underground for most of the day, but still it will be good to see blue sky when we emerge.'

'Before you leave, I hope you'll have time to enjoy the countryside,' Nancy said politely. 'I take it you've never visited before?'

Francisco laughed. 'It would be difficult, don't you think? Brazil is a little far for a day trip, no?'

'I was surprised you had even heard of Cornwall when you live so far away.'

'Anyone who mines the tin has heard of Cornwall, Mrs Tremayne. Once upon a time this area was the most important producer in the whole world.'

'Though not now,' Leo interjected.

Was her husband hoping for a clue as to what was driving this man to buy Wheal Agnes? Nancy would like to know herself. She was sure there had to be some hidden motive, and Almeda's scowl suggested she was right.

'What you say is true. Mining has fallen on sad times. But it does not have to be so. It could once again be the very best, could it not Perry? With the right energy, the right equipment, the right people.'

'And a great deal of money,' Leo said.

'Yes, that is so. And I have it.' Senhor Silva's smile was angelic.

'And you want to spend it on the Tremayne mine?' Nancy couldn't stop herself asking the question and sounding incredulous at the same time.

'It is my dearest wish,' Francisco said. 'I believe there is only one other working tin mine in Cornwall, so if I want to make this industry great again, this is where I must start.'

He seemed sincere, she thought. Misguided perhaps, but sincere. It was an honest ambition that he held, and she was glad she had liked him from the outset. Perhaps selling Wheal Agnes might after all be the best thing Perry could do, as long as Mr Silva could be persuaded to take on the Port Madron miners as his workforce. She thought he might—he appeared a genuinely decent person. But then she looked at the man sitting to his right. Almeda's face wore a heavy frown, his dominant brow making him look more like an angry chimp than the mole Kitty had called him.

He doesn't like the idea of buying the mine, Nancy thought. Or if he does, he'll want it for a rock bottom price, with any local men taken on paid subsistence wages. Pure speculation, she recognised, but nevertheless she felt it strongly.

'If you're happy, Francisco, we'll leave for the mine early,' Perry said. 'Catch the morning shift before they start work.'

'Mr Tremayne, you think it a good thing that these men know why we are here?'

This was beetle-brow as Nancy had christened him in her mind. He seemed to have as good a grasp of English as his employer, yet Perry had spoken of language difficulties between them. Why would that be? Deliberate deception on Almeda's part?

Perry looked taken aback by the man's remark and Mr Silva was swift to intervene. 'It is right they know that a sale may happen and if it does, I will be the "boss".' He beamed his smile around the group, then spread his hands in a supplicating gesture. 'It is their future, Tomas, is it not?'

'I'll introduce you as a visitor from South America,' her brother-in-law was quick to say. 'Someone who's interested in the way we mine. I don't think it's the right time to mention a possible sale. I hope you agree, Francisco.' It was clear that for Perry things were moving too swiftly.

'My friend, I am at your disposal. If you do not wish to speak of it, my lips are closed.'

'And you, Mr Almeda?' Perry was being unusually forceful, Nancy thought.

Beetle-brow merely grunted, and she had a fair idea that the man had already spread rumours of a sale around the village.

'Have you met any of the miners, Mr Almeda?' she asked innocently. 'You've been in Port Madron for quite a while now.' She was rewarded with another grunt.

'He will meet them tomorrow.' Mr Silva gave her a warm smile. 'And I will be with him.'

***

Archie had found a sheltered corner in the Tinners Arms and sat nursing a pint of beer while he waited for his eldest brother. He'd come directly from dropping Leo off at Penleven, his second trip to the Truro hospital that day. It looked as though Ned Tremayne was going to pull through despite the panic his seizure had caused. Archie hadn't gathered much from his boss on the journey back—Leo had been tight-lipped and evidently feeling the strain from what had been a tumultuous day. But it was clear that something untoward had happened. Since when could pumping the wrong stuff into a very sick patient be an accident?

Archie had suspected the Tremaynes were in some kind of trouble from the moment his employer had woken him in the middle of the night and demanded he find an aircraft at short notice. Yes, Leo's father was an ill man, but his boss's agitation had been extreme and instinctively he'd known there was something else, some other trouble that Leo wasn't telling. Archie was still to discover what it could be—village gossip hadn't been as helpful as he'd thought. Treeve Fenton seemed to be part of it and now Ned himself. Something to do with Wheal Agnes, Archie was sure. No doubt with Nancy on the case, he'd soon know a lot more.

His smile went a little awry. He'd hoped that whatever trouble there was in Port Madron would pass her by, but no such luck. Especially after her encounter with Clem Hoskins this afternoon. It had felt strange seeing her in his old home— he hadn't a clue why he'd invited her to come back with him. Perhaps because she'd looked so shaken after that desperate scene in the hospital? But though strange, it had felt right. She'd fitted in to his mother's kitchen as though she'd lived there forever. In London, Nancy seemed always to perch. Never quite belonging. Never quite permanent.

He drank up and went to the bar for a second beer. Rich

was late but he wasn't too worried. His brother would turn up eventually. He'd have his men to pay this evening after two days at sea and he'd need at least to say hello to his wife and daughters. Probably to Ma as well.

As he was delving into his pocket for change, he felt a tap on his shoulder and, turning, saw Rich's wide grin. 'Wasson, Arch. Sorry, I'm a bit late. Stuff to do.'

'I reckoned that. Good to see you.' He gave his brother a slap on the back.

'So what's goin' on with you?' Rich asked him, when they'd settled back into Archie's corner. 'I heard from Ma you flew a plane down 'ere.' He laughed aloud. 'My little brother flyin' a plane, eh?'

Archie grimaced. 'I'm likely to have to fly it back sometime, too.'

'Your boss not goin' back to Lunnun then?'

'He will, but he'll take the train. And not until his father is more stable.'

Rich took a long draught of his beer. 'I heard old Tremayne was doin' okay. Isn't that right?'

'He seemed to be doing well, but there was some trouble at the hospital today and it's put his recovery back. So... I'm likely to be here for a while longer.'

'I know someone who'll be pleased with that. Ma never stops talkin' about you makin' a visit.'

'How is Ma, Rich? I can't get a truthful answer from her.'

'She's doin' fine. Gracie keeps an eye on 'er when I'm not around. But the old lady's been missin' Lowen these last few months. You're a bonus.'

Archie leaned forward. 'But the problem with her heart?'

'Seems to have settled.' Rich gave him a friendly tap on the arm. 'You can't worry, Archie. Your life's elsewhere now. And thank God for that.'

'I take it the fishing is still bad?'

'Diabolical. Two days out and all we 'ad to show fer it were some pilchards I dropped off at Newlyn, a miserable few bass, not much more mackerel, and pollack. And pollack don' get a decent price, you know that. If Grace didn't work, we'd be buggered.' Rich scowled. 'I hate she has to go cleanin' but there's nothin' else.' He began twisting his tankard in his hands. 'Port Madron don' 'ave a future, that's the truth. Think of my little maids. What future 'ave they got 'ere?'

'Linda's only what? Ten? Plenty of time for things to get better.'

'Eleven. Goin' to school in Truro come the autumn,' Rich said proudly, his gloom temporarily lifting. 'But now Gracie's lost the job with Treeve, she's goin' to have to look fer another.'

Archie waited for his brother to mention the items missing from Fenton's house, but Rich said nothing. Grace had evidently decided to keep her worries to herself—at least for the moment.

'Did Gracie work a lot for Treeve Fenton then?' he asked.

'Most days she were there. Kept the place spotless. But poor old Treeve. That's a strange 'un. Gracie reckons there's been some malarky about his death, but I dunno. He was an old chap.'

'Not that old and pretty fit by all accounts.'

'The police are 'appy. Best not to rake over what can't be changed. There's enough trouble in the village as 'tis.'

Archie looked across at his brother, his expression serious. 'Jory Pascoe, you mean?'

'The man's a shit-stirrer if ever I saw 'un. I'll tell 'e what, 'e came creepin' round me just before I sailed, arskin' for work. And after 'e's been blackballed by every skipper in the district. I was fair jumpin'.'

Archie looked surprised. 'He's given up mining?'

'Seems like. But not till after 'e's caused trouble there, too. How's Mr Perran copin' with it all?'

'I haven't spoken to him properly since I got here. There's a dinner going on at Penleven right now. They're entertaining some foreign bloke who's interested in Wheal Agnes. His sidekick is staying here in the pub.'

'You mean the little short bloke?'

'Probably. I haven't met him.'

His brother whistled. 'Looks like the Tremaynes are goin' to sell the mine.'

'It's not definite and for God's sake, Rich, don't say anything. The village is awash with rumours already.'

His brother shook his head. 'It'll be a sad day if that mine goes foreign. There are men workin' at Agnes that 'ave been there all their lives. I thought the plan was to dig further out. Pascoe's been shoutin' about it. Saying it were dangerous, though I dunno if that's true. Probably not, knowin' 'im'.

Archie gave a characteristic shrug. 'Who knows what's going on?'

'That young lady must.' Rich looked slyly across at his brother. 'What's 'er name? Nancy? Fancy Nancy!'

Archie glared across the table at him. Ma had evidently been talking to her daughter-in-law, imagining stuff that wasn't true. He'd known she wouldn't be able to resist. But he could trust his brother. Rich wasn't one to spread stories. But Grace?

Seeming to sense Archie's annoyance, Rich changed tack. 'Ma said that Clem Hoskins came on strong to the poor maid.'

'Hoskins is a tuss.'

'He's got a point, though,' Rich said mildly. 'With the Tremaynes at least. If they extend Wheal Agnes like Pascoe says they will, it could bugger up Clem's livelihood.'

'Then he'd be compensated,' Archie said abruptly, half rising from his seat. 'Do you want another?' He gestured to his brother's almost empty glass.

'Best not. Gracie is waitin' fer me.'

Archie sank back onto the settle. 'Hoskins will get more if he's compensated than he'll ever make fishing.'

Rich nodded. 'He's pretty 'opeless,' he agreed. 'But this Nancy –?'

He never finished his question. A loud noise had both brothers jump up from their seats and look towards the bar where a heated altercation had broken out.

'That's Pascoe,' Rich said, peering across the room.

Jory Pascoe was poking his finger into the chest of an older man and shouting into his face. 'You're a lackey, tha's what you are. A lackey to the Tremaynes,' he bawled. His victim tried to take a step back but cannoned into the bar's wooden counter.

'What's 'e doin'?' Rich asked. 'There's no more 'armless man in the village than Tallack.'

'Tallack probably dared to defend the Tremaynes. For Pascoe, that's a red flag.'

'Should we stop it, do you think?' But before Rich could make any move, a younger man had stepped between the two antagonists.

'That's enough, Jory,' he said. 'Tallack's done nuthin' wrong. Leave him be.'

Pascoe turned on him, his face blotched with rage. 'Done nuthin' wrong! 'e works for a c'rrupt family tha's what. A c'rrupt family,' he repeated, slurring his words. 'And 'e don' just work—'e defends 'em. 'e needs a poke in the eye.'

'Well, you're not givin' 'im one,' the young man said. 'Go 'ome and sober up.'

'Who sez?' Pascoe swayed dangerously forward, then

regained his balance.

'I do.' Tallack's defender straightened his shoulders and rolled up his sleeves.

'You're a tuss, tha's what you are. I could scat you down.'

Despite his words, Jory's wish to fight seemed to have waned. He took one last swig from his glass, then smashed it against the counter. Fragments of glass scattered across the floor in a wide circle and the men who'd been quietly drinking at the bar made haste to move back.

'Phone the police,' someone called out to the landlord.

The young man who had defended Tallack bent to pick up the larger pieces of glass and Pascoe, still swaying, leaned forward and punched him on the back of the neck, sending his adversary flying. Then bending down himself, he picked up a large shard of glass and, to the horror of his onlookers, drew it across his arm. Blood gushed from the wound and began dripping onto the bare floorboards.

'I bleed, d'you see. I bleed,' he shouted incoherently and staggered to the door just as the publican lifted the telephone.

Chapter Fourteen

Nancy woke with a start. There was something tickling her cheek. When she turned over, it was to see Leo smiling down at her, his fingers gently stroking the side of her face.

'Come on, sleepyhead. It's past nine o'clock.'

She pulled herself upright, bunching the sheets around her. 'Mr Silva. Breakfast,' she said, sounding aghast.

Leo climbed onto the bed beside her. 'There's no panic—Perry did the honours, though it was simple enough. Our friend, Francisco, looked distinctly green when confronted with cornflakes. Instead, he drank three cups of what I'm afraid was mediocre coffee, then said he was fit to go.'

'They've both left for the mine?'

'About ten minutes ago.'

'You should have woken me earlier.' Nancy pushed long strands of hair behind her ears and tried to force her eyes open.

'You were tired, sweetheart. You were the one doing most of the running around last night—apart from Kitty—and *you* were late to bed.'

It had been past midnight before Nancy had cleaned the kitchen to her satisfaction and crawled up the stairs. Even then she had found it difficult to sleep, replaying the evening in her mind several times over. Her feelings about it were decidedly mixed. While Francisco Silva appeared genuine, Nancy had serious doubts about his assistant, yet Silva appeared to trust Tomas Almeda completely. It was an uncomfortable paradox. At least Almeda had left for the Tinners reasonably early, refusing Perry's offer to walk with him to the village or to lend him a torch. A torch was something he wouldn't need, she thought tartly. Almeda was a man of darkness.

She threw back the covers, submerging Leo beneath a flurry of bedclothes. 'I must get up. I promised Kitty Anson I'd return her serving dishes. She said it wasn't urgent, but it's possible she'll need them sooner than she thinks.'

Leo extricated himself from the swathes of linen and swung his legs off the bed. 'Will you want help carrying them to the village?' He sounded hesitant. 'If not, I've work to do. I'd planned to get on with a paper I need to write.'

Nancy looked blank.

'The conference at St Martins,' he reminded her. 'If I could knock it on the head in the next day or two, Archie might be able to dig up a typewriter from somewhere. It's a cursed nuisance—the conference is scheduled for early next month. I'd expected to be back in London in good time for it, but with Dad being so poorly...'

'You must get on with your work, Leo. I'll be fine.'

Yesterday's near disaster was affecting them both. It had certainly played a part in her restless night. Could a rogue medic have been responsible for that poisoned drip? It hadn't taken her long to dismiss the idea as highly unlikely, and become convinced that someone was out there who hated Ned Tremayne enough to deliberately injure him or worse. Hated him enough to devise a complicated plot that could easily have led to the perpetrator's immediate arrest. While Leo slept, her mind had leafed through the names she knew, searching Port Madron for the person responsible for her father-in-law's seizure.

After Clem Hoskins' outburst yesterday, he filled the role of prime suspect very neatly. If he could rant at Nancy, a Tremayne by marriage, in the way he had, he was surely capable of hurting a true member of the family. But how could he have done it?

He would have to find transport to Truro—it was too far to cycle—walk into the hospital, presumably as a visitor, and visiting hours were limited, then find his way into Ned's room, undetected. If the medical staff were engaged elsewhere and Ned himself asleep, it might be possible. But once in the room, Hoskins would need to have with him a drug that was certain to poison the drip. More than that, he'd have to know how to administer it. Holes, Leo had said. Small puncture holes made by a syringe. How would Hoskins find a syringe? How administer it without Ned being aware he was in the room, and pressing the alarm button?

Leo was looking quizzically at her. 'Sorry,' she said. 'I was daydreaming. I better wash.'

'I'll see you downstairs then.'

Nancy conjured up a smile as best she could, though her mind was full to bursting and, standing beneath the hot shower a few minutes later, she went on thinking. And thinking. Pascoe was a more likely suspect, she decided. Crucially, he'd not been at work yesterday *and* he had a car— Perry had half joked about the man's earlier absence: that it might be due to his taking the day off for a scenic tour of the countryside. And Jory Pascoe hated the Tremaynes as much if not more than Hoskins. But it wasn't enough. She still faced explaining the poisonous drug, the syringe, the opportunity to commit murder.

Her husband had already started work when she arrived

downstairs, his books spread across the dining room table and a heap of papers by his side.

'A cup of tea?' she offered.

'Not just now, darling. I need to get on. I have to go back to the hospital later.'

Nancy heard the beginnings of irritation in his voice and backed out of the room. Sitting alone at the kitchen table with a cup of tea and a slice of toast, she gazed through the window at a lowering sky. Despite Leo's love for Penleven, she found it difficult to like the house. No doubt it had felt very different in Rachel Tremayne's day, but Nancy had never found the place welcoming. Even less so this morning. All trace of yesterday's beautiful weather had vanished and a sky of several hues of grey meant that little natural light permeated the kitchen.

She would go outside. Take a walk to the village. Fresh air would make her feel brighter. First, though, she must make an important call. It was a perfect time to telephone—Leo was immersed in his work and oblivious to anything she was doing.

Nancy had rung her mentor at the studio the morning they'd left London, apologising for the very early hour, but explaining that her father-in-law had suffered a major heart attack and she was needed in Cornwall. She had dreaded asking for time away from a job in which she was still relatively new, and when there was a mountain of work waiting for her. But Connie had been amazingly understanding and Nancy would have liked to hug her over the telephone. Now, though, she had to ring again, this time to tell her mentor that Ned had suffered a setback and she wouldn't be returning as soon as she'd hoped.

She went upstairs to fetch the small notebook in which she kept important telephone numbers, certain she had left it on the bedside table. It wasn't there. In her handbag perhaps? Though why she'd decided to carry it with her, she couldn't remember. But the notebook wasn't in the bag or in the second handbag she'd brought from London, still packed away in her suitcase. Nor in any of the drawers of the bedroom chest.

Perplexed, Nancy retraced her steps. Had she taken it into the sitting-room? A quick search proved unsatisfactory and, walking back to the kitchen, she was about to give up when she noticed the lid of the flour bin sitting slightly askew. She hadn't used flour in any of the cooking she'd done and Mrs Cheffers, who yesterday had made a rudimentary attempt to clean, was unlikely to have been so thorough that she'd removed the lids of storage canisters.

Nancy experienced an odd sensation. As she walked across the room, it was as though she'd fallen into a dream, her legs seeming to move in slow motion, her hand making a lazy arc before it landed on the half-open lid. It was as though she knew already what she would find. She had been here before. Not in this kitchen. Not at Penleven. But in her old London bedsitting room—the one Philip March had violated. She peered inside the bin and there it was. Her notebook and the pen Concetta had given her as a farewell present from Venice.

Feeling nauseous, she pulled the book from its hiding place, dusting the flour from its cover, then fished out the pen, now rendered useless. Her legs were too shaky to do more than slump into a chair, the phone call forgotten. She sat for a long time, staring into space, waiting for her pulse to return to normal. How could this be happening again? Surely, it couldn't. But it was, and the knowledge that once more someone had her in their sights—was trying again to send her mad—was terrifying. Archie had dismissed her fears, but who else could it be but Philip?

Gradually, though, her courage returned, and she pulled herself to her feet. She couldn't let this start again. Whoever this person was, he mustn't succeed in destroying her. She would call Connie later, she decided, when she could trust herself not to break down. In the meantime, Connie had the Penleven telephone number and could ring herself.

Desperate now to get out of the house, Nancy pulled on her raincoat and picked up the basket she had packed earlier. She would walk to the village as she'd originally planned and take the china back to Kitty.

The basket was heavier than she'd expected, and she arrived at the village store flushed and out of breath.

'What on earth are you doing, my luvver?' Kitty asked her when she puffed through the door. 'Give that here and come upstairs. Hedra can watch the shop.' She waved a hand at a middle-aged woman busy filling a long shelf with tins of baked beans.

Once in Kitty's kitchen, Nancy got her breath back sufficiently to say, 'That was a splendid meal you cooked last night. Mr Silva praised it to high heavens.'

Kitty filled the kettle and lit the gas. 'Glad to hear it. You never quite know how things will turn out.'

'Well, they turned out brilliantly and I can't thank you enough.' Nancy sank gratefully down onto the nearest chair.

While her friend made tea, she looked around her. Kitty's kitchen could not have been more of a contrast to the bare space at Penleven. It was small and cosy with blue gingham curtains at the window and blue cushioned chairs around a scrubbed wooden table. A tall dresser standing in the alcove next to the window was filled with delicate china: shelf upon shelf of cups, saucers, plates, some plain, some patterned in florals, often with gilded edges. It was a splash of luxury in what was a simple room.

'You don't like cooking then?' Kitty asked, filling the teapot.

'To be honest, I've never really tried. To cook properly, I mean. My mother never let me near the kitchen and when I lived in London—before I was married—I had a bedsit with a single gas ring. It didn't really lend itself to culinary experiment.'

'And now?' Kitty carried two mugs of hot tea over to the table.

'Now, I have Mrs Brindley standing guard. She's been Leo's housekeeper for years and she never lets me forget it.'

Kitty grimaced. 'Old bat,' she said, with a grin. 'But I know what you mean about bedsitter land. I've been there, too. It's always the same, though, isn't it, for working women? Poor wages and lousy homes. Catch the bosses living like that!'

'This was when you worked in London?' Nancy felt surprised that Kitty hadn't lived more comfortably. The girl had mentioned she'd worked in a high-class jeweller's— but then shop wages were notoriously low even in the most expensive establishments. 'Which jeweller's did you work for?'

'The shop was in Bond Street. You wouldn't know it.'

'You're right.' Nancy was rueful. 'If it was a Bond Street shop, I wouldn't. I imagine you gave up work when you married?' That was the common experience of women. Most were glad to exchange poorly remunerated work for the security of an agreeable home and a family, but not all. Not Nancy.

'I did. Trevor didn't like the idea of me working. Anyway, after the wedding we moved out to the suburbs and I couldn't have travelled to the West End every day. It would have been much too far.'

'Where did you move to?' Nancy asked, more from a desire to be companionable than any real wish to know.

'You wouldn't know the place. It was the back end of nowhere. Though I was happy enough living there.' Kitty gave a loud laugh.

Nancy liked the young woman sitting opposite and it would have been good to build a more complete picture of her, but Kitty obviously didn't want to talk of the past and that was understandable. She had lost her husband at what must have been a very young age.

'You spent a lot of time in Cornwall, I think you said.' Nancy hoped this might be a happier topic. 'Did you have a favourite place for holidays?'

'Probably Port Madron,' Kitty answered easily, 'though Trevor loved the whole county.'

A little puzzled, Nancy nodded. Kitty must have forgotten that she'd visited Port Madron alone, before she took the job at the shop. But that would have been just after her husband died and grief could affect the mind and memory.

'It's rather a lovely story that you came back,' she said sympathetically.

Kitty shook her head of tight blonde curls. 'You get on with life, don't you. Now, tell me, how's that father-in-law of yours? I did hear he'd taken a turn for the worse. Such a shame for the poor man.'

'He seems to have got through whatever it was, thank goodness. Leo is going to the hospital later today and we'll know more then.' Nancy was deliberately vague. She liked Kitty a great deal, but thought it best not to share what could be shattering news. Best that her friend and the rest of the village thought Ned's current difficulties simply a setback on the road to better health.

She pushed her empty mug to one side. 'Thank you, Kitty, that was just what I needed, but I'd better get going. Your assistant downstairs won't thank me for taking you away from the shop floor.'

'Oh, Hedra will be fine. She only started work a few days ago but she's already picking it up.'

'Does she live in the village?'

'Yeah. It's convenient for both of us. The Pascoe house is just a few doors down.'

'Pascoe? Hedra is Jory Pascoe's wife?

'That's right. The old bugger got himself a cushy berth there, I reckon. Hedra was a widow and was left her cottage by the dear departed. But she wasn't a widow for long. Enter Jory.'

'You talkin' 'bout me?' A belligerent voice sounded from the landing and in a second Jory Pascoe was standing in the doorway.

'Come in, Jory. You after a cuppa?' Kitty asked cheerfully. But her eyes, when Nancy caught a glimpse of her face, were decidedly unfriendly.

The man glared across at Nancy sitting at the table, and at the empty cups between them. 'I could do with one,' he said, his voice surly. 'Now the missus is 'elpin' you out, no one to put the kettle on.'

'Then you'd better learn to do it yourself,' Kitty said tartly. 'It's right there.' She pointed to the kettle sitting beside the gas stove. 'I'm taking Mrs Tremayne downstairs.'

Jory's chin jutted forbiddingly. 'Best place for 'er. Even better would be as fer as I can throw 'er.'

Nancy felt her heart sink. Port Madron seemed to harbour so much hostility against the family into which she'd married, and much of it plainly unfair.

'Be polite,' Kitty warned him. 'Nancy's nothing to do with the mine. Her husband is Professor Tremayne.'

'It's 'is family though, innit? The bloodsuckin' Tremaynes with their big cars and big 'ouse. Livin' in comfort 'stead of lookin' after the men who make the money for 'em.'

'You're like a scratched record, Jory. C'mon, Nancy, I'll walk you down.'

Pascoe leered at her. 'It's alright fer you, innit, Kitty? You're sittin' pretty. Rakin' it in with the shop.'

'You're talking nonsense. I've no more money than you.'

He sucked in his teeth. 'Doubt it. You like money and yer a canny one.'

'Make yourself tea. I'll be back in a few minutes,' was all Kitty said.

Pascoe sniffed and reached forward to grab the kettle. As he did so, a deep scarlet slash was exposed, covering half of his bare arm. Nancy gave a gasp. 'Your arm, Mr Pascoe! You've hurt yourself badly.'

He swivelled round. 'It don' need no attention—not from the likes of you leastways.'

'Keep a civil tongue, or you can leave.' Kitty had jumped up and gone to a cupboard high up on the wall, retrieving a small square box from its depths. 'That looks nasty. You could get an infection. You best let me sort it for you.'

Pascoe muttered something unintelligible but submitted to having his wound dressed. Nancy watched as her companion expertly bathed the wound, drying it with a clean towel. Opening the box, Kitty unloaded a tube of disinfectant cream, a thick pad of lint and several rolls of bandages onto the kitchen counter. 'You should rightly go to hospital,' she told him as she peered down at his arm. 'Get that stitched. It's very deep.'

'I aint' goin' to no 'ospital,' Jory said angrily. 'Leave me alone, woman.' But he let Kitty smother the wound in cream and expertly bandage it.

When Kitty began to repack what must be her first aid box, Nancy jumped up from her seat and made for the door.

'I best be off now,' she said. 'And thanks again for the tea.'

'Thank you for bringing the china back, sweetie.'

Jory Pascoe gave Nancy another fierce glare, then unexpectedly followed her down the stairs. His wife had finished filling shelves and was standing behind the till. Nancy saw the woman give her husband a weak smile when she caught sight of him. She appeared uncomfortable. Was that Hedra's newness in the job or was it something else? And why did Kitty need an assistant anyway in what was a very small shop?

***

Nancy had walked only a few yards from the store when it began to rain. It had been threatening all morning, but now the sky was almost black overhead and the slight breeze had become a powerful wind, whirling an empty paper bag down the street towards the harbour. It was fortunate the walk back to Penleven was a short one, but part of it ran uphill along a narrow lane with tall trees on either side. Their branches, still almost bare, began to creak ominously as she walked between them, her shoulders brushing against vegetation already dripping water.

The track ahead was growing darker and a shiver chased through Nancy's body. Was it the rain? The wind? Or had there been movement behind her? Swiftly, she turned to look down the lane, but it was quite empty. Nevertheless, she couldn't shake off the feeling there had been someone or something closing in on her and several times she turned abruptly to check. But there was no one, not even a shadow. This was the second time in days that she'd felt she was being followed. She tried not to think of the terror she'd suffered in London before she married, telling herself that it was the wind she sensed—it was rising still—and scolding herself for being foolish. It did nothing to banish her unease.

Just as she emerged from the wooded lane, a figure crossed her path only yards ahead. It was that of a man, head bent and swaddled in gabardine. The rain had begun in earnest and Nancy peered through the drizzle, trying to make out who would be walking in such bad weather. She was sure it was Clem Hoskins. Had he been the one following her? Both he and Pascoe had shown her animosity, but Pascoe would be drinking tea in Kitty's kitchen by now. Why, though, would Clem be following her, and if he were, how had he contrived to get ahead? It was nonsense, she told herself—the man was simply going about his daily business and she was clutching at straws.

When she opened the front door of Penleven, it was to see Leo pacing the hallway, walking back and forth along the runner that covered the polished floor, his hands furrowing through his hair.

When he turned, his face was ravaged. 'You're home. Thank goodness. Where have you been?' He sounded frustrated, even angry.

'I told you. I took Kitty's china back to the village shop.'

Her remark appeared to pass him by. 'I've had a phone call from the hospital. An hour ago.' His eyes were dark in the gloom of the hall.

'Is it your father?' She rushed over to him, holding out her arms.

'Dad's okay. He's doing well, in fact, and I'm off to see him this afternoon. But—'

'What?'

'I can't believe this, Nancy.' Once again, he furrowed his hands through his hair. 'They said… the hospital said…' He took a deep breath. 'They've investigated what went wrong with the drip. It wasn't an accident.' Leo drummed his fingers against the grey stone wall.

'I think we knew that,' she said gently.

'It wasn't one of the hospital staff either.'

Why had Leo expected that to be the answer? Perhaps it was more comforting to think that a doctor or nurse had run amok than to accept there was someone who hated his father so much that he or she would run the risk of being arrested for murder.

'You get rogue medics sometimes,' he said defensively. 'Think of John Bodkin Adams. He's been all over the papers these last few months. Charged with thirteen murders.'

'If it wasn't any member of the hospital staff,' Nancy said calmly, 'do they have any idea who it was?'

'Of course, they don't. They can't make sense of it.'

So what was the news from the hospital? What couldn't her husband believe? Nancy was riven with impatience but tried hard to keep her voice calm. Leo was evidently furious and bewildered, and it was making him lose his customary clear-sightedness. It was also making him look ill. His skin had taken on the same whitish-grey hue she'd seen when he had panted his way up the hill from the ruins of Wheal Harmony.

'Come and sit down,' she said, turning towards the sitting room. Leo remained standing where he was, his body stiff with tension.

'They've told you what it was?' she prompted, turning back to him. 'The stuff that was added to the drip?'

'Disinfectant.' He almost choked on the words, his breathing irregular.

Disinfectant. The thoughts tumbled through Nancy's mind. An everyday substance. Something anyone could buy. Something anyone could administer if they found a syringe. Jory Pascoe, for instance.

Chapter Fifteen

That afternoon Leo came back from the hospital a good deal happier than he'd gone. His father was making progress, the doctors were delighted to say, far more quickly than they could have hoped. If Ned continued to do well during the week, he would be allowed home after the weekend. As for the disinfectant that had found its way into the drip, Matron had taken Leo into her office after visiting hours and apologised profusely. She could offer no explanation of how it had happened and was unsure whether or not Leo wanted it reported to the police.

'It was clear Matron was hoping the matter could be glossed over,' Leo told her. They were in their bedroom where Nancy had gone to change for supper. 'The hospital would avoid any kind of scandal then. But if I wished, she said, she would take the facts of the case to the local constabulary, though it might take some time for them to investigate and come up with an answer.'

'But you'll insist she report it?'

'I don't think so,' Leo said slowly. 'I know I railed against whoever was responsible but, with hindsight, the publicity the affair is bound to attract could do Dad more harm than good. Now that he's come through and come through better than I could ever expect…'

'Someone deliberately set out to harm him, Leo,' she protested. 'How can you dismiss it?'

'It could have been accident.'

'You must know that it wasn't.'

Nancy was sitting at the dressing table, brushing her waves into a semblance of order. She watched in the mirror as her husband came towards her, putting his two hands on her shoulders and gripping them tightly. He bent his head to speak to her.

'You mean well, Nancy, I know, but sometimes it's necessary to be pragmatic. Apart from the unwelcome publicity, Dad couldn't cope with a police investigation, not at the moment, while he's still recovering. The best thing we can do for him is get him home as quickly as possible, nurse him well and keep him safe.'

Nancy swivelled to face him, the hairbrush still in her hand. 'And Perry? What does he think?'

'Perry is of the same mind. He considers it best that we put the event down to an unfortunate accident.'

Nancy shook her head in disbelief, prompting an irascible response from her husband. 'Perry has his own problems to deal with. He doesn't need more.'

'Problems such as?' She raised her eyebrows.

'It's been difficult for him at Wheal Agnes. Francisco Silva appears to have liked what he saw, and the suggestions he's made for improvements in the supply chain chime with Perry's own thinking. But some of the miners were less than polite to Silva. I guess they're realising the sale of Wheal Agnes is a real possibility now.'

'Poor Mr Silva—he doesn't deserve that.'

'I agree. It's Pascoe, I think, that's still stirring up trouble. One of Perry's most trusted workers stopped him on his way out and told Perry he'd seen Tomas Almeda talking to Pascoe a few days ago and the man was sure that money changed hands. It's left Perry in a quandary. If the chap's right, and there's no reason to doubt his word, then Almeda could be working against his boss, paying Pascoe to make trouble.'

'Why on earth would he do that?'

Leo sighed. 'I've no idea. And neither has Perry.'

'Do you think Perry will mention it to Mr Silva?'

'He hasn't decided. To be honest, he's still unsure about selling. Things are galloping ahead at a frightening speed and Perry is struggling to keep up. And now I've come back from the hospital saying Dad is making excellent progress, he's even more unsure. It's clear Silva likes the mine and is keen to buy, but if Dad recovers fully, it will be difficult for Perry to make the case to sell. It all adds up to a confusing situation.'

There was no confusion for Nancy. Perry might be tying himself in knots over Wheal Agnes, but his father's 'accident' had been a deliberate attempt to kill and only the medical staff's quick action had saved him. The would-be murderer was at large and, if neither Leo nor his brother were willing to investigate, Nancy would. It was Treeve Fenton's death that held the clue, she was sure. That had been the first link in the chain of tragedy. Tomorrow she would speak to Grace Jago again and Kitty, too. Both women had seen the old man on the day he'd died. They might know something, might have seen or heard something, without realising its significance.

***

In the morning, though, it appeared that Leo had other plans for her.

'I forgot to say last night that the docs are doing more tests on Dad today and visitors aren't welcome on the ward. I thought we might take a trip out. I could do with putting aside the paper I'm writing—for a few hours at least.'

It wasn't how Nancy had envisaged spending the day, but so far she had seen little of Leo since they'd been at Penleven and she was happy to agree. His next words, though, had her reconsider.

'I telephoned Archie earlier. He can drive us.'

'Drive us where?'

'St Michael's Mount. Everyone must see the Mount at least once in their life—and this is your moment! What do you think?'

Nancy's smile was weak. 'It sounds wonderful,' she said, as brightly as she could.

A day closeted with the two men who had divided her heart so completely was not one she could look forward to, but escape was impossible.

Downstairs, she found Perry stacking breakfast dishes and about to leave for the mine. Nancy wondered if she should raise the issue of the poisoned drip, but then thought better of it. Perry seemed happy to push the matter to the far corners of his mind, and she should let it rest there.

'Great idea, to have a day out,' he said cheerily. 'I wish I could join you.'

Nancy wished it, too. Another person to break up the trio, another presence to dilute the tension, would be welcome. Not that Leo appeared to sense any. It was she who felt awkward. And Archie, she guessed. It was different if the three of them travelled together for Leo's business. There was a formality to it that eased the occasion. But off duty, on a pleasure trip…

'Oh, there's a letter for you, Nancy,' her brother-in-law said, shrugging himself into an ancient waxed jacket. 'A big one, too. Hope it's as big a surprise.'

Nancy glanced down at the large brown envelope that he'd left on the kitchen table. It was certainly addressed to her but bore neither stamp nor postmark. Hand delivered? Who would be delivering a letter to her at Penleven? Who even knew she was here?

While she waited for Leo to join her, she took hold of the envelope and shook it. It seemed unusually heavy and must surely contain more than a letter. Curious, she tore the envelope open and plunged her hand inside. Then quickly shook her fingers free. Something sharp. She shook the contents onto the table and small strips of pale pink wool spread themselves across its wooden surface. Nancy felt the blood drain from her face. They were small strips of a garment she recognised. Her lost cardigan. And amid the ruins, something glinting. Almost against her will, she stretched out her hand and took hold of it. It was small and very sharp. A knife, dagger-shaped, its serrated blade dripping red. Blood! No, not blood but paint.

Beads of sweat drenched her forehead and, trembling, she rushed to the sink and felt her stomach heave. For minutes she stood, head bowed, not daring to look back at the table. But then hearing Leo's footsteps on the stairs, she pulled herself together and swept the dreadful contents back into the envelope, shovelling it roughly to the back of the broom cupboard behind a motley collection of worn brushes.

'Ready?' Her husband put his head round the kitchen door. 'Archie's outside in the car.'

***

Archie looked at her in the driving mirror. Nancy had lost whatever colour she'd gained when he'd seen her at his mother's two days ago. And her lips were compressed into a tight line. What the hell was going on with her? He didn't want to know, but he couldn't bear that she was in trouble. Why the blazes did he have to do this trip, stuck for the day between the two of them? The sooner he got back to London, the better. A call had come through from Croydon airport early this morning. The firm who owned the Cessna had a list of clients wishing to hire and the aircraft was already massively overdue. There was a fine in place and mounting by the day. Just when was this plane being returned?

Leo had mentioned some paper he was writing for a conference in a few weeks' time, something he needed Archie to type. Did his boss really expect him to produce a typewriter in Port Madron? He'd speak to Leo today about going back to London—he could kill two birds with one stone— return the Cessna and get some work done. Get some peace, too. Leo and his wife could catch the London train as soon as Ned Tremayne was well enough.

Once he was back in Cavendish Street, Archie decided, he wouldn't be returning to Cornwall for some time. He'd be sorry to say goodbye to Ma, of course he would, but the strain of having Nancy so close and having to pretend indifference was too severe. He'd shut Rich up the other night and so far Ma had been too wary to speak her mind, but he knew what his family were thinking, what they were imagining.

In any case, Nancy was better when he wasn't around. More relaxed, happier even— unless she started back on her wretched sleuthing. But he didn't think she would, not if Ned was getting better and the police weren't interested in Treeve's death. Why would they be? There was virtually nothing to go on, not even for Nancy.

Within the hour, they were driving into Marazion along a narrow, winding road, with grey stone houses on either side. He saw Nancy crane her head to see what was beyond the row of buildings and, when the car finally emerged onto the seafront, her eyes open wide. The Mount was a magnificent sight. No matter how many times you saw it, it took your breath away. An island of granite, topped by a castle that belonged on the covers of a fairy story.

At high tide it was surrounded by water, white-crested waves dashing themselves against the grey rocks and splashing over the harbour wall. But today the tide had pulled back and the ferry was redundant. Leo would be able to walk his wife across the causeway—Archie had no intention of accompanying them. He'd stay with the car, maybe drop into the Goldophin Arms for a quick pint.

But when he pulled into one of the few available parking spaces behind a row of palm trees, he was disappointed. Leo had a different idea.

'The car will be fine here,' he told Archie. 'No need to stay, and a walk will do us all good. Even one under grey skies. The rain looks as though it will hold off.' For an instant, a faint sun had broken through the louring sky, sending a sheen of brightness across the wet sand.

Reluctantly, Archie walked round to the car boot and found his raincoat. Looking up at the grey blanket of sky, he thought he would probably need it. The small beam of sunlight had disappeared as quickly as it had arrived, and the atmosphere felt stormy. Nancy, he noticed, had wound a thick scarf around her neck. Cornwall could be chilly. It wasn't always the Riviera, and it was never the Caribbean where she'd walked bare-legged and bare-armed. He could see her now, a slim tanned figure in that splashy red sundress she'd bought at some London market. Dogged, determined, stupidly brave.

'Let's walk,' Leo urged, and the three of them set off across the cobbled causeway.

'The castle used to belong to the monks of St Michel in Normandy,' Leo was saying. 'Round about the time of the Norman conquest. They're sister islands. It was the monks that built the church and the priory that are the heart of the castle.'

There was a pause before Nancy asked, 'Are there monks still living here?' To Archie's ear, her voice sounded strained. As though making conversation was a wall she must climb.

He saw Leo shake his head. 'I think the monks abandoned ship after a few hundred years. This place has a huge history—it's changed hands so many times. The first beacon was lit here to warn London of the approach of the Spanish Armada.' Leo had almost to shout, his words swept away by the fierce wind blowing across the causeway.

Archie trudged behind them, saying nothing, hands dug deep into his pockets. For several minutes there was silence, but as they approached the island's harbour wall, the wind died a little and it seemed to rouse Nancy into making another effort.

'Who owns the island now?'

'The St Aubyn family. Since the seventeenth century, I believe.'

Leo knew a little about the Mount, Archie thought, but not much. Why would he? He'd spent most of his life out of Cornwall—at prep school, boarding school, university. Then five years in the army fighting a war none of them had wanted.

Leo couldn't know the Mount as he did. He'd loved the place from the moment when, as a small child, he'd seen it for the first time. His grandad had taken him on a long bus ride, another first since he'd never left his fishing village before. The bus had been exciting enough, but when he'd stood on Marazion beach and looked across at this wonderful island and its amazing castle, he'd been without words. His grandad had walked him over every inch of the island and told him the most magical stories of the place. Archie would have liked to tell Nancy some of those tales. But it wasn't for him to do. He was the assistant, the one who followed, and he better remember it. Remember Leo's kindness, his decency, the loyalty he owed the man.

Chapter Sixteen

By the time they had climbed the winding path to the top of the island and reached the castle entrance, Leo had stopped talking. His shoulders were slightly hunched, and he seemed to drag his feet.

Archie gave him a concerned look. 'Are you okay, boss?'

'I'm fine, thanks,' Leo managed to say, though he was breathing heavily and his face was pale. 'It's quite a climb, that's all. I think I'll go into the church and sit down a while.' The mediaeval building, granite-stoned and slate- roofed, lay adjacent to the castle.

'I'll come with you.' Nancy sounded worried.

'No, don't. No need to fuss. Now you're here, you must have a look around. Archie can walk with you.'

He had disappeared into the church before Archie turned to her. 'Is Leo really okay? The breathlessness, I mean.'

'I hope so, but I'm not sure. It happened a few days ago, too. When we were walking on the cliffs.'

'Persuade him to see a doctor once you're back in London.'

Nodding a silent agreement, she walked to the edge of the path. She seemed to be gazing blindly into the distance.

'And you?' Archie asked. 'What is it with you?'

'Nothing.' She twisted round to face him, her mouth, he saw, trying very hard to smile.

'Come off it, Nancy. It's me you're talking to. What's wrong?'

She looked down at her feet, then said very quietly, 'My lost cardigan turned up.'

'See, I said it would.'

'In pieces.' She looked up at him and her eyes were wide and staring. Beautiful grey eyes. He forced himself to concentrate.

'In pieces? How exactly?'

'Cut up into fraying ribbons of wool and posted through the letter box in a brown envelope.'

'Jesus. Who would do something as weird as that?'

'There's only one person in the world who would.' He saw a shiver pass over her shoulders and wanted to put his arms around her.

Instead, he was dismissive. 'That's nonsense. I told you—' he began.

'There was a knife in the envelope, too,' she interrupted in a flat voice. 'Covered in red paint. I was supposed to imagine blood.'

Her shivering had become fiercer and, desperate to comfort, Archie grabbed her and pulled her close.

'He's here, Archie, I know.' She gave a small sob. 'Philip March. I don't know how he's found me, but he has.'

Archie cradled her head against his shoulder, letting his lips brush the top of her head. 'It could be some other joker,' he said, without much hope. 'Was there a postmark on the envelope?'

She shook her head and he felt her move closer to him. 'Just my name and address but no stamp and no postmark.'

For several minutes, they stood with their arms around each other. Then, as if they had both come to their senses at the same time, they parted abruptly.

Nancy delved into her pocket for a handkerchief and gave her nose a short, sharp blow. 'He's been following me these last few days,' she said dully. 'I've felt him there, behind me, several times. I thought it might be someone else, but now I know it wasn't.'

'If the bastard *is* back, he'll have me to deal with this time.'

'That's if he doesn't get to me first.' Her voice sounded faint and wavering.

'Nancy!' He took her by the shoulders, holding her at a distance. 'You're braver than this.'

'Usually,' she sniffed. 'But Philip terrifies me.'

'Have you told Leo? He should know.'

'Not yet.' She looked down at her feet again.

Archie wasn't going to let it go. 'Why not?' he demanded.

'Because …'

'Yes – ?'

'I don't want to worry him, not with his father so ill. I'll tell him when I find the right time.'

'Like you were going to find the right time in Malfuego to tell him you'd lost the baby?'

It was a cheap jibe, Archie knew, but she was hurting and that hurt him, too. He felt a frantic need to lash out. 'Sorry,' he said inadequately.

She turned her pale face to him, the wind whipping the long waves of her hair into a halo around her head. 'It's okay, you're forgiven. Why don't we do as Leo suggested and look around?'

She began to walk uphill, following the line of the ancient church towards a large clump of stone. 'This looks interesting. What is it?' she called back to him.

In a few minutes he was standing beside her. 'It's called the bedrock,' he told her.

'It must mark the highest point of the island. But is it more significant than that?'

It was, but he wasn't going to tell her. People believed that if you touched the stone while wishing for a love that was true, your wish would be granted.

'There were some miracles back in the day,' he said vaguely. 'The island attracted a lot of religious pilgrims. Plenty of airy-fairy people, too.'

Nancy looked bewildered.

'Ley lines. Spiritual energy or some such guff. The lines are supposed to travel under the sea and cross at the heart of the Mount.'

'Let's hope we've imbibed some of it,' she said lightly, though he saw her eyes were shadowed. 'Time to go?'

Together, they wandered back to the church door.

***

The walk along the causeway to Marazion took only a short time and, as they neared the car, Leo suggested they find a café in the village for a quick snack. His voice held a new weariness.

'It might be best if we return to Penleven,' Nancy was quick to say.

Archie could see she was concerned for her husband, and rightly so. But even if she suggested he visit a doctor locally, he knew his boss would refuse. Leo would insist on waiting until he could see his own practitioner in London.

'Definitely time to go home,' Archie agreed. 'The mizzle is getting worse and we'll get soaked. Even the mad artists are packing up.' He pointed to several scurrying figures, pulling off their painterly smocks and hastily loading palettes, brushes and easels into the back of their cars. 'In any case, I've arrangements to make,' he added.

Surprised, Leo stared at his assistant.

'Croydon have been on the telephone this morning,' he explained. 'They want their plane back. We've incurred quite a fine already.'

'Then we'll have to incur a heftier one,' Leo responded, opening the car door for his wife. 'I've not yet finished the paper I'm writing and I need you to take it with you.'

'Couldn't you send it to me in the post?' Archie asked, when they were settled in the car.

'It's too much of a risk.' In the driving mirror, he saw Leo give a rare smile. 'I've one or two gems hiding in its pages and I've no copy. A few more days and I'll be finished. Tell Croydon they'll have to wait.'

It wasn't great news. Archie was eager to be off and beyond temptation. The feelings Nancy stirred in him were wrong and getting stronger every day they'd been here. He needed to be away from her. But before he went, he would insist she tell Leo about the cretin who was stalking her. Philip March, if indeed it was him. Her husband, forewarned, would know what to do.

They were back at Penleven within the hour and Leo immediately disappeared into the house. Archie was climbing into the car again when Nancy caught hold of his sleeve. 'There's something else. Something I haven't told you.'

He gave a small groan.

'It was disinfectant that poisoned Ned Tremayne's drip.'

He almost laughed. 'You've got to be joking.'

She shook her head. 'No. Ordinary household disinfectant, not some amazing drug whose name you can't even pronounce. Which means—'

'Don't tell me.'

'Which means that anyone could have done it if they bought a syringe or picked one up in the hospital. There must be plenty of those.'

'Hardly lying around,' he objected.

'Maybe not, but you've got to agree it's not something that would be difficult to get hold of. Not difficult to fill it with disinfectant either. Jory Pascoe could have done it.'

'Only if he became another person entirely. What you're suggesting would need careful planning and Pascoe is a hothead. He'd be quite incapable of anything so sophisticated. He's the kind of bloke who starts a pointless brawl in the pub and ends up cutting his own arm open.'

Nancy's mouth opened slightly. 'So that was how he got it,' she said thoughtfully.

'You've seen Pascoe?'

'He turned up at Kitty's when I was having a cup of tea with her. He was lucky — she was an expert with the bandages. But if it wasn't Pascoe, who did it?'

Archie planted his feet firmly in front of her and stared down into her face. He was going away, and he needed her safe. 'Forget it, Nancy. You have other worries, remember. If Leo isn't concerned to find who's behind the tampering, you shouldn't be. No one has died.'

'Treeve has.'

'That was an accident.'

She looked obstinate and he grabbed hold of her hand and held it tightly. He hadn't meant to touch her again, but he had to stop her from taking risks. 'Repeat after me, it was an accident.'

'It was an accident,' she said, a small smile on her lips. 'But it wasn't, Archie. And you know it.'

***

Leo had already returned to his papers when Nancy walked into the dining room. He was looking a lot less ashen than he'd done all morning and she felt relieved.

He looked up as she came through the door. 'Sorry the day was a bit of a damp squib.'

'It was fine,' she reassured him. 'I enjoyed the trip.'

'We could have done with some sun.'

'We could, but even under clouds the island was magnificent. I loved the priory church. How beautiful it was—brimming with light, and that rose window amid all the stone.'

'Nancy, I've been thinking.' Leo stopped shuffling papers and looked directly at her.

'Yes?'

She was surprised. He sounded unusually serious. She was even more surprised when he walked over to her and took her in his arms.

'I'm not getting any younger and we spend very little time together,' he said. 'It doesn't work, does it?'

Nancy had sometimes thought that if they lived their lives more closely, it might smooth the bumps in what was often a difficult relationship.

'I think we might be happier if we shared out lives more,' she agreed, nestling against him. 'What do you suggest?' She looked up expectantly.

'Why don't we try for a baby again?'

Her mouth fell open and she pulled back abruptly.

'I know, I know,' Leo said quickly. 'It must sound odd, particularly after the last few months when we haven't, well … we haven't been a properly married couple. But maybe if we made an effort to share our life more, we'd get back to the way we were, and things would follow on from there. '

Nancy walked over to a chair and sank down. This was something so unexpected that she needed time to think.

'It's my fault entirely,' Leo went on, 'but after what happened in Malfuego, your losing the baby, then me nearly losing you in that terrifying eruption, I didn't think it was the right time to start thinking of another child. Not then. And not since either. I've been involved in so much travelling — more than I've done for years. Maybe now, though, is the time to start over. What do you say?'

'Won't you be travelling as much this year?' she ventured.

'I'll make sure I don't. But you have to play your part, too. You've been working as much as me.' To Nancy's ear, that sounded like an accusation. But she knew she could be too sensitive on the topic and tried not to think it.

'You were never at home when I was,' he went on. 'Or you were tired. That job exhausts you at times.' She wasn't being overly sensitive after all, it seemed. 'But now with Dad getting sick like this, it's made me realise he isn't going to live for ever. He'll get better this time, I'm sure, but eventually… And Perry is unlikely ever to marry. He's over fifty and has never had a serious relationship except when he was very young, and that fizzled out. Wheal Agnes is his great love.'

'What are you saying, Leo?' She was grappling with what exactly her husband was driving at.

'I'm saying that when Dad dies, when Perry dies and me, too, that's the Tremaynes gone. I'd like to think that wouldn't happen. That someone will follow in our footsteps and bear our name.'

'We're to have a baby to carry on your family name?' She couldn't help sounding incredulous.

'In part, but that's not the whole of it. I think you'd love a baby. In fact, I'm sure of it. You're a caring woman, Nancy, and you'd make a wonderful mother.'

Where had he got that idea? She wanted to scream that being a caring woman didn't automatically qualify you for mother of the year. And that perhaps she felt as much passion for her work as Leo did for his. Had he given any thought to the apprenticeship for which she was diligently studying? To Leo, her work was expendable. It didn't matter. It was a stop gap until she fulfilled her real destiny of being a wife and mother.

'Well, what do you say?' He was looking at her eagerly.

'I think we should allow your father to get truly better, see him back home again and go home ourselves.'

'But after that?' he persisted.

'We'll talk about it later, shall we?'

She saw his lips tighten and, when he spoke, his voice was brusque. 'We'll talk later,' he agreed.

Chapter Seventeen

Nancy mounted the stairs to the bedroom and slumped down into the old nursing chair, its blue velvet worn grey with age. Through the window she could see the weather worsening by the minute. The mizzle, as Archie had called it, had turned into a downpour, water bouncing off the gutters and flooding the small patch of lawn she could just glimpse from where she sat. She felt stunned. She'd told Leo she would talk later. But how? He had shocked her so completely that she'd be hard pressed to string a sentence together.

A baby had been the last thing on Nancy's mind. On her husband's, too, she'd assumed. Ever since that wretched miscarriage in Malfuego, she'd buried the thought of another child. The idea, it seemed, had been forgotten by them both. For Nancy, it had been important to forget. There was something she hadn't told Leo. Another secret she'd kept from him.

As soon as they'd arrived home from the Caribbean trip, her husband had insisted she see a doctor and, when she returned from the appointment, had quizzed her thoroughly. She'd insisted over and over again that she was fine and there was nothing to tell, and eventually Leo had seemed happy. Happy to leave plans for another baby to some unspecified time in the future. But though she'd been pronounced fit, the doctor had made clear to her that the miscarriage was unlikely to have been bad luck, that she could be one of a small band of women who found it difficult and sometimes impossible to carry a child to full term. When she'd asked fearfully whether, if she'd sought medical attention at the time she'd miscarried, it would have made a difference, he'd told her no. In fact, she had been lucky to conceive in the first place, he'd said. And Nancy had believed him.

For a long time, she'd sensed that she was destined never to bear a child, and when the doctor had confirmed it, she hadn't known whether to feel glad or desperate. Her mother had suffered multiple miscarriages—Nancy had been the miracle child, though she doubted Ruth Nicholson had ever thought so. The choice for Nancy was stark: either she ensured she never became pregnant again or she risked a new pregnancy and a new trauma.

As the months had passed and Leo made no mention of another child, she'd been content to let things drift, made easier by the fact that their lives had become increasingly separate. She'd told herself that it was better to keep silent, better not to upset him all over again, when a baby was no longer something he craved. But she had been wrong. His desire for a child had not gone away; it had simply been sleeping and now, once more, she had to disappoint him. Break it to him that his wish was unlikely ever to be granted.

***

It was a good few hours before Nancy felt able to walk down the stairs and face her husband again. Leo was still in the dining room, head bent and scribbling furiously, and she thought it best not to interrupt. Perry, though, had arrived home and she went to join him in the kitchen. He was staring morosely at a heap of vegetables.

He turned as she came through the door. 'Mrs Cheffers has left us these,' he said gloomily. 'And there's a small chicken in the refrigerator. I really don't know what to do.'

'A roast perhaps? It might brighten up the evening.' When she saw his face fall, she said quickly, 'I'll help, Perry. I'm not Marguerite Patten but I can manage a simple roast… if you'll give me a hand with these.' She picked up a knife from the cabinet drawer and pointed to a cauliflower and the heap of carrots. 'There are potatoes in a sack outside, I think.'

'In the scullery,' he said. 'I'll fetch some.'

As soon as they were launched on the potato and carrot peeling, she asked him how his day had gone. 'Better than ours, I hope,' she said. 'The weather was miserable at the Mount.'

'I didn't see much of the weather. I spent most of the day in my office or below ground. Silva wanted to inspect the under-sea workings.'

'Was he impressed?'

'He seemed to like what he saw.'

'I wondered if he might be staying with us again tonight.'

'I offered him the room, but he'd found a hotel in Truro. I think he thought with negotiations at a delicate stage, it was better to be living elsewhere. And the Tinners evidently didn't appeal. Can't think why.'

Perry gave her a grin. When he smiled, Nancy could see Leo in him and imagine them as boys together here. With a mother they'd both adored.

'So, Mr Silva is enthusiastic about Wheal Agnes?'

'He is. Very. And enthusiastic about my plans to extend. He thinks it could be the way to go.'

'Does that surprise you?'

'A little. It wasn't something he knew about before he arrived.'

'Can you fetch down that roasting tin?'

'To be honest,' he said, handing her the dish, 'I thought he might want to buy up the mine, get what he could from it, and then sell it off. That would kill me, you know. For Dad, the mine is part of his inheritance and something that speaks to his Cornishness. But for me, it's the mine itself.'

Perran stood, knife in hand, an almost mystical look on his face. 'It's dark and unknowable, Nancy, exciting and wondrous—all those things rolled into one. A place where treasure is brought from the bowels of the earth. And the camaraderie is second to none, each man's life depending on his fellows.'

Perry stopped abruptly and looked embarrassed. Then in a different voice he said, 'If Silva is really serious about extending beneath the sea, it will need commitment. It's very much a long-term project.'

'Didn't you say you've plans already prepared?'

'Mostly. They were completed way back. My grandfather used some of them for the existing workings, but there are drawings to extend much further out. Francisco thinks they're pretty good and the mining surveyor I consulted agrees. Whoever drew them up, knew what they were doing.'

Nancy tipped the potatoes into the pan of sizzling fat and emptied the carrots into a colander. 'I thought your idea was to develop the workings yourself. As an alternative to selling.'

'Originally. But since then I've done my sums. I've been in talks with a manufacturer of the kind of drilling equipment I'd need and totted up just how much I'd have to spend, plus materials to support the new passageways that would need constructing. I'd have to borrow a huge sum to make it possible and the bank is unlikely to lend me that amount.'

'But Mr Silva has the money?'

Perry stood still, holding the colander beneath the cold

water tap. 'That's the rub. I may not have the money, but I have got the know-how. I'm convinced the deposits are big and the tin should be excellent quality. At the moment, the ore we produce isn't good enough to attract a high price. But Silva has the cash for a large extension and contacts with importers worldwide.'

'There must be a mid-way,' she suggested.

Her brother-in-law sat down on one of the kitchen stools, his elbows resting on the wooden table. 'I'm thinking a partnership might work,' he said in a sudden burst of confidence.

Nancy considered it for a moment. 'It might,' she said, 'but what does Francisco Silva think? Have you broached the idea?'

'We haven't talked in detail, but he seems to be leaning that way. It would solve the problem of finance. And solve my problem of what I'd do if we sold the business. I'd still have a job, I imagine. Silva would want someone he could trust running the mine. He's got his own business in Brazil to look after. Best of all,' Perry swept up the vegetable peelings and dumped them into the kitchen bin, 'Wheal Agnes would rise again.'

Nancy loved how passionate Perry was for the work he did. She understood it perfectly. She felt the same passion. But though she didn't want to puncture his enthusiasm, she felt she should sound a note of caution.

'A partnership would be quite a turnabout,' she said. 'I'm wondering how your father would react.'

Perry's face clouded. 'I'm not at all sure. Ordinarily he'd be dead against it, but after his illness he may be more flexible, more willing to relax his grip a little. If I show him the balance sheet, really make him confront the problems we face, I might be able to persuade him. I've never done that before, you know. Shown him the figures. I haven't wanted to worry him unduly, but I think the moment has arrived.'

'Well, it's a problem you don't have to worry about just yet. Mr Silva has to make the offer first.'

Perry gave a loud sigh. 'Indeed. Things are going on that could easily dissuade him.'

'Is Jory Pascoe still giving you trouble?' Nancy took a seat beside him.

'Not just me. Francisco, too.'

'Leo told me that some of the miners had been openly rude. Cold-shouldered the man.'

'It's more than that. There was some real nastiness at the mine today. Pascoe turned up halfway through the afternoon, drunk as a lord. He must have been holding up the Tinners bar for a couple of hours. Then he had to start a fight. With Tomas Almeda.'

'Almeda? How odd. Do you know why?'

'He said the chap owed him money. When Almeda told him in no uncertain terms to go away—it turns out he has a great command of English after all—well, a certain kind of English,' Perry couldn't help another grin, 'Pascoe told Francisco to his face that his assistant had been bribing the miners to spread stories. To spread a lie that I was conspiring to sell the mine for a song and then walk away, leaving Francisco to sack all the men.'

'No wonder the miners are so angry when Pascoe has already stirred them up over the cut in pay.' Nancy got to her feet and walked over to the Aga, rearranging potatoes and the chicken, now turning a golden brown. 'But Almeda must have denied it.'

'Naturally, he did. But Francisco is a tough boss and he insisted on speaking to every miner present, asking them one by one if they'd been approached by his assistant. A good half dozen said they had. None of them, I'm delighted to say—except Pascoe—had agreed to take the money.'

'But that's crazy. Why on earth would Almeda do that? Try to sabotage the sale his boss is negotiating?'

Perry pushed back his chair, seeming agitated, and began pacing up and down the kitchen. 'I asked Francisco that and he muttered something about a cartel back in Brazil trying to stop him developing his business, and that maybe Tomas was in their pay. It all sounded incredibly murky. It did make me wonder if I was wise in trusting Silva.'

'Perhaps that was part of the plan, to make you suspicious and pull out of any deal. But Mr Silva will discover what's been going on, won't he? Hopefully, he can reassure you.'

'It sounded to me as though he'll be on the rampage the minute he lands back in Brazil.'

'And Almeda? What will he do about him?'

'He's done it already. He dismissed him on the spot.'

'Phew!'

'Phew indeed. Silva doesn't mess about. The chap is probably queuing for the next plane back to Rio as we speak. Have we done enough veg, do you think? I'm not too hungry myself.'

'It's more than enough,' Nancy said decidedly. 'I'll put the water to boil. I'm not too hungry either.'

When they were later seated around the kitchen table, having silently agreed among themselves that the dining room was too depressing on such a miserable evening, Nancy found it difficult to clear her plate. She sat quietly, eating little, while Perry recounted to his brother the stirring events at Wheal Agnes.

'But those plans,' Leo said, 'Can you use them? Wasn't there some kind of kerfuffle over them? I seem to remember Grandpa steaming for months.'

'There was a court case,' Perry said. 'I was too young to understand all the detail, but Dad told me later that the chap who drew up the plans swore he'd been promised a share of any profit they made. Grandpa evidently thought not and, since there wasn't a written contract, he won the case. The chap disappeared after that, but the row seems to have put an end to any further extension.The plans are still there, though, and they belong to us. I think they're feasible and Silva does, too.'

'So, a partnership seems the best way out?' Leo returned to the crucial point in Perry's long monologue.

'It could be. If I can persuade Silva.' There was a pause before Perry finished wearily, 'And then persuade Dad.'

***

That evening none of them were late to bed, Perry because he had another early start at the mine— Silva was leaving for London in the afternoon and there were important talks to be held beforehand—and Leo because he seemed intent on getting Nancy alone. She knew why. She had said they would talk later, and he would hold her to her promise. It was likely to be a difficult conversation.

But when, lying side by side in bed, she explained to him as gently as she could the doctor's findings, he turned to her, wrapping her in his arms and gave her a long, warm kiss.

'You should have told me before, Nancy. You shouldn't have had to carry that burden alone.'

'I should have said something and I'm sorry. But it was such an upsetting time— remember? I didn't want to make things worse.'

'You wouldn't have done. I reacted badly on Malfuego, I know, and I couldn't be more regretful. It's made me determined to be there for you in the future. Determined that

142

you never again have to go through such a thing on your own. To be honest, I was so relieved to find you safe at the foot of that dreadful mountain that nothing would have upset me—then or now.' He gave her another long kiss.

Wriggling free of his embrace for a moment, Nancy propped herself up on her elbow. She had to say this. Had to make sure he understood the true situation. 'Leo, you do see that it's unlikely we'll ever have a child? I'm so sorry this is the way it is. I didn't think about it when I married you.'

'Or you wouldn't have married me?' he teased.

Nancy couldn't have said that. She had married for protection. Protection that had been desperately needed.

He leaned over and gave her a quick squeeze. 'It doesn't matter, sweetheart. We have each other, and from now on, we must value that. Make sure we spend as much time together as we can. And you never know, the doctor might have painted the very worst picture. So as not to disappoint you.'

Nancy was about to protest that the doctor had been measured in his diagnosis, but before she could say anything, Leo spoke again, his tone arch. 'He didn't say it was impossible, did he?'

'No, he didn't,' she conceded, 'but he did say that if I became pregnant again, it was very likely to end in miscarriage.'

Leo took a long strand of her hair and wound it round his finger. 'Very likely isn't definite though, is it?'

'As near to definite as a doctor can be. Miscarrying was horrible and I wouldn't want to risk it again.'

Leo pulled away from her slightly. 'If there was a next time, I'd be with you, Nancy. You wouldn't have to face it alone. Now I'm aware there's a possibility that things could go wrong, I'd know what to expect.'

'And so would I.' Nancy's voice shook. 'I'd be thinking that any moment, I could lose this baby, that every small twinge might sound a death knell.'

'That's a trifle dramatic, darling, even for you.'

'I don't think so. You seem to forget that it's my body we're talking about.'

She felt his figure stiffen beside her and move even further away. 'Are you saying you're not even prepared to try?'

'I'm saying that I can't imagine in the circumstances you would expect me to try.'

He was silent for a long time. When he finally turned back to her, she saw in the lamp's dim light that his mouth had hardened into a thin, straight line.

'It's that job, isn't it?' His voice was clipped and cold and Nancy felt utterly lost.

'What do you mean?'

'I think you know very well what I mean. You won't even consider a baby because it will stop you working. That's the truth, isn't it? At least, be honest with me.'

It was an echo of Archie's words a few hours ago, but they had been said out of concern for her. There was no concern here. Leo had decided he wanted something and that was good enough. It was his need to control, his need to order the world in a way that gave him comfort and certainty. Nancy understood a little—Leo, as a small boy, packed off to boarding school miles from the home he loved, the mother he adored dead before her time—but understanding didn't soothe the pain she felt. She turned away and buried her face in the pillow, hot tears trickling down her cheek.

Chapter Eighteen

Nancy woke with the sun in her eyes. The curtains had been partly opened and the room was as bright as a stage set. She turned over to see the bedside clock and then relaxed back on the pillow. Plenty of time. Not yet eight o'clock. But Leo wasn't beside her, she realised, and after she'd washed and dressed and walked downstairs, he wasn't there either. Instead, there was a scribbled note. The brothers had been asked to call at the hospital early that morning for a meeting with the consultant who was treating Ned. It was Perry who had written the note, she saw, and felt the gulf with Leo stretch wide.

She poured herself a bowl of cornflakes—really, she must find a different cereal—but before she'd unearthed the milk from the refrigerator there was a loud knocking at the door. Panic sent her heart tumbling and the breath catching in her throat. Philip March. It was Philip March, come finally to end their tortured relationship. And she was alone and isolated. Penleven wasn't far from the village, but it might as well be across the ocean for all anyone would hear her cries for help.

On shaky legs, she walked to the front door and peered through the small side window. Its opaque glass made it difficult to see anything clearly, but then suddenly a face loomed up in front of her, pressed against the other side of the window pane. Nancy jumped back, terrified, then slowly came to her senses. The figure was wearing a policeman's helmet. Shamefaced, she pulled back the heavy oak door.

'Good morning, Constable.' She hoped she sounded reasonably sane.

'Aiden Bolitho, Mrs Tremayne, your local policeman.'

'Bolitho?' She looked vacantly at him, thinking the name was in some way familiar.

'My folks own the village store,' he offered cheerily. 'May I come in for a minute?'

She stepped back to allow him to enter, puzzled as to what he might want with her, then ushered him into the kitchen. He took off his helmet and lay it reverently on the scrubbed wood table. It looked utterly surreal, perching there beside the uneaten bowl of cornflakes, but Constable Bolitho appeared not to see anything odd and sat himself comfortably down on a kitchen chair.

'Is Mr Perran around by any chance?' he asked.

'I'm afraid not. He's at the hospital with Professor Tremayne. They're visiting their father.'

'Ah, yes. Sad business. I hope the old chap is doin' okay.'

'Much better thank you. But as they're not here…'

'Mebbe you can help, Mrs Tremayne. I'm arskin' around — as a matter of routine, you understand.' He paused and sucked in his cheeks a little. Nancy waited for him to continue.

'Were you by any chance in the vicinity of the harbour last night?'

She almost laughed. 'We had torrential rain, Constable. I'd hardly be out walking.'

'True enough. But Mr Perran and the Professor? You were all together?' he persisted.

Nancy looked bemused. 'We were home all evening, keeping dry.'

'Sorry for the questions, but I have to arsk, just in case you were down in the village and saw somethin'.'

'Such as?'

'Such as Mr Pascoe. Though I'm not sure if you know the gentl'man.'

'I've met Jory Pascoe.'

'That's him. Well, I won't bother you further.'

Aiden got to his feet and picked up his helmet, but Nancy was not going to let him go that easily. Pascoe was her number one suspect.

'Mr Pascoe was at Wheal Agnes yesterday,' she said. 'Mr Perran told me there was some trouble between him and a man who was visiting.'

Aiden nodded. 'So I understand. I went over to the mine first thing and arsked his workmates about it. Former workmates,' he corrected himself.

Nancy was getting impatient. Pascoe had fallen into more trouble, it seemed, and she wanted to know what. 'Has something happened to Mr Pascoe?' she asked innocently.

'I think you could say so.' The constable's tone was ponderous. 'The gentl'man was found this morning on the harbour beach. Looks like he drowned—it was high tide last night and the water deep—but we've got detectives on it. They're down there right now. It's my job to carry out the routine enquiries.' He said this with pride.

Nancy's mind was working rapidly. Pascoe drowned! It could easily be accidental. The man had been drunk all afternoon, so goodness knows what mood he'd been in by evening. Foolish? Reckless? In a moment of bravado, he could have waded into the sea and lost his balance. It was unlikely anyone had seen him—there were no street lights at that point, she recalled—which meant rescue by a passer-by was nigh impossible. On the other hand, if it wasn't an accident…

Aiden had been edging towards the front door and now had his hand on the latch. 'I won't take up any more of your time, Mrs Tremayne.'

'I'm sorry I can't be more help.'

He gave her a brief smile and whisked himself out of the house, leaving Nancy to return to the unloved cornflakes.

She no longer had any appetite and, pushing them away, bent her mind to think over the news she'd just heard. It was yesterday that Pascoe had quarrelled badly with Tomas Almeda, and because of him Almeda had lost what must have been a well-paid job. More than that. This shadowy cartel Perry had spoken of—if they had been paying Almeda to stir trouble, he'd be no further use to them. Wouldn't they want to disassociate themselves from him, now that he'd been found out? So Almeda would be returning to Brazil without a job and possibly with little chance of finding another, at least in the region he called home.

Wouldn't he want to pay Pascoe back before he took the train to London and travelled to the airport? Nancy thought it likely. How easy it would be for Almeda to lure the man down to the harbour. The promise of the money he was owed or taunts about his cowardice would work equally well. Then while Pascoe was drunk, unstable on his feet, perhaps only semi-conscious, how easy to push him into the sea and hold him beneath the waters, leaving a retreating tide to wash him up the next morning like so much flotsam.

According to Aiden Bolitho, the police were taking the death seriously, yet Nancy had a hunch they would eventually come down on the side of an accident. Another accident. One of far too many. First Treeve Fenton, then Ned, and now Pascoe. Frustratingly, there seemed nothing she could do to prove that villainy rather than fate was at work. It was all so subtle, so easily explained, so swiftly forgotten.

Her inability to get to grips with what was going on in Port Madron, and the thought that Philip March could even now be close, made Nancy jumpy and restless, uncomfortable to be alone in the house. She would walk down to the village, she decided. At least there would be people there—no doubt a fair sprinkling of onlookers gathered at the harbour to watch the police at work.

She found a light jacket and slung her handbag over her shoulder, but when she opened the door it was to see a small yellow van in the driveway. Kitty Anson jumped out.

'I've brought you your pasties,' she said. 'Sorry they're a bit late, but at least you'll have lunch today.'

'Thank you, Kitty. I'd completely forgotten them.'

'Me, too,' the young woman confessed, throwing back her head in a laugh that made her curls bob.

Nancy took the pasties back into the kitchen while Kitty followed her. 'Seems a bit quiet around here,' she remarked.

'Leo and his brother are at the hospital.'

'But not you?' There was understanding in Kitty's eyes or so Nancy thought.

'They're speaking to the consultant this morning, and it's better for Ned to see his sons alone,' she said lightly. 'If I were there, he'd have to make conversation.'

'And so would you.' Kitty burst into another laugh. 'Don't worry. I know Ned Tremayne. He's a crusty old bugger. I don't suppose you went down too well as the new bride.'

It wasn't a subject Nancy wanted to pursue and she was quick to say, 'I thought I'd walk down to the village.'

'Do you really want to? Wouldn't you rather come with me? I'm making deliveries this morning—it would give you the chance to see more of the local area.'

Nancy was surprised at the invitation. Kitty had said nothing of the police presence in the village.

'We can find a nice pub,' her friend went on, 'and there *are* some—they're not all like the Tinners—and have a drink and a bite to eat.'

It was an appealing prospect, and Nancy found herself saying yes. For a moment, she wondered whether she should leave a note for Leo. But only for a moment. She had cried herself to sleep last night and today he had done nothing to make her feel better, leaving without even saying goodbye.

'Where are we going? she asked, once they were settled in the van.

'Here and there. We've quite a distance to cover. Cadgwith's our first stop, then Coverack and St Keverne and then back to Port Madron.'

'And we're delivering groceries?'

'No, my luvver. The villages have their own stores for that. It's my pasty delivery.'

When Nancy looked puzzled, she said teasingly, 'Didn't you know? I've got quite a name in these parts. Wait until you taste one of those lovelies I've left you and you'll understand. Villages around here are desperate for my pasties! Well, the nobs anyway. They're the only ones who can afford them. I don't come cheap.' There was another gurgle of laughter.

'Do you do this trip every week?'

'Every week, come rain or shine. Tuesday is baking day or baking evening rather—I have to watch the shop in the day. Then Wednesday, I've been closing in the mornings so I could deliver these little darlings. Until Hedra started work, that is.'

'It sounds a lot of effort. You must find it worthwhile.'

'Money-wise? Definitely. And I like to think it's my small contribution to human happiness!'

'You'll have had to close the shop this morning, I suppose. Mrs Pascoe won't have come to work.'

'How do you mean?' Kitty steered the van expertly around

two double bends.

'You haven't heard?'

'Oh, Jory, you mean. Him drowning like that. Yes, I heard.' She glanced across at her companion. 'Don't look so shocked, Nancy. The man was never sober. He was an accident waiting to happen. You saw what he did to himself when he came barging in on us last time I saw you. He was bound to end up in a mess.'

Nancy thought her friend harsh. Jory Pascoe was an unpleasant man, but he was still a man and he'd left a loving wife behind.

'Have you seen Mrs Pascoe today?'

'I'm planning to call on her when we get back. See how she's doing.'

'The poor woman must be in shock, but I guess work will be a lifeline for her—eventually—once she feels she can cope. Keeping busy in the shop, talking to people every day.'

Kitty shook her head. 'Hedra won't be working for me anymore.'

Nancy turned to her in surprise. 'I thought you needed help in the shop.'

'She's been useful enough, but really I can manage on my own.'

That seemed to wrap up the conversation and they sat in silence until they reached Cadgwith, Kitty steering the van carefully down its narrow streets and eventually stopping by the sea wall. She jumped out and opened the back of the van. Nancy watched as she balanced a basket on one hip and took two more in each hand.

Kitty nodded towards the main street of the village and called out, 'I'll be back soon. All my customers live on this hill. Only the best for them!'

Nancy looked over her shoulder and saw what her

friend meant. Neat, white-washed cottages, one or two with thatched roofs, unusual for Cornwall, lined the hill leading up from the sea. Their front gardens were beautifully tended, and in a few weeks' time would be filled with flowers. The view from their windows must be stunning, she thought—a small picturesque cove with a shingle beach playing host to a spread of colourful small boats.

After yesterday's storm, the sea was now a mill pond and, when later they drove into Coverack, another charming fishing village, they found the harbour equally calm. From there they travelled inland to St Keverne and Kitty's last delivery. By the time they pulled into the Square at St Keverne, Nancy was feeling decidedly hungry.

'This is a nice place,' Kitty said, parking outside the Three Tuns. 'They do some of the best crab sandwiches around.'

Nancy dutifully ordered a crab sandwich at the bar and with glasses of cider in hand, they settled themselves at a table in the snug.

'So, Mrs Tremayne, when you are back to London? Can't be long now.'

'I hope not.' Nancy tried not to sigh. 'Cornwall is beautiful, but I have a job to go to and I'm worried that I'll lose it if don't return soon.'

'They let you take time off then?'

'I explained about Mr Tremayne being so ill and my mentor said I was to go immediately. But she can't be happy that I've been away over a week already, and Leo hasn't once mentioned returning.'

'A mentor? Sounds fancy.' Kitty bit into her thick sandwich, spraying a fair amount of crab around the plate.

'It's not really fancy. I'm doing an apprenticeship—in art restoration. It can be gritty work sometimes. Other times it's slow and painstaking, but very rewarding. I'm learning on the job, you see, and it's why my mentor is so important. She's amazingly knowledgeable.'

'You love it, I can tell.'

'I do, Kitty. To be honest I can't wait to get back to it.' She took a long sip of cider.

'Then get back to it. I bet that husband of yours will be getting back to *his* work as soon as he needs to.'

Nancy thought about the paper Leo was writing for the forthcoming conference and knew he'd make sure to get back to London for that.

'I can't just leave though,' she protested.

'Why not? I'll run you to Truro station. Plenty of trains to London from there.'

Nancy laughed. 'You're preaching sedition.'

'What else is there?'

'Do you miss London?' she asked, when they had pushed their empty plates to one side.

Kitty looked at her askance. 'Why would I? When I live in a beautiful spot, have a lovely flat and a job I enjoy?'

'I just wondered if you found Port Madron a little quiet,' she said mildly. 'Particularly in the winter. '

Kitty shrugged. 'It's only quiet if you let it be. London may be busy, but it's soulless. No one cares for anyone there.' The edge to her voice suggested a well of unhappiness.

'But your job? Working for a high-class jeweller must be glamorous. You must have enjoyed it.' Nancy was curious to know what was behind that edge.

'You don't go home to glamour though, do you? You go home to a miserable bedsit, overrun with mice.'

'Surely not when you married? When you moved to the suburbs?'

'Oh, that,' Kitty said off-handedly. 'It was okay, but not a patch on Port Madron. Trevor would have agreed with me.

153

The pity was he never got to enjoy living here.'

'It is a lovely place,' Nancy agreed, 'but I can see that making a living can be hard.'

'It's true the fishing is bad right now, but mining is always hard. The tinners know that and accept it. It's a filthy, dangerous job, but they go down those tunnels every day because it's the only thing they can do.'

'Do you know any of the miners well? Apart from Jory Pascoe, I mean.'

'They come into the shop from time to time. Decent men. All they ask is decency in return.'

Nancy frowned. 'You don't think they're treated well?'

'How would I know?' Kitty spread her hands. 'Bosses make promises, don't they, but are happy to shrug them off. It's the same the world over. C'mon—we should be getting back.'

They had walked to the van and were about to get in when Kitty suddenly stopped.

'Damn! The pasties. I had some for the pub and clean forgot. Here, you get in and I'll take them to the kitchen.' She reached into the back of the van for a small covered box. 'The Three Tuns is a good customer of mine.' She winked. 'It's why we got a quid off the bill.'

Nancy climbed into the front seat, still wondering at Kitty's words. Her friend was a strange mix, she thought, but it had been an interesting morning. She wished she'd had a map with her to trace their journey from village to village. Kitty did a lot of travelling—perhaps she had one. Nancy opened the glove compartment and shuffled her hand around. There was a map, just as she'd thought. She'd have a quick look while she waited for Kitty to emerge.

She unfolded the large square of paper onto her knee, draping its top half across the compartment lid. In doing so, something fell into the well of the van and she picked it up.

It was a small, square photograph of a young woman taken against a plain blue background. It looked like a photograph you'd have done for a passport, except it was in colour. It was slightly blurry, but even so the woman bore an astonishing resemblance to Kitty, the same cluster of small, tight curls, though dark brown rather than blonde. If it was Kitty, Nancy guessed that it had been taken two or three years ago. She turned it over to see if there was a date. People often wrote that on the back of photographs. Instead there was just a name: Sally Crouch.

Kitty opened the door and plumped down into the driver's seat. She stared at the photograph Nancy was holding. 'What are you doing with that?' she demanded.

'I wanted to look at a map, see where we'd been today. This photo fell out.'

Kitty took it from her, then turned to her smiling. 'My cousin, Sally.

'You're very alike.'

'My mother always said we could be twins.'

Identical twins, Nancy thought, and wondered about the photograph. But Kitty had started the engine.

'Ready for the long trundle back? Sorry the old van isn't more comfortable.'

The once firm leather seats had sagged and Nancy was already suffering backache, but the morning had been a treat, and she said so.

'It's been a wonderful trip and I'm sure your van never lets you down, even if it is old. I hope not anyway. I wouldn't like to break down on any of these country roads.'

'I have done once or twice in the past—the van's an old girl, after all—but I coped. I'm pretty good with machines.'

'You're a miracle woman,' Nancy said warmly.

'You bet!' And Kitty snorted with laughter.

Chapter Nineteen

Waving goodbye to Kitty, as the van chugged its way down the Penleven drive, Nancy heard the front door open and turned to see Leo standing in the doorway.

'Been out and about?' he asked.

'Kitty was on her delivery round. She invited me to go with her,' Nancy said quietly, glad that at least they were talking to each other.

'I'm sorry I had to leave so early this morning.' Leo stood back to let her pass into the house. 'Sorry we didn't get to speak. I didn't want to wake you. You looked so peaceful.'

Did Leo really believe she'd been at peace? If so, he'd managed to sweep aside last night's painful disagreement. Nancy wished she could, too.

Conjuring up a smile, she asked, 'How did you find your father? Is he still doing well?'

'He is, yes.' Leo walked with her into the kitchen. 'In fact, he seems a great deal stronger. The hospital asked for a meeting with Perry and myself first thing, but only to discuss the best way forward for Dad. They're discharging him after the weekend, if all continues well.'

'That is good news.' She felt genuinely happy for Ned. Most of all for his sons.

'He'll need to make adjustments to his daily routine,

mind,' Leo went on, 'and he's not going to like it.'

'Are you thinking he won't be able to go to the mine?' Nancy crossed to the sink and filled the kettle. 'Do you want some tea, Leo? I had cider for lunch and it's made me very thirsty.'

Her husband gave a vague nod. 'Work is a big concern,' he agreed. 'Dad has to learn to put his feet up.'

'I can see that won't be easy.'

'Not remotely easy. Plus getting him into the habit of taking medicine regularly for the first time in his life. He's been given a whole regiment of pills and we'll need to make sure he takes every one of them and at the right time of day. Perry—he's gone to Wheal Agnes, by the way—will have to find more reliable help than Mrs Cheffers. Someone who'll keep the house clean and cook every day for them. Maybe supervise the pill schedule.'

'That's a tall order.'

'Don't I know it! I want to stay and help Perry as much as I can, but I've got this conference coming up at the end of next week and I need to be back in London for it.'

Nancy filled the teapot and arranged cups and saucers. No mention of my work, she thought, but if it meant she would be back in London very soon, she was happy. Cornwall was heart-stoppingly beautiful, but she was chafing to be in the studio again.

'I was wondering...' Leo sat down at the kitchen table and cradled his cup in his hand. 'How would you feel if I bobbed back to London, did the conference and then came back to collect you?'

Nancy put her own cup down with a thump, not sure she had heard aright. 'You want me to stay here, but you leave?'

'It would help Perry enormously. And help me, too. I feel bad trotting off and leaving him to it. Whereas if you were here, he'd have back-up. It would only be for a few days.'

Or would it, she thought? What was the likelihood that Leo would find other calls on his time, as essential as this conference, and she'd be left here until… until it suited him?

She gave him a straight look. 'No,' she said.

'No?' He seemed shocked, his head jerking backwards as though someone had punched him on the chin.

'I don't want to stay here on my own, Leo. I want to go back to London, too. I have a job as well.'

'But it's not – '

Nancy interrupted him before he could finish the hateful sentence. 'Go on, say it. It's not important.'

'Well, is it really that important, darling?'

She jumped up from the table and scooped the empty cups into the sink. 'It is to me,' she said in a furious voice. 'And to you, I think, since you seem intent on making sure I can't do it.'

Leo jumped up, too, and walked over to stand behind her. 'That's unfair, Nancy. I'm just surprised it means so much to you.'

More than a baby was what he didn't say, but she knew he was thinking it.

'It means a great deal. Connie has been very understanding in allowing me to take so long away, but I don't want to abuse her kindness—I need to begin work again as soon as I can. If you're going back to London once you've seen your father settled at home, I'm coming with you.'

'If that's how you feel, you can leave earlier still. Archie is flying the Cessna back the day after tomorrow. You can go with him, then you'll be sure to get back for Connie.' Leo almost snapped out her mentor's name.

Going back with Archie was the last thing Nancy wanted to do. Being alone together in the Cavendish Street house was a very bad idea.

When she spoke again, she tried to keep the anger she still felt from her voice. 'I'll stay here until you leave, Leo, and we'll travel home together.'

He seemed to relent a little and put his hand on her arm, drawing her closer. 'I'm sorry I'm a bit of a grump. Your job— it's just that I—'

But he never finished whatever explanation he was about to offer since Perran burst through the kitchen door.

'Have you heard?' he asked, a trifle wildly, his expression deeply troubled. 'About Jory Pascoe?'

'Sit down, Perry.' Nancy drew out a chair for him. 'It's a shock, isn't it? A policeman—Aiden Bolitho, he said his name was—came here just after you'd both left this morning and told me the news.'

'I can't believe such a thing could happen.' Perry drew a hand through his hair.

'Well, I can,' Nancy said firmly. 'You told us how drunk Pascoe was yesterday. But I agree that to drown like that is horrific.'

'Pascoe's dead? At least he won't cause you any more trouble,' Leo said brutally.

Perry sat staring at the kitchen table. 'That's true,' he said, reluctantly. 'I certainly don't need any more problems. I've five days in which to find a more or less full-time housekeeper. That's in addition to getting Dad to understand what pills he needs to take and when.'

'And persuade him that he no longer belongs at Wheal Agnes,' Leo put in.

'What about approaching Grace Jago?' Nancy had had a flash of inspiration. 'She wouldn't be able to live-in, but she could cook for you and clean. Maybe even take on the pill schedule. Mr Fenton was one of her best customers, so she might be looking for new work.'

'I don't know.' Perry sat in silent thought for a while. 'She must have other people she works for and I don't like to ask her to give them up. And she'd have to—Dad is going to need a lot of looking after.'

'Don't dismiss the idea completely,' Nancy told him. 'Grace might be willing to do it if she knew the job at Penleven was permanent—and paid well.'

When he still hesitated, she said, 'I could sound her out if you like. I've met her a couple of times and we got on well together.'

'Would you?' Perry's eagerness showed he was gradually coming round to the idea. 'The truth is I don't think I've ever spoken to her. I know Archie's mother a little, of course. She comes to the door to sell fish, and one of his brothers—Lowen, wasn't it? He was a great friend to Treeve. But none of the rest of the family, and I'd feel a bit awkward approaching her.'

'I'll walk to the village now if you like. She'll be home, I think. She has to collect her young daughters from school.'

***

She remembered Grace's house from the time Archie had dropped his sister-in-law at her front door, the first full day Nancy had been in Cornwall. The day she'd found her way to Treeve Fenton's house. The cottage was down a narrow side street, a short walk from where Morwenna Jago lived. Was Archie at home with his mother, after driving the Tremayne brothers to Truro and back early this morning? For a moment, she toyed with the idea of asking him to walk back with her to Penleven. A stupid idea! There was no need for her to be scared. She wouldn't be at Grace's more than an hour and it would still be light when she left. She could walk home the long way round, avoiding that narrow lane.

She was welcomed at Grace's door with a smile and a cup of tea. As soon as her hostess heard of the Penleven offer, she jumped up from her chair, upsetting a basket of knitting in the process, and flung her arms around Nancy in a fierce hug.

'That's amazin',' Grace said breathlessly. 'Thank you fer suggestin' me. I reckon it were your suggestion, weren't it?'

'It was,' Nancy admitted, smiling up at her, 'but I wasn't sure whether it would be something you'd want to consider.'

'Consider? I'm goin' to jump at it feet first. Permanent hours and a decent wage.'

'Perry was concerned about your other customers. That you'd have to let them down.'

Grace regained her seat and gave a loud sniff. 'Apart from one old dear, they blow hot and cold. Sometimes they want me. Sometimes they don't. And I can always fit the old lady in one evenin'. Treeve were my mainstay and since 'e's been gone I've been scratchin' around to fill the gap.'

'Mr Tremayne will need a lot of looking after,' Nancy warned, 'and he might not be the easiest person to deal with.'

'Don't you fret, my dear. I know Ned Tremayne. He were often at Treeve's and 'e can be a pussy cat if 'e wants.' She broke off to shout at a rustling that had started in the kitchen. 'Put those chocolate biscuits back in the cupboard, Heather, and you, Susie.'

'It's my birthday, Mum,' a small voice wailed.

'Not until the day after tomorrow, it isn't.' Grace turned back to her visitor. 'Wait till I tell Rich the news. He'll be over the moon. He's been that worried.'

'The fishing is poor I've heard.'

'Poor isn't in it. Rich works so hard, takes risks—sails too long and too far. I don' like to dwell on that, but nothin's worked. I wanted 'im to think about pottin'. Crabs and lobster and so on but 'e's too proud. Says it ain't proper fishin'.'

'That's what Clem Hoskins does, isn't it?'

Grace nodded. 'Ma told me Clem laid into you. So sorry about that. He's not usually mean—not like Jory Pascoe— just kinda weak. But the fishin' bein' bad and the mine bein' uncertain, everyone in the village is on end.'

'Perhaps the dust will settle now.'

'Now that Jory's gone? Mebbe. Let's hope so. Did you hear what the police found?'

'All I've heard is that he was discovered on the beach this morning and the police are investigating. Though I didn't see any of them when I walked here.'

'You won't, they're long gone. As soon as they found out he'd been drinkin' fer most of yesterday, they put it down to an accident. They arsked around, to be fair, but no one 'ad seen anythin', so I guess that's it.'

'It seems a little early to decide it was an accident.'

Nancy was disappointed but not surprised. She'd hoped that when they investigated Pascoe's death, the police would realise the significance of what was now a string of accidents.

'I can't blame them not botherin' too much,' Grace said. 'When you think about it, it were bound to be an accident. It were high tide last night and the silly bugger 'ad been drinkin' fer hours, so the boys told me. But no, what I meant was did you know what the police found when they went to the house to tell Pascoe's missus the sad news? It's taken a load off my mind, I must say.'

'How do you mean?' Nancy was confused.

'Remember the clock and the porcelain bowl that went missin' from Treeve's?'

'Yes, you were wondering whether or not to report it.'

'Well, in the end, I did. Leastways I told Aiden—casual like. Anyways when he went to Pascoe's house this mornin' to break the news to Hedra, he saw this bag open on the sittin' room floor. He asked 'er what it was, suspicious like. And she said she'd found it at the back of the cupboard and she were goin' to ask Jory when 'e came in. But then she remembered 'e weren't comin' in and started howlin'. Aiden took the bag and ran.'

'The bag contained Treeve's clock and bowl?'

'Absolutely. That slimy toad, Pascoe, 'ad walked into the house and stolen them. Then hid them in the back of a cupboard. The only reason Hedra had gone to the cupboard was her carpet sweeper weren't working and she thought she 'ad a tool somewheres that would release the rollers. She found something a bit more valuable, eh?'

Nancy felt dazed. She was trying hard to make sense of Grace's recital, grasp what it could mean for finding the would-be murderer.

'Are you all right, my luvver?' Grace asked anxiously. 'You look awful pale.'

'There's been a lot of things happening, that's all, and this is just the latest.' Then on a sudden thought, she asked, 'Do you know a Sally Crouch?'

Grace shook her head. 'Should I?'

'I'm not sure. I saw a photo this morning and wondered if she lived in the village.' That must sound odd, she thought, but she had to stay vague. She'd no wish to inflame Grace's curiosity by being more specific, particularly as it concerned Kitty Anson, a woman for whom Grace had no love.

'There's no Sally Crouch in Port Madron, nor in any village round 'ere, I doubt. Not ezactly a Cornish name, is it? But where are my manners? Let me get you another cup of tea.'

'It's kind of you, Grace, but no thanks. I must be getting back, and your girls will want their supper. Your husband, too.'

'Not Rich. He's off fishin' somewheres. He better be back fer the party, though. It's Suzie's tenth and her Nana is giving her a big tea. You're invited.'

'Me?'

'Yes, you. Why ever not? You're one of the family—sort of. Bring your husband, too.'

'That's so nice of you. But a birthday present—'

'Forget that. Just bring yerself.'

***

As she'd promised herself, Nancy took the long way round to Penleven. It gave her time to analyse what she had just learned. Pascoe was a thief, which meant that at some point he had crept into Treeve Fenton's house unseen. Had it been the night Mr Fenton had died? Had Treeve disturbed him in the act of stealing and there'd been a struggle? Nancy's mind raced on. Maybe he'd knocked Treeve out. Perhaps he thought he'd killed him and then set about making it look like an accident. Except that Treeve could still have been alive. From the start, it had been assumed that Treeve had died accidentally, his age a clear factor in the tragedy, and as far as Nancy knew, there had never been a pathologist's report to establish the actual sequence leading to his death. She could visualise the scene distinctly. Jory, panicking he'd killed a man, running the water and then tipping Treeve into the bath without checking for a pulse, thinking he had a dead body on his hands. Jory Pascoe wasn't the brightest of men.

If Pascoe was guilty of Treeve's murder, what about the attack on Ned? The timing fitted—the man had gone absent from the mine that day—and the method was just about possible, even for someone who wasn't a great thinker. But why do it, if Treeve's death was accidental and not part of a plan? Had it given Pascoe the idea? He hated the Tremaynes, may have waited for months to get his own back on them, then suddenly he found he'd killed the closest person to Ned

Tremayne. Someone, who until a few years ago, had been essential to the running of Wheal Agnes.

When Ned had suffered the heart attack, did Pascoe feel jubilant, reckoning that he'd been the cause of it? Nancy could imagine him boasting to himself that, by killing Treeve, he'd brought Ned Tremayne to his knees. So why not finish the job? From what Nancy knew of Jory Pascoe, it was an act of vengeance he'd enjoy. But the poisoning had failed, Ned had begun to recover, yet Pascoe hadn't tried again. Or so it seemed. Instead, he appeared to have switched tack and gone for the Tremaynes in a different way—by conspiring with Almeda.

Then fresh in her mind, another idea… and with it a small spurt of relief. Pascoe could be her enemy, too. He would consider her as much a target as Ned and attacking her would be another way to attack the Tremaynes. Yesterday, as she'd scurried along that narrow lane, feeling a hunted animal— could that have been Pascoe? And before? It seemed he could walk into people's houses with impunity so why not people's summerhouses? The ripped cardigan and the painted knife could have been his attempt to intimidate. A last attempt, as it turned out. If so, the fear was over. Pascoe was dead and there would be no more threats. It was a thought she must cling to.

Chapter Twenty

The next morning, Perry greeted the news that Grace Jago was happy to take the job at Penleven with the biggest smile Nancy had seen on his face since she'd arrived. He must have thanked her half a dozen times before she said laughingly, 'Let's hope it works out, Perry. If not, you won't be thanking me!'

'It will, I know. It's marvellous news and I could do with a boost after that—' He stopped abruptly.

'After what?'

'It's nothing. Nothing to worry about. Just one of those letters again.'

'An anonymous letter?'

'They're ridiculous, aren't they?' Perry gave an unconvincing laugh. 'About time the idiot who's sending them stopped.'

Ridiculous maybe, but deadly serious. Treeve had received one and died. Ned had nearly died. When had Perry received the note? She didn't want to upset him further by asking, but with Pascoe dead, she'd expected the letters to stop.

Perry put on his bright smile again. 'The best thing this morning is that I can go to work not worrying about Dad. Leo is coming with me. How about you?'

'Leo is going to Wheal Agnes?'

166

'You sound surprised. But, of course, you don't know. After you'd gone to bed last night, I had a phone call from Brazil. It was Silva and he's offered that partnership. I've come to the conclusion, if I can get Dad to agree, that it's the best way forward. But I don't just need to talk to Dad. The men are involved in this, too, and they're restless after Jory Pascoe's death. I've got to talk to them again. See how they'd view the mine being partly in foreign hands.'

'And that's why Leo is going with you?'

'Moral support,' her husband said, coming into the kitchen, his jacket slung over his arm.

'Then I think you can probably do without mine. I'll stay home.'

A degree of strain still existed between them. Perry's sudden appearance yesterday had interrupted the conversation they needed to have. About work, about a baby. And the subject had not been mentioned since.

In any case, it was best the two men went alone. The miners were more likely to listen if they felt the family were consulting them, and she was still an outsider. She always would be. And not just at Wheal Agnes. Not just at Penleven either. Sometimes it seemed to Nancy that she'd been an outsider from the day she'd been born. Hers had been a solitary life in London when Leo had scooped her up and married her, and before that she'd led a lonely existence at home in Riversley. At school she'd made just one true friend—Rose was still in her life and she was glad of it.

A few years ago their friendship had almost ruptured. She'd been angry with Rose for warning her against Philip March—but how right her friend had been. When she'd offered a heartfelt apology, Rose had been magnanimous, enough for Nancy to feel she could again share her deepest feelings. And after the miscarriage in Malfuego, she had needed a woman friend, someone who'd known her from a young age, someone who had children of her own and would understand. She'd written to Rose then, pouring out her pain. Her distress at her husband's angry response.

Later, when she'd returned to London, they'd had tea at Simpsons—Nancy's treat—and talked and talked, past problems forgotten. It transpired that Rose and her husband were thinking of moving out of London, to Dorset, where Mike had family. *You must come and visit*, Rose had said, seizing Nancy's hand. *'I might be miles away, but I'll always be there for you, you know that.*

She wished Rose was here now. Being alone in this house never felt easy, but at least this morning it offered a rare chance to phone her mentor—without irritating Leo. Earlier, she'd been too panicked by the theft of her notebook to make the call. Now, though, she dusted down the book and hoped she'd made out the studio's telephone number correctly. Hoped, too, that Connie was willing to excuse her long silence. Dialling the number, she felt apprehensive, but when her mentor answered, she could not have been more charming. Nancy mustn't fret over her prolonged absence, she said—they would catch up on the work together as soon as she returned. Nevertheless, Connie sounded glad that she was likely to see her apprentice back in the studio after the coming weekend. Nancy crossed her fingers as she agreed. No definite day had yet been fixed for their return.

The telephone call took only a few minutes and she was faced with what to do for the rest of the morning. Leo would be home for lunch, she imagined, but that was hours away. She walked to the kitchen window and looked out, hoping for inspiration. The view was dreary, the garden looking bedraggled. Perry had mentioned he employed a part-time gardener, but judging by the state of the lawn, the man must be very part-time. There were still heaps of autumn leaves scattered across grass and flower beds. Spring bulbs had pushed their way through the mulch, but these too had been left to their own devices. Dead snowdrops, dying daffodils, and a new batch of tulips, their multi-coloured display making a brave attempt to brighten the space.

She made a decision. She would spend a few hours working in the garden. In such a short time, it was unlikely she'd manage much of an improvement, but even a small one was welcome. And if she made sure to stay working at the front of the house, she could avoid going anywhere near the summerhouse. Her dread of the place was continuing, even with Pascoe dead. That made her sad, since she was sure it had been Rachel Tremayne's favourite hide-away.

Nancy hadn't worked in a garden for many years, not since she'd lived at home in Hampshire, and that was a long time ago. She'd left Riversley at seventeen, much to her parents' alarm, determined to carve out a life for herself away from the village, away from parents for whom she felt little closeness. She had gone to London, determined on a career in the art world, and after several dead-end jobs, had managed to land a post in one of the capital's prestigious auction houses. Her progress, though, had been hampered—a male hierarchy had seen to that—and any hopes she'd still cherished of climbing the career ladder had been ended abruptly by Philip March's inhuman pursuit.

Walking through into the scullery, she looked around for the gardening tools she remembered having seen there. Some worn gloves and a trowel had been stored on a top shelf and, in a corner, she found a wire leaf rake. That would be the first thing she'd need.

Gathering the implements together brought a vivid picture into her mind. Of her father's allotment. It had been his pride and joy and, when she'd been a small girl, Nancy had tried to help him whenever he let her, tried to be the son he'd so much wanted—pulling out weeds, ridding cabbages of caterpillars, shaking dirt from newly dug potatoes. Would Harry Nicholson still be digging or was age making it impossible for him now?

For an instant, a wave of guilt overwhelmed her. She had not seen her parents for over three years and the single contact she'd made had been at a distressing time, not long after she'd miscarried. And then only because Leo had nagged her that she should at least let them know she was alive and well. She had agreed, but reluctantly. Her parents had not been kind. They had endorsed Philip March's version of events, taken his side against her, and been furious when she'd rejected him. Without their support, she had been left alone to fight a man who was intent on destroying her—until Leo had ridden to the rescue.

Nancy had always had the fear that if she got in touch with her parents, they would lead Philip to her, and in her letter she'd made no mention of her marriage and given no address, simply stating they were not to worry about her— not that she thought they would. The Nicholsons still had no idea of who she was and where she lived, so Archie must be right in saying it was impossible for Philip March to be behind the threats that had blighted her stay at Penleven. It had to have been Jory Pascoe.

After a brief survey, she decided to work on a small patch of ground slightly to one side of the house. It appeared to be the most neglected, possibly because it was invisible from any of the windows. It would give her a partial view of the drive so that she'd see Leo when he returned home, and it was a small enough area to be able to finish in a morning and feel some pride in a job well done.

Walking around the corner of the house, she stopped dead. Someone had cleared the leaves, but not from any benevolence. They had been gathered into a heap in the middle of the square patch of grass and formed into a definite shape. The shape of a coffin. There was no mistaking it and, as if to ram home the message, a rough cross had been made out of twigs and driven into the earth at the head of the makeshift grave.

Nancy's hands went numb. The rake tumbled to the ground. The trowel and gloves fell with a thud. She felt a churning in her stomach. How long had this dreadful thing been here? Was it another instance of Jory Pascoe's malice, a legacy he'd manufactured before he died? Or was there someone other than Jory involved in her persecution? The old terrors were returning in full strength, locking iron bands around her chest and choking her lungs so that she struggled to breathe. She had to get inside, sit down, before she fell.

A noise made Nancy lift her head for an instant. Kitty Anson's yellow van was rolling up the drive and, through a haze of tears, she saw her friend wave a hand, then jump out of the van and drag a cardboard box from its interior.

'Perry ordered these on his way over to Wheal Agnes,' Kitty called out. 'The shop is as dead as a dodo this morning, so I thought I'd nip out for a few minutes and deliver them. He said you were pretty low on supplies.'

She began walking towards Nancy, but then stopped abruptly and dropped the box on the grass, rushing the rest of the way with arms extended for a warm hug. 'What's the matter, my 'ansome? You look fair stricken.'

Nancy managed to raise a trembling hand and in silence pointed to the heap of leaves.

Her companion stared at it in amazement. 'Someone having a laugh?'

Nancy found her voice at last. 'I don't think so,' she said shakily.

'Here, you need to sit down.' Kitty sounded more concerned than Nancy had ever heard her. 'Let's get indoors.'

Once in the kitchen, Nancy sank into a chair, staring blankly at the opposite wall.

'Tea,' Kitty said briskly. 'No. Brandy. As it happens, I've a small bottle in the van, but don't tell anyone!'

She was gone a few seconds only and, when she returned, poured a tot into one of the china mugs left to dry on the draining board.

'This is what you need.' She handed Nancy the mug and when Nancy shook her head, urged her to drink. 'Believe me, you'll feel better.'

The action was so reminiscent of Archie, that Nancy could have cried all over again. If only he were here. If only she had him beside her. But obediently she sipped the brandy and the colour gradually returned to her cheeks.

'Where's your husband?' Kitty demanded. 'You shouldn't be on your own in this state.'

'He's at the mine with Perry, but he'll be back at lunchtime—I think.'

'Good.' She paused for a moment, frowning heavily. 'So, what's all this about? That stuff outside—it's a bit gruesome, but most people would have shrugged it off. Why didn't you?'

Nancy took another sip of brandy before she felt able to talk. Then in a quiet voice she recounted, one by one, the threats she'd suffered since coming to Penleven: the ruined portrait, the loss of her notebook and pen, the mangled cardigan and the blood-stained knife.

'Phew.' Kitty blew out her cheeks. 'Someone in this village really doesn't like you. But who would want to terrorise you in this way?'

'I simply don't know. '

It was the truth. Nancy might suspect, but she didn't know, and it seemed wrong to mention her belief, strong though it was, that Jory Pascoe was the villain. The grave could have been constructed by him days ago and lain undisturbed ever since—no one visited that side of the house, as far as Nancy knew. It was sheltered from the wind, and the rain had only served to mulch the leaves further into the grass.

'A bogey man, my dear,' Kitty said rousingly. 'Or a bogey woman. Someone who's a coward leastways. You're not to think about it. Sweep it from your mind, otherwise they win.'

'I know I should, but when you feel so threatened, it's not easy.'

'I can imagine. But tell the professor—and Perry, too. Then they can be on the lookout. If you're all on the case, you should catch the blighter red-handed. How about some sweet tea to put you right back on your feet?'

Nancy smiled weakly. 'I'm okay, Kitty, really. And thank you for looking after me. You're a real friend.'

'I hope so.' Kitty looked at her quizzically.

Nancy thought for a moment and then, quelling any misgivings, asked, 'Was that photograph I found in the van really of your cousin?' It had been a small niggle from the day she'd seen the picture.

Kitty gave her a stern look. 'You don't believe me?'

'I do,' she said desperately. 'It's just that the girl looked so much like you.'

'I told you why.' Kitty's voice had grown hard. 'Families can throw up that kind of weird likeness. You either believe me or you don't. And while we're on the subject of lies, what about yours? That you're an apprentice in an art studio.'

'I am,' Nancy protested.

'Then why did I overhear Grace Jago say to another

customer that you were an investigator? That woman is a terrible gossip, by the way. Is this apprenticeship just a cover for what you really do? If so, apparently, you're investigating me now. Which is a strange thing to do to a friend.'

Nancy reached out for her companion's hand, but Kitty withdrew it sharply.

'It was a stupid thing to say,' she admitted. 'I work in an art studio. I'm not a proper investigator and I'm not trying to stir trouble. If I'm truthful, I had a fleeting thought when I saw that photograph that maybe you'd changed your name and your appearance because you'd been abused.' When Kitty began bouncing in her seat, Nancy held up her hand. 'We all have our stories and I thought it possible.'

Her friend burst out laughing. 'Trevor abuse me? The man adored me.'

Nancy smiled in relief. 'I've been foolish. I think this scary stuff has got to me. I've had to deal with an abuser myself, a fiancé who wouldn't accept our engagement was over.'

'Is that why you married Leo Tremayne?' Kitty asked shrewdly.

'I love Leo.'

'Right on, but did you marry him as a way of protecting yourself from the creepy fiancé?'

Put so baldly, it sound dreadful. Mercenary and uncaring.

Kitty patted Nancy's arm. 'Don't worry, my love. Like you say, we all have our stories. We do what we need to. Right now, though, you shouldn't be on your own. How about I drop you at Wheal Agnes on my way back to the village? It's only a small detour. Then Professor Leo can play the concerned husband.'

She said it lightly, but Nancy got the distinct feeling that Leo had not made the best impression on Kitty.

Chapter Twenty-One

Kitty drove through the gates of Wheal Agnes at full speed, pulling up sharply outside the row of offices situated to one side of the headgear.

'Do you want me to come with you?' she asked.

Opening the van door, Nancy smiled back at her. 'I'll be fine, Kitty, and you have a shop to run. But thanks again for being such a good friend this morning.'

'If you're sure... See you around the village then.' Kitty waved a hand, putting her foot heavily down on the accelerator and driving noisily back through the gates.

Nancy had only the haziest notion of the mine's layout. When she'd visited with Perry, they had met the group of men outside the offices where she now stood. Leo and his brother could be anywhere. But she was lucky. Walking to her left, a little way past the headgear, she found them deep in conversation. They looked up when they heard her approach, surprise on both their faces.

'You're here,' Leo said, a question in his voice. 'What happened to your morning at home?'

For an instant, the image of the leafy grave crushed Nancy's mind and she struggled to suppress it. 'Kitty called with the groceries Perry ordered,' she said as casually as she could. 'When she offered me a lift, I decided I'd come to meet you.'

She wanted very much to confide in her husband, grasp the nettle and speak of the fears that haunted her, but she knew he would insist it was her imagination to blame. An imagination that was too vivid, he always maintained. Leo was convinced that in marrying Nancy, he had put a stop to her persecution, and it would be difficult ever to persuade him otherwise. Nevertheless, it was important he knew what had been happening to her. Not here, though, not now.

Perry laid a friendly hand on her shoulder. 'It's good to see you here, Nancy. I wonder, would you like to look around?'

'I'd love to, but tell me first how did the meeting go? You've spoken to the men?'

'I did, as soon as we got here. We were just talking about it when you arrived. I think it went okay.' He looked across at Leo for confirmation and his brother gave a small nod. 'The men were willing to listen, at least. Jory's death appears to have had a calming effect. They seemed resigned more than anything. It can't be easy for them having no real say in what their future holds.'

Nancy knew how that felt. 'I'm sure you'll do the best for them,' she said warmly.

'One thing's for sure, I won't be signing any contract until I know their jobs are safe. But come on, let's start in the Mill. The compressor house won't interest you and I can't take you into the Dry. Strictly men only.'

'The Mill?' she queried.

'It houses the processes the materials go through, except for the actual drilling. And the tramming and hoisting. All the surface operations, in fact.'

Perry had already lost her and by the time she'd been taken to see the Mill Feed, the shaking tables, the Froth Flotation and the Magnetic Separator, Nancy was completely bemused, a host of strange words and strange procedures dancing through her head.

'Feeling tired?' her brother-in-law asked, smiling at her beneath his helmet as they walked through the far exit of the Mill. 'Or are you willing to brave the underground workings?'

They had travelled downhill in a series of steps as they'd made their way through the different levels of the Mill, and now the sea seemed very close, a sheet of deep blue water that spread itself invitingly before her. In comparison, the underground workings lacked appeal.

'I don't think she should—' Leo began to say. He had been following in their footsteps, his expression one of subdued boredom.

'It's quite safe,' his brother interrupted, trying to reassure.

'I'd love to go, Perry, if you'll take me.' It was Leo's desire to control that stirred rebellion in Nancy. 'But you don't have to come, Leo, if you'd rather go back to Penleven.'

'I'll come,' he said grumpily.

'Good. First, though, we need to get you both kitted out.' Perry ushered them back uphill towards the row of offices. 'Overalls, a hard hat and a head torch. I'll bring them to my office and you can get yourselves sorted there.' He looked down at Nancy's feet, encased in low-heeled leather pumps. 'I've boots for Leo, but you'll have to manage in those, I'm afraid.'

'It's what I said,' Leo muttered. 'It's not a good idea for Nancy to go underground.'

'I'm going,' she said with a bright smile. 'I'll just walk carefully.'

It wasn't only footwear that proved difficult. The overalls were a struggle for Nancy's slender figure, overwhelmed as she was by yards of heavy, thick cloth, but eventually once she was equipped to Perry's satisfaction, her brother-in-law walked them to the Landing House. From here, they would take a cage down to the mine workings.

'There are different compartments for services,' he explained. 'For the air and water pipes, the electric cables. And an additional shaft for hoisting the skips of ore—they're big, two tons—but the main shaft is kept for the miners. You can get to the Landing House the way we've come or along the passage from the Dry. Having a connecting walkway makes things easier for the men.'

When Nancy saw the cage that would take them some fifteen hundred vertical feet below ground, she felt her first shiver of apprehension, but told herself that it was nothing to what she had left behind at Penleven. And it *was* fascinating. Perry pressed a button to one side of the cage and three bells sounded. An answering three bells came from the winder's cab close by. With a flick of a lever, they were slowly lowered to the bottom, passing horizontal tunnels at different levels that had been driven out from the main shaft, large enough to allow men and machinery to pass safely.

'Those are the main tunnels,' Perry said. 'Cross cuts we call them. But they'll be others, driven off of them, to follow any tin-bearing lode we find.'

'What do you think?' Leo asked her, seemingly resigned to the expedition.

'It's vast.'

Vaster than anything Nancy had imagined. A cathedral of arches and cloisters, but instead of black-garbed clerics, there were groups of white-suited miners intent on the tasks set them for that day. As the cage dropped slowly, foot by foot, she felt the air change, growing warmer and thicker until, when the cage finally came to a stop, she stepped out into a thick soup of hot air. Perry had warned her she would find it noisy below ground as well as hot, and given her a pair of ear muffs to wear alongside the protective suit and helmet, but the noise echoing through the chambers that ran to the right and left of them was brutal, and became utterly deafening when Perry led the way along a smaller tunnel.

'The men here are developers,' he said, his words barely audible. He pointed to the two workers ahead of them, hammering drills into the rock face. 'They work in pairs, as you can see, to drill a pattern of holes in the face of the tunnel. It's tough work. The drills are heavy, but it's the vibration that's the worst. In later life, they often suffer from white finger.'

They had moved back a little from the drilling and Nancy asked, 'It sounds horrible. What is it?'

'Damage to the nerves and blood vessels in the hand, caused by holding a heavy drill for hours on end. It's a miserable legacy, but unfortunately the work has to be done. The blasters will come after them and fill the holes with gelatine to be fired by electric detonators. A normal round of explosives will break nearly twenty tons of rock.'

'They won't be blasting right now, I take it?'

'Don't worry. You're not about to go up in smoke,' Leo said.

Perry grinned at her. 'The blasting produces poisonous gases, so it's carried out at the end of the working day. That allows time for the ventilation system to get rid of the noxious stuff before the chaps begin work the next morning to "muck out". Clearing the rock,' he explained.

As the minutes passed, Nancy found the mine increasingly oppressive. The thought of all that rock pressing down on her head was becoming more and more uncomfortable. But what must it feel like to have fathoms of water over one's head?

'Are we near the sea here?' she asked, a trifle nervously.

'For that, we'd need to walk a good quarter of a mile further on,' her brother-in-law said, 'and those shoes of yours wouldn't be up to the terrain. We'll go back the way we came, then you can see the rock being loaded onto wagons ready for hoisting to the surface.'

Nancy had seen the rail lines when they'd first stepped out of the cage and wondered where they led. Now, as they reached the end of the track, she saw a line of skips filled with large rocks.

'They'll be on their way to the grizzly. That's the machine that crushes the rock. The ore will be hoisted to the surface in those skips, then pushed through the grizzly's parallel steel bars and fall into storage bins. Anything too large for the grizzly has to go to the jaw crusher.'

Perry turned to them, bright with enthusiasm, but then seeing their faces, said, 'You both look as if you've had enough. It can be pretty overwhelming, I know.'

'The noise is immense,' Nancy said. 'And the heat—I'm finding it difficult.'

'Thank God for ventilation shafts,' Leo put in.

They turned around and began to retrace their steps to where they had started, Nancy feeling a surge of relief when she saw the cage waiting to deliver them back to the surface.

'What happens if the ventilation system fails?' she asked. A shudder passed through her. Without it, this place would surely become an airless tomb.

'Simply put, we wouldn't be able to work.' Perry shut the cage door behind them and rang the bell. 'The ventilation system is crucial for the miners to stay safe. The fans draw foul air out of the mine at the same time as fresh air is drawn down the main shaft. We have air doors to control the direction of the airflow, and we can use them to seal off parts of the mine if we need to.'

'Even with ventilation, it was very warm down there,' Nancy said.

'The deeper the mine, the hotter it gets and the fouler the

air. Ventilation is essential to keep the air breathable, and to get rid of the smoke and the gases after blasting.'

'As essential as pumping out water to make sure Wheal Agnes stays dry,' Leo added wryly. 'I hope you're remembering all this, Nancy.'

She might not remember the details, but she'd not forget the overwhelming sense of entombment she had felt. The passageways were huge, but still the sense of hundreds of tons of cliff over her head, bearing down on her, the air being squeezed from her lungs, was frightening. She felt a new respect for the men whose daily work took them down this mine shaft.

'Do the miners often face a dangerous situation?' she asked.

'Mining is always going to be a dangerous business, there's no getting away from it,' Perry responded. 'But we have a team of rescuers trained to deal with any kind of accident or any outbreak of fire. In a confined space, a fire can mean disaster.'

They had reached the surface and Nancy walked out of the Landing House and breathed deeply. The air felt sweet. She wasn't sorry to have gone underground, but she hoped never to do it again.

'I'll drop you both home, if you like,' Perry said. 'I can spare half an hour to have lunch with you. Hopefully, Kitty's delivery includes a plate of pasties.'

Chapter Twenty-Two

A rchie made his escape from the kitchen as soon as he could. His mother and Grace had commandeered the room from early this morning and he was definitely in the way. It was only a small birthday party and surely it didn't need so much preparation? He climbed the narrow stairs to his bedroom and sat down on one of the single beds. He'd shared this room with his brother, Lowen, for years and more lately whenever he came back to Port Madron. This time he'd had the room to himself and it felt strange. He'd never been particularly close to Lowen—it was Rich, his eldest brother, he'd adored as a child and whom he still found easiest to talk to. But Lowen had been part of his life, an unchanging, unmoveable part, until suddenly he was no longer there.

A few hours more, Archie thought, and he'd be away from Port Madron himself. He'd leave early tomorrow, driving first up to Penleven to collect Leo's precious conference paper and then on to St Mawgan where he'd hand in the keys to the hire car. A flight to Croydon was waiting for him, and a very large bill when he arrived back at the airfield. Then off to central London and Cavendish Street in whatever transport he could find.

He wasn't sorry to be leaving Port Madron. He would miss Ma certainly, and miss drinking with Rich. Miss his nieces and Grace, for that matter. But this last week he'd felt suffocated. He wasn't sure why—it hadn't happened other times he'd come home—but he suspected it was Nancy's presence in the village that he found so unsettling. It was a paradox; he lived closer to her in London than he did at Port Madron. Except that in London they were rarely together. He was either travelling abroad with Leo or buzzing around town on various errands, and now that Nancy had a job she loved, she was rarely at home during the day.

But here there was no escape from each other. In Port Madron, he ran the risk of meeting her whenever he walked out of his front door. Inevitably, it reminded him of their journey to the Caribbean, where they'd been constantly thrown together. What had happened between them there lay deep in his memory. He should forget it, but he couldn't.

In Port Madron, though, it wasn't only the danger of proximity. It was seeing Nancy with his family for the first time. She had felt closer to him than ever, as though she could have stepped into his life without a second thought. As though she and he were a fit. But despite that infamous kiss last year, they weren't. Nancy was a fit for someone else.

When his mother had told him this morning that she'd invited the Tremaynes to Susie's party, he'd taken her to task.

'You shouldn't have done that,' he'd said, and seen his mother give Grace a knowing smile.

'Why not?' Morwenna had said airily. 'Nancy is a nice woman. Don't worry—she won't eat you alive. Her husband will be with her.'

Almost certainly Leo wouldn't come, but in any case his mother and Grace had it all wrong. Thinking that Nancy was some kind of black widow, ready to pounce. They didn't know her. Didn't know she was fighting demons, too, and had done her best to keep out of his way since they'd arrived in the village. She'd been in his company only when she'd had to be—the journey to Truro, the trip to the Mount, for instance—and when he'd inexplicably invited her home. It had been a bad decision, he could see that now, and Nancy was probably regretting it as much as he. It was as though they were constantly dancing around the inevitable, with every minute they spent together bringing that moment closer.

She would come alone this afternoon, Archie was pretty sure, but the house would be full and she'd be lost among so many. And he'd have Rich to talk to. His brother had arrived back from his trip late last night, calling at the cottage and seeming more cheerful than Archie had known him for days, with a decent catch of mackerel to report. His mother had been hoping that Lowen might make it back, too, but he'd phoned early this morning to say sorry. He was having to work an extra shift, but would be home at the end of the month for a few days and Susie was to look forward to the best ever birthday present then.

'Archie!' That was Morwenna's voice. 'Can you come down and help, my luv?'

'Dreckly, Ma,' he said, using the age-old Cornish expression, that meant he'd come but in his own good time.

'Now, Archie, please.'

There was no escape, it seemed. Abandoning the empty suitcase and the small pile of folded clothes, he ran down the stairs to join his mother.

'It's the lights,' Morwenna explained. 'We want them decorating those two walls, but I've no head for heights and Grace has gone off to buy more sweets for the prizes. Can you fix them?'

For the next hour, Archie was kept busy hanging strings of coloured lights—where had Ma found these? he wondered—

nailing a birthday banner to the mantelshelf and fixing a clutch of balloons over the front door. Then it was a climb into the cottage's miniscule loft to search for extra furniture.

'Do you think these will bear anyone actually sitting on them?' he asked his mother, pointing to the two chairs he'd found, their legs scratched and sagging at a slight angle.

'They'll do,' Morwenna said briskly. 'The little ones can sit on them if they get tired. Now where did I put that blancmange?'

***

'We're invited to Susie Jago's birthday party this afternoon,' Nancy reminded her husband over breakfast.

Leo frowned, a slice of toast halfway to his mouth. 'Susie Jago?'

'Archie's niece. She's eleven today. It's an important age. She'll be off to senior school soon.'

'Yes,' Leo said vaguely. 'Remind me, why are we invited?'

Nancy stared at him, for a moment taken aback. 'Archie works for you. She's his niece and it was a kind gesture of his mother's to invite us to the party.'

'Very kind,' Leo agreed.

'So are we going?' Nancy persisted.

'I don't think so, darling. Archie's family is his own and we shouldn't intrude.'

'But we're invited. And you know Morwenna Jago.'

Leo nodded. 'I do, and she's a good-hearted woman. I've always liked her—she was kind to me as a child—but I think it's best not to confuse the personal with the professional. My only real connection with the Jago family is through employing Archie. In any case, I need the conference paper ready for tomorrow and I've still a few revisions to make.'

Nancy stood up and began clearing the breakfast dishes.

Her silence seemed to sink into Leo's consciousness because he said over his shoulder, 'You go, by all means, if you'd like to.'

She turned to face him, her head tilted to one side. 'I will.'

There was a note of reproach in her voice and Leo's response was to push back his chair and walk quickly to the door. 'I'll be in the dining room if you need me,' he said, and disappeared.

Washing up the breakfast bowls and plates, Nancy wondered if she would ever truly understand the man she'd married. Archie was his assistant, true, but he was surely more than that. He'd shared the house in Cavendish Street with Leo for years, had worked for him for as many, had, for goodness sake, served with him during the war and, by Leo's own admission, had saved his boss's life. They came from the same village, Morwenna Jago sold fish at Penleven's kitchen door. Perhaps that was it. In Leo's mind the Jago family belonged at the kitchen door.

But she was being unkind. Leo was more generous than that. Nancy found it strange, though, that he couldn't see how right it would be to accept the invitation and for an hour or two play the gracious guest.

After she'd stacked the dishes, she went up to her bedroom. Grace had said not to worry about a present for her young daughter, but Nancy didn't want to go the party empty-handed. There was only one possible shop in Port Madron, though—Kitty's village stores— and she was unlikely to find anything suitable there. With no easy means of travelling to Helston, the nearest town, it would have to be something she already possessed.

She pulled out her suitcase from beneath the bed and looked through the few items she'd left unpacked. Bits and pieces of clothing, a spare pair of slippers, several pieces of jewellery—not at all suitable for an eleven-year-old—and a pristine notebook. Nancy had bought it months ago, then stuffed into her suitcase at the last minute, thinking that if she had the chance, she might make a record this time of her visit: a few sketches perhaps, a few notes about the places she'd seen. But there had been so much upset since she'd arrived, that she'd never found the right moment to begin.

She smoothed her hand across the notebook's jewel-coloured cover. It was a Florentine design, perhaps a little sophisticated for a young girl, but she hoped Susie would appreciate it. Archie had that appreciation—an innate sensitivity to art—though his life before working for Leo had given him little chance to follow it. Flicking through the blank pages, each with its gilded edge, she thought what a beautiful notebook it was, and was pleased she could offer it as a gift.

As a young girl, Nancy had loved stationery. Not that she'd ever possessed much, but on the few occasions she had been given a new pen or a fresh writing book, she'd been thrilled. How to wrap the present, though? A few sheets of tissue paper lay at the bottom of the case. She had used them to stop her clothes from creasing on the journey but now, she thought, they would do nicely. A page torn from the old notebook and folded several times made a small tag.

Delighted with having solved her problem so neatly, she picked up her copy of *Wildfire at Midnight* and settled herself into the nursing chair. A novel by Mary Stewart was always a surefire escape from present troubles. But her mind had other ideas, constantly wandering, unable to absorb the words in front of her. Had she made the right decision to go to the party? Archie would be there, surrounded by his family, and she worried that it would feel too close, too intimate. Worried that he would feel it, too. He couldn't excuse himself from his niece's birthday celebrations, but she could. Perhaps she should walk down to the village, wish Susie a happy birthday and simply hand her the present. She could invent an excuse as to why she couldn't stay.

She made Leo a sandwich for his lunch and took it into the dining room along with a cup of tea.

'Thank you, darling. Most thoughtful. I would eat with you, but—' he waved his hand at the scattered papers—'I'm desperate to get this finished and I can eat while I work.'

'That's fine,' Nancy said brightly, and retreated to the kitchen.

She was too nervous to eat. The excuse she'd concocted sounded flimsy and she couldn't see herself making it. At a quarter to three, she packed the present into her handbag, slipped on cardigan and shoes and called out a brief goodbye to her husband. She had changed into the one good dress she had with her, a deep red silk, and hoped it looked celebratory enough.

When the door of Morwenna's cottage opened, Nancy realised it was the least important thing. The party had already begun, loud laughter flowing out into the street as a blindfolded Susie attempted to pin the tail on a donkey. Then shrieks of alarm as her pin found a balloon instead. From the kitchen beyond, there was a hum of activity, Grace and her husband busily setting up the table for what looked a mammoth birthday tea.

'You look fair lovely,' Morwenna said, opening the door to her. 'Come on in, my 'ansome.'

Chapter Twenty-Three

Nancy hovered in the sitting room doorway, feeling slightly dazed. The room had been decorated within an inch of its life, coloured lights hanging from the walls, an enormous banner that read *Happy Birthday, Susie,* attached to the mantelpiece and balloons everywhere. Several young girls were lining up for their turn at pinning on the donkey's tail.

'Come and meet Mrs Tremayne, Susie,' her grandmother said, pulling a young girl dressed in pink organza to one side.

'A very happy birthday, Susie,' Nancy greeted her.

'This is her big sister, Linda.' The lanky teenager gave Nancy a shy smile. 'And the little one here is Heather.'

Heather, who seemed already to have consumed a fair amount of jelly judging by the state of her party dress, began jumping up and down, then clutching at herself frantically.

'Grace,' Morwenna shouted to her daughter-in-law in the kitchen. 'Heather needs the bathroom.' Then turning to her granddaughter, she wagged a finger. 'We don't want an accident, do we? Not like last year.'

Once Heather had been despatched, Morwenna took Nancy's arm. 'Come and sit down, my dear. Unless you fancy joining in the game.'

Nancy smiled but shook her head and sank into one of the

armchairs that had been pushed to the side of the crowded room. Susie must have invited at least half her school class, she reflected. So much buzz and noise and laughter. She had never known a party herself. The nearest she'd come to celebrating her birthday was a visit with her parents to the local cinema, to see a film chosen by them. She couldn't even remember its name now.

'Thanks for coming.' It was Archie's voice in her ear. He'd slipped into the sitting room unseen.

'I'm glad to,' she said, and meant it. 'The party seems a great success.'

Nancy smiled up at him and, in response, he pulled his mouth down into a grimace, but his eyes were laughing. At that moment, Morwenna came back into the room with a tray filled with objects for the next game, and her gaze travelled between them before she busied herself clearing a small side table.

Nancy felt a shock. That had been a knowing gaze. Abruptly, she got to her feet. She would join the line of children, along with Archie's brother, Rich, waiting to guess the mystery objects on the tray. She would become as anonymous as possible and leave as soon as she politely could. The guessing game took some time to finish but, immediately afterwards, she joined the eager circle of young guests waiting for Pass the Parcel, relieved to have melted into the background.

***

Halfway through Pass the Parcel, Clem Hoskins came through the door and Archie, standing guard by the wall, felt himself tense. He glanced swiftly across the room at Nancy, who was in the midst of tearing off yet another sheet of wrapping paper. She was laughing and relaxed and he wanted her to stay happy.

He glared at Clem who had sidled up to him. 'Come for a bit of birthday cake,' Clem muttered. 'Thought I would. I mind when young Susie were born.'

'If that's all you came for,' Archie said sharply.

'What else? Oh, 'er,' Clem nodded towards Nancy. 'I was wrong about 'er. I've nuthin' against 'er. She aren't like any Tremayne I've known.'

'Probably because she isn't one,' Archie said, realising as he spoke how true that was.

Nancy bore the Tremayne name, but that's where it ended. She didn't fit the family into which she'd married. He had only to look at her now, sitting cross-legged, unmindful of the creases in her beautiful silk dress, laughing with Susie, who sat beside her wearing a slightly askew paper crown that Grace had made for her daughter.

Clem looked as though he was going to disagree, but instead walked through into the kitchen to speak to Morwenna who was counting out candles. From where he was standing, Archie could just glimpse his mother. He saw Morwenna smile at Clem in her usual generous manner, but she looked tired. Older, Archie realised, with a sinking feeling in his stomach. She'd been up since dawn getting ready for this party and, really, she shouldn't do it. She loved her grandchildren to pieces, but there had to come a time when she handed the reins over to the next generation. Grace was quite capable. Nancy, too, he thought, then pulled himself up. Nancy was no more a Jago than she was a Tremayne.

And Grace's parents did damn all. They weren't even here this afternoon. His pent-up anger landed squarely on the absent in-laws. They were strict Chapel goers and parties were frowned on, even eleventh birthday parties for their own granddaughter. 'Preachy' Ma called them, and about as much fun as a wet weekend in Newlyn. No wonder Grace could be flighty at times. All that chit chat and gossip. It was escape—from a miserable childhood. But they were all escaping from something, weren't they?

'Time to eat,' Morwenna called out, 'once that dratted parcel's unwrapped.'

'It is,' shrieked Linda. 'I've got the prize. Look, it's a new pen.'

'That's not fair,' Susie began to wail. 'It's my party.'

'And that's why you'll be first at the table, my luv.' Grace swooped down on her daughter and swept her into the kitchen.

It was a small room for such a lot of people, but his mother had emptied it of chairs and spread the party food across the table and on every available kitchen surface.

'You'll have to load up your plate and find a space on the floor next door, children,' she told Susie's excitable classmates. 'The chairs are for the grown-ups. Here, Clem, take this plate and find yourself a seat. You, too, Rich.'

His boss would have hated it, Archie thought. He'd heard Nancy apologise for Leo's absence as soon as she'd arrived, citing pressure of work. His mother had merely smiled understandingly. She had never really expected Leo to show, Archie knew.

The table and kitchen counter were crammed with every kind of sandwich—cheese, jam, meat paste. It looked as though the family would be eating them for weeks, while sausage rolls, pork pies, a plate of ham and a box of cheese quarters sat proudly at the other end of the table. How much had this cost Ma, he wondered? There were individual jellies of various flavours and a large pink blancmange with two platters full of small iced cakes. In the middle of the table sat a resplendent iced sponge with Happy Birthday blazoned

192

across its top.

'We'll light the candles later,' Morwenna said, hushing Susie who was fidgeting with excitement.

By the time the children had mowed their way through a large portion of the food, his youngest niece, Heather, was looking decidedly sickly. Her mother took hold of her plate.

'Enough,' she said firmly. 'You'll need space for the big cake. And the rest of you—if you're done with the food, Susie can open her presents now.'

Nancy's gift was the first to be opened and Archie watched as his niece peeled back the tissue paper and saw her face glow. 'Is it fer me? Honest?' she asked Nancy. 'It looks real grown-up.'

'I hope you like it,' Nancy said. She seemed touched by the child's evident pleasure.

'It's some beautiful. I'm goin' to write it in every day, and none of you are goin' to read it,' Susie announced defiantly to her sisters.

While the child tackled the pile of presents still to be opened, he glimpsed Nancy going into the kitchen and joining Grace at the sink.

'Let me help,' he heard her say.

'You can't,' Grace protested. 'You're a guest.'

'Nonsense. Guests need to be useful. I'll wipe while you wash.'

'It would be a help,' Grace admitted. 'I want Ma to have a rest. Far more of the little blighters turned up than I expected.' She scrubbed the blancmange bowl with vigour. 'Plus, we invited several of the villagers who've known Susie most of 'er life. It's a big birthday for 'er. We asked Hedra. She only lives a few doors along, and Ma thought the poor soul must be lonely. Jory weren't a nice man, but Hedra loved him. Goodness knows why.'

193

'She couldn't have felt able to cope with a party.'

'It were a daft idea, but we thought we'd best offer. Show sympathy. Most of the village feels sorry for 'er, though they think she's well rid. Jory was a no-good. Chucked off every boat he sailed on, then making trouble at the mine. He was lucky Mr Perran gave him a job. And what does 'e do? Abuse it.'

Nancy's face wore an expression that Archie had come to know. It was what he called her 'dog with a bone' expression. She would encourage Grace to talk, hoping his sister-in-law might provide evidence against Jory Pascoe or against someone else. Please don't do this, he prayed. Not when I'm going away, and Leo knows sod all about what's been happening. Pascoe might be dead, but what else—who else—lay below the surface?

'Do you think Mrs Pascoe will be okay?' Nancy asked. 'I don't suppose her husband had a pension and now she's without his wages.'

'I'm sure she will.' Grace began to put away the dishes Nancy had dried. 'She were left the house, you know, by 'er first husband. Not ezactly a wealthy widow, but she's got enough, I think. And she's got the job at the stores. That will help if she's pinched.'

'I don't think so.' Nancy carefully hung the tea towel to dry.

'What do you mean?' Grace demanded. 'She's not working at the stores?'

'I believe Kitty didn't need her.'

'Kitty Anson sacked 'er?'

Hedra's dismissal from the village stores was a quixotic move, an unkind move, Archie thought. It was one that would concern Nancy.

'Not really sacked. Just that she didn't need help anymore.'

'She never did.' Grace snorted. 'That shop has always been managed by a single person. Bolitho ran it on 'is own for years. Aiden—that's 'is son—didn't even help as a young boy, except mebbe to go round in the van with 'im.'

'Perhaps she was trying to do Mrs Pascoe a favour, but it didn't work out. Kitty seems very popular in the village.'

Nancy was trying to defend someone she considered a friend, but his sister-in-law wasn't having any of it. Grace tipped the washing-up bowl to one side and poured the suds away. Then, putting her hands on her hips, she faced Nancy directly.

'Kitty Anson's popular because she's smarmed her way round the Bolithos and fawns on the vicar, doin' fund raisin' for 'is church, that sort of thing. And she gives folks credit in the shop before pay day. She weren't employin' Hedra fer the woman's sake, she were doin' it fer Pascoe, that's what. Now 'e's not around no longer, she don' want 'is wife.'

'Doing it for Pascoe?' Nancy sounded mystified.

'Don' ask me what, but somethin' was goin' on there. Pascoe was in and out of them stores like a lamplighter.'

'I don't think it could be anything of that nature,' Nancy said, a laugh in her voice.

'You never know.' Grace raised her eyebrows. 'In this village anythin's possible.' And then joined in with the laughter.

Archie's mother bustled past him into the kitchen, evidently rejuvenated by her rest. 'What's all this then?' she asked. 'Come on you two. We're going to cut the cake. We'll take it into the sitting room. Now, where did I put those blessed matches?'

Susie doused all eleven candles with one enormous blow and, to loud cheers, Morwenna plunged the knife into the cake and begun to cut large slices for everyone.

'Last decent piece of cake you'll have for a while,' she said over her shoulder to Archie, who was busy handing out laden plates.

'When are you leavin', Uncle Archie?' Linda asked him.

'Tomorrow, early, before you've opened your sleepy little eyes,' he replied.

'D'you have to go?' Susie's lip had begun to tremble. 'It's been fun with you 'ere.'

'He's goin' to be flyin',' Rich interrupted. That would stave off the party tears, Archie reckoned.

Susie's mouth fell open. 'Flyin'? How?'

'In a plane, stoopid,' her father said, and flapped his arms energetically up and down.

'Are you goin' with 'im, Mrs Tremayne?' the young girl asked.

Nancy shook her head. 'I'll be staying in Port Madron a while longer.'

'But d'you live in London, too?'

'I do.'

'With Uncle Archie?'

'Nancy is married to Professor Tremayne,' Archie cut in quickly. 'You remember him. He sketched you one year in the garden when I took you up to Penleven.'

Susie nodded. 'But you all live together?' she persisted.

During this exchange, he'd sensed Nancy grow gradually more tense. They might be a child's natural questions, but Nancy's cheeks were flushed, and he saw the flustered way in which she brushed back her hair. At that moment, his mother and Grace exchanged a look.

Nancy pushed back her chair—the look had evidently proved too much. 'I'd better go home and see how the professor is getting on with his work,' she said brightly. 'It's been a lovely party and thank you for inviting me, Susie. I'll remember it for a long time.'

'Do you have to go just yet?' Morwenna asked, clearly disappointed.

'I should. But thank you again.'

Archie watched as she picked up the cardigan she'd left draped across a chair and made for the door.

Chapter Twenty-Four

Once outside Morwenna's front door, Nancy paused, not wanting to return to Penleven immediately. If Leo had finished his conference paper by now, he'd naturally want to know how the party went, but she didn't feel able to talk about it. Not at the moment. The sense that everyone in the room was watching her, watching how she behaved towards Archie, had made her die a little inside. But she was cross, too. She shouldn't have let herself become so ruffled. It was really only Morwenna and Grace who'd shown awareness. Morwenna was naturally curious, she was Archie's mother after all, and Grace—she was simply being Grace.

In truth, it was the whole situation Nancy was struggling with. The necessity of pretending to herself, to Leo, to Archie and his family, had become an immense strain. It was as well Archie was leaving first thing in the morning. By the time she and Leo returned to London, there would almost certainly be another foreign trip in the offing and she would be left alone in the Cavendish Street house once more. It was the best outcome she could hope for.

The late afternoon was still bright and the air fresh and salt-laden. A walk along the headland, the same path she had taken with Leo days ago, should clear her head. The climb up the hill leading out of the village was slow, but her pace quickened as she took the narrow path that branched towards the sea.

This afternoon had given her a good deal to think about. The conversation with Grace about Kitty Anson, for instance. When Grace had mentioned that *somethin' was goin' on* between Kitty and Jory Pascoe, Nancy had been uncomfortably reminded of how he'd walked into the village stores the day Kitty had invited her for a cup of tea, shambling up the stairs to swagger into the kitchen as though he had the freedom of the building. But any suggestion of an affair between them was comical. Putting aside the fact that Pascoe was a married man, Kitty was far too young and far too attractive to look twice at him. Not to say still wedded to the memory of her poor dead husband. Grace's insinuation must owe more to her dislike of the young woman, who'd made a successful home in Port Madron, than from any truth.

It was a long climb to the headland and Nancy emerged at the top of the grassy cliff slightly out of breath. She wouldn't walk for too long, she decided. A half hour would be enough. The sea was as deeply blue as when Leo and she had walked this way, but the wind blowing from the south-west was much stronger today, the waves smashing angrily against the rocks below. It would make for hard walking.

In any case, she needed to be back at Penleven when Perry arrived home from Wheal Agnes. The hospital was discharging Ned Tremayne after the weekend and she'd promised to help her brother-in-law ensure that everything in the house ran smoothly. She had suggested they make the dining room into a temporary bedroom—they hardly ever used the room for meals and, being on the ground floor, it would make life a good deal easier for Ned. And for his helpers. Perry had leapt at the idea and he and Leo were to start shifting furniture this evening. Tomorrow, Grace would come to clean and make up the bed, and discuss with Nancy what best to cook for an invalid. Not that Nancy had much idea, but between them, she thought, they should be able to concoct a sensible menu.

She had reached level ground, the point at which the headland became a flat plateau that stretched for miles beyond. Ahead, she could see the granite stone path. It followed the line of cliffs into the distance, winding its way around the rock face, around the crevices and fissures created over centuries by wind and tide. Nancy stood for a moment, her cheeks now thankfully cool, and watched as the sea danced to the tune of the wind, white-pointed waves tumbling into shore, crashing loudly against the boulders below, the sea froth hissing at the base of the rocks, then gradually dissolving before the next onslaught. The rhythm of the rolling, pounding waters was mesmeric.

A movement below suddenly cut short her reverie. The back of a head appeared over the rim of the cliff, then the outline of a pair of shoulders. There must be some kind of path beneath her, she guessed. Or a ledge scoured out of the rock face. To venture down the cliff on a day like this was extraordinarily dangerous, but she wouldn't wait to meet this foolhardy person. Whoever it was had disrupted the solitude she'd sought. It was time to make her way back to Penleven.

'Don't go, Nancy,' a voice said. 'We should have a talk.'

She froze on the spot, unable to move, every limb rendered useless. Cold, heavy, paralysed, her stomach the only part of her in motion, lurching so violently that she thought she would vomit. Her very worst nightmare was coming true.

The figure had emerged fully now, and the sound of his footsteps on the stone path as he crunched towards her seemed inordinately loud. She must move, Nancy thought stupidly. Make her legs work. Run. But he would follow, she knew. He would catch her. The only way to face this was with courage.

Philip March had changed little in the three years since she'd escaped him. His hair was perhaps a little duller, his form a little more bony. But his eyes as he drew near were unchanged. They wore the same malicious glint.

'Did you think I'd forgotten you?' he taunted, his mouth twisted.

Nancy couldn't speak. A multiplicity of questions was whirling through her mind and none of those questions made sense. What was Philip doing here? How had he found her? Had he been hiding in the village, and where? Was he the one responsible for the threats against her?

But, of course, he was.

'Surely you've something to say.' He moved forward again, so close now that she could feel his breath on her cheeks. 'I find your silence a little odd. As I remember, you had plenty to say when you gave me my ring back.'

'I don't know why you're here, Philip,' she managed at last, trying desperately to keep the shakiness from her voice. 'But please go away. Please leave me alone.'

'I will.' His mouth formed itself into a smile, but his eyes were cold and shark-like. 'That's the good news for you, Nancy. I will go away. But only when I've finished what I came for. Perhaps not such good news?'

She stepped back in an effort to free herself of his intimidating closeness.

'How long have you been in Port Madron?' she asked.

If she talked to him, heard out his grievances, they might come to some resolution and he would disappear forever. It was a vain hope but the only one she had.

'A fair few weeks. And you had no idea I was here! It's what I'd call intelligent planning. I'm good at it. I was clever

enough to find a bed and breakfast just outside the village—
near enough for what I needed, but distant enough not to
cause gossip. This place is a hotbed of gossip. A stranger
making too many appearances on the village street would
have been ripe for tale telling.'

'But how—?' she began.

'How did I know I'd find you here?'

March's posture had subtly changed. His body had
relaxed, his shoulders loose and one leg slightly bent, as
though he'd be happy to stay talking on this cliff top for the
rest of the day. He is enjoying this, Nancy thought. Enjoying
my fear and he wants to prolong it.

'You wrote a charming letter, didn't you? Not before time,
I must say. Your poor parents not knowing whether their
daughter was alive or dead.'

She gave a small gasp. 'You saw the letter to my parents?'

'Not exactly, but I knew you'd written.'

'They told you!' Nancy's tone was accusing. She had
always feared the Nicholsons' championship of March might
lead them to betray her, but how could they have done it—
actually done it—knowing how she felt about this man?

'They have been good friends to me,' Philip said. 'Unlike
their daughter. And we had common cause. They feel as
much cheated by you as I do. They know how badly you've
behaved. They know you have to be punished.'

The Nicholsons had thought Philip special, a great catch
for a daughter who'd stubbornly remained unmarried.
Gradually, he'd smoothed his way into their confidence so
that when Nancy had ended the engagement, they'd been
furious with her, refusing to believe how frightened she was.
Her relationship with them had never been easy but, even so,
the knowledge that her own mother and father had delivered
her to this monster was devastating.

Nancy bit her lip hard and tasted blood. Angrily, she brushed it away. 'How could my parents tell you where to find me? They didn't know.'

'They didn't know, not precisely. You were a clever little girl, weren't you, disappearing so suddenly and not leaving an address? It was as though you'd be magicked away. But not that clever. There was a postmark, London W.1. And, of course, there were people who had known you at the auction house. Remember Brenda Layton?'

'That bitch.' Nancy shocked herself. Swearing did not come naturally to her.

'Tut, tut. Not the language of a lady. What would Professor Tremayne say if he heard the woman he'd condescended to marry talking like a fishwife?' March put his head on one side. 'A fishwife,' he repeated. 'What could be more apt in this benighted place? But you should have tried to cultivate Brenda, you know. Or at least pretended to. She really doesn't like you. She told me some story about your leaving Abingers to get married. The rumour was that you'd hooked one of their art experts, a professor. She thought she knew which one, but I had to be confident she was right. It didn't take long for me to put together a list of all the experts that Abingers use—I'm a journalist, after all—then gradually winnow them down. I asked questions, made phone calls, scoured old newspaper articles. Research skills can come in useful at the most unusual times.'

It was ironic, Nancy thought, that she had done exactly the same when she'd been on the trail of a wrongdoer, but in her case it had been to bring the guilty to book and win justice for the innocent. For Philip, it was wholly malign, an activity designed to hurt, to destroy.

'Most of the men on my list,' he continued, 'were either too old—you weren't likely to settle for a pensioner, unless of course he was very rich—or they lived in the Home Counties or in completely the wrong area of London.'

Nancy had begun to sidle further back during this recital. Any idea of placating this dreadful man had gone and she had a wild idea that if she could put some distance between them, she could surprise her attacker by darting to one side and running as fast as she could to safety. But with every step she took backwards, Philip March took one forward.

'There was only one likely candidate,' he went on. 'A Professor Tremayne, just as Brenda had prophesised. I looked him up in *Who's Who*. You shouldn't have married such an eminent man, my dear. His address was there in black and white. Cavendish Street, W.1. He fitted the bill perfectly.'

'And you went to the house,' Nancy said dully. It was a statement of fact, not a question.

'I went to the house,' he repeated. 'You *have* done well, my dear. Very impressive. But a dragon of a housekeeper. *The family is not at home,* she announced. So where could you be? Abroad perhaps or maybe in Cornwall, at the Tremayne family home. *Who's Who* is really most comprehensive.'

'If you've been here for weeks, you must have arrived in Port Madron before us.' Nancy's mind seemed now to have absorbed the terrible shock of March's appearance and was slowly coming back to life.

'It was complete chance. Serendipity, if you like. I'd booked into my cosy cottage and started nosing around, then less than a week later what should happen? Gossip in the village. Thank God for gossip. Apparently, the patriarch of the family had had a massive heart attack and the younger son was expected to arrive at any moment. The dragon had misled me. You were still in the house in London when I called. In the end, it didn't matter. Because here I am. And here you are.'

'You were the one who slashed the portrait.' Nancy's mind ranged over the past few weeks.

'Indeed, I was, and it was strangely sad. The painting was really quite well done, but it had to go. That man is not your true husband. His image had to be destroyed.'

She stared at him. During their engagement, she'd come to realise that Philip March's need to control was extreme, extending to physical threat. Now, though, he seemed to have tipped over the edge into madness. But she needed to keep him talking. If she could only get him to relax his guard for an instant...

'And my notebook and pen?' she asked

'The notebook was boring and the pen cheap. Neither at all interesting, but they served a purpose. What I really liked, though, was the knife and the red paint. I thought you'd appreciate the artistry. And then the grave of leaves. Now that *was* a beautiful gesture.'

'You are quite mad.' Nancy said aloud what she had been thinking ever since he'd started to speak.

'Foolish, not mad,' he rejoined. 'Foolish to think I could trust you. To think that when I asked you to be my wife, the only proposal I have ever made to any woman, and you agreed, I believed that you actually meant it. You made me a solemn promise and then you broke it.'

'I had every intention of keeping my promise,' she said defiantly. 'But then I found you out for what you are.'

He took an aggressive step forward. 'And what am I?' His face loured over her and he caught her chin in his hand, painfully forcing back her head.

'Why can't you leave me alone?' She was finding it difficult to speak, her face contorted by his ruthless hold. 'You have a good job, a good future. I'm nothing to you.'

'On the contrary, you are everything—you always have

been. It's why I can't allow you to belong to anyone else. My situation is not a happy one, Nancy, and I need to resolve it. I no longer have you. I no longer have a job.' He gave what sounded like a small giggle. 'Too much of my time given to searching for you and not enough spent writing articles the newspaper wanted to print. So, I'm jobless now. Almost homeless. And all because of you. You do see, you have to be punished?'

'You are utterly insane.' She wrenched herself from his grip, her face hot and stinging. The sudden movement brought her close to the edge of the cliff.

'Maybe a little. But not so insane that I can't plan to perfection. You see, I can disappear from the village without anyone knowing I was ever here. And when *you* disappear, it will be put down to misadventure. There have been so many accidents in Port Madron lately, so I hear.'

Nancy found herself teetering on the slippery grass as he lunged forward and grabbed her by the arms. 'I'm tired of this chase and you must be, too. Let's finish it now. The sea is so conveniently close.'

He had her in a stifling bear hug, pulled tight into his chest, lifting her almost bodily and shuffling her backwards until she was inches from the cliff edge.

His face broke into a hideous smile. 'I've waited for this moment so long. Once or twice I've even thought of coming with you. But now I believe I'd like to stick around. Enjoy the fruits of my hard work.'

Struggling free was impossible. He was far stronger and his arms had imprisoned her in an unbreakable lock—until he chose to let go. Then she would tumble to her death. Nancy dared not look down at the rocks below. It was sufficient for the pounding sea to fill her ears. One more push and she would be gone.

Chapter Twenty-Five

Out of nowhere, March was crumpling at the knees. His grasp slackened and Nancy felt herself falling backwards. A hand shot out and grabbed her by the forearm, pulling her upright and back onto safe ground.

The sound of a fist on bone, then Philip March was sprawled on the grass, his face a mess of blood. 'I should kick you into the sea.' Archie's voice was razor-edged and his foot hovered over his victim. 'You are vermin.'

'Don't!' Nancy tried to shout, but her voice cracked beneath the strain. 'It would be murder.'

'Murder wasn't something that worried *him* over much.' Archie's foot was still lifted. 'As this low-life said, who would know he was even here?'

'Please don't.'

Archie gave the recumbent man one hefty kick. 'Get up and get going,' he snarled. 'But if you ever come near Mrs Tremayne again, I'll make sure it's the last breath you take.'

Philip March crawled to his knees, struggling to breathe. Then, with difficulty, staggered onto his feet. For an instant, he swayed dangerously close to the cliff edge, hatred in his eyes, then turned from them and slunk away.

Nancy stood dazed, immobile. 'You followed me from the village?'

Archie gave a brief nod and took her by the hand, leading her back to the safety of the granite path. He waited a few minutes before he asked, 'How did that rat find you?'

Relief coursed through Nancy's veins, bringing her body back to life and her mind out of chaos. Slowly and precisely she told him how Philip March had tracked her down.

'An enterprising specimen of vermin,' was Archie's judgement.

'Do you think he's gone?' She managed to sound calm.

'I'd be surprised if he hadn't.'

'I mean gone forever—not just from the village.'

'I reckon it will be a long time before he pulls that stunt again. If ever.' Archie was looking at her with concern in his blue eyes 'Are you okay?'

She was shivering badly, though trying hard not to. 'I can't believe… I can't think what would have happened if .. if you hadn't…'

'But I did. Hey, it's all right.' He took hold of her trembling form and held her tightly, his hand stroking her hair. 'It's okay' he murmured. 'It's over.'

Nancy lifted her face. 'Thank you,' were the only words she could say. But her lips did the talking, searching for and finding his. And then he was kissing her, deeply, tenderly as though he couldn't stop. As though neither of them could.

Shocked by the sudden torrent of feeling, they broke apart.

'I think you're okay,' Archie said thickly.

'I'm sorry,' she said in a whisper, 'that was my fault. It was this that made me—' and she waved her hand at the cliff and the sea beyond. 'It was Philip, and his threats… I'm not making sense, am I?'

'Not much.' He gave a lopsided smile.

'Being in danger, I mean. That's what made me behave badly. Made us… in Malfuego, too.'

Archie's face cleared. 'Ah! The volcano.'

'I suppose it's a natural reaction to danger,' she said desperately, knowing in her heart that it wasn't.

'I suppose it is.' Archie seemed keen to agree. There was a pause before he said, 'I'm off tomorrow,' as though this could offer a solution to the gaping chasm that stretched before them.

This afternoon, the fiction she'd been telling herself ever since that kiss in Malfuego had been laid bare—that it had been an aberration, a momentary misstep. It hadn't. The feeling that flowed between them was real, urgent, and it wasn't going away.

Nancy cast around for something to say. Anything that would keep her from thinking. 'Did Grace mind you leaving the party early?'

'I told her I'd be back in a jif. That I needed a cigarette. She doesn't like me or Rich smoking near the girls. She's funny like that.'

'You must have missed your slice of cake.' Nancy was trying for distraction, though not succeeding very well.

'The cake will keep,' he said shortly. 'But we should be getting back.'

Together, they turned and began the stroll downhill to the village.

'I heard a bit of March's boasting,' Archie said, as they walked. 'Was he responsible for the stuff in the summerhouse?'

'He was. He got into the garden and found the place unlocked, took my cardigan and destroyed Leo's portrait.'

'He must have been watching Penleven for days. He'd have to know people's movements, to make sure he wasn't caught.'

Nancy felt the nausea rising in her throat. 'He's been living just outside Port Madron and creeping into the village to spy.'

'He was the someone who delivered that brown envelope, I take it?'

'I got it all wrong. I knew someone was following me, but it seemed too fantastic to think it was Philip. I reckoned it had to be a villager and that the envelope had come from one of them. Jory Pascoe, in fact. When he died, I felt guilty because I was so relieved he'd gone.'

'And the grave? I caught the mention of a grave on the wind. What was that about?'

'You didn't see it,' she said, attempting to follow Archie's lead. The conversation had taken on a surreal edge.

It was as though they had stepped out for a pleasant stroll in the evening sunshine. Yet a few minutes ago, a vengeful man had tried to kill her. A few minutes ago, she had been in Archie's arms and so thoroughly kissed that her body still glowed.

'Philip must have scooped a pile of dead leaves together and moulded them into the shape of a coffin,' she explained. 'It was in a part of the garden that no one normally visits. I suppose he hoped I'd be the one to find it since I'm home most of the time. And he was right. I did find it and it frightened me badly, but Kitty came by and rescued me.'

'Kitty Anson? She seems to be getting a bad press—from Grace, at least. My sister-in-law doesn't like her one little bit, does she?'

Nancy shook her head. 'I like Kitty. She's been a good friend to me. I've no idea what went on between her and Jory Pascoe, if anything, but I doubt it was the affair that Grace was suggesting. Of course, I could be wrong. I was monumentally wrong about Pascoe. I thought he was targeting me as part of his campaign against the Tremaynes, when it was Philip March all the time.'

They had reached the lane leading up to Penleven and

Archie stopped. 'You weren't wrong, not initially. Don't forget, it was me who tried to convince you it wasn't March. And you could still be right about Pascoe—that he's Port Madron's villain. He stole Treeve Fenton's possessions, didn't he, so he must have crept into Fenton's house at some point.'

'I wondered if Treeve discovered him stealing and there was a struggle in which the old man died.'

'And Pascoe panicked and decided to drown him for good measure?'

'It's possible.'

'You always like to complicate things.'

He looked at her hard and she looked back at him. She had a grip on her emotions now—talking had proved a useful diversion.

'I don't see how that complicates anything. It seems a sensible explanation. Pascoe would want to make Treeve's death look like an accident.' There was a pause before Nancy went on, 'He could have gone to the hospital, too, and tampered with Ned's drip. That was something a layman could do, and Jory Pascoe was absent from work the day that Ned had his seizure.'

'And afterwards, Pascoe drowned himself in remorse?' Archie was laughing.

'No,' she said firmly. 'Someone else drowned him. My money is on Tomas Almeda. I hope the police drag him back from Brazil for questioning.'

'They won't be able to. We don't have an extradition treaty with Brazil.'

She gave a wry shake of her head. 'You are a fount of knowledge, Archie.'

'Like I once told you, I read—actual books. Pascoe is well and truly dead, so if he *was* targeting the Tremaynes, life should become a lot more peaceful now. Until Ned gets

211

home, that is!'

'Only two more days before he's discharged.' Nancy gave a heavy sigh. 'His homecoming won't be easy. At least, you'll be well out of it.'

'Come back with me.'

She looked at him, startled. She had schooled herself to say an unemotional goodbye, but now as she looked into his eyes, her stomach hollowed. *Come back with me* had only one meaning.

'I can't,' she said shakily. 'You know I can't.'

'Your choice.' His tone was casual, though the situation was anything but. A terrifying choice was splitting her life open. It had hovered there for the last two years, threatening, enticing, and now she was stuttering on the brink, heart thumping and breath coming too fast.

To cover her confusion, she said, 'When you get to London, will you do something for me?'

Chapter Twenty-Six

Archie made sure he was at Penleven the next morning before the household was up and about. His knock brought Leo to the front door, bleary-eyed and still in pyjamas. He clutched a sheaf of papers in one hand and a battered attaché case in the other.

'I didn't expect you this early,' he said, handing them both to Archie.

'Thought I'd get a good start, boss.'

And avoid meeting Nancy, he could have added, but didn't. He'd spent a nearly sleepless night trying to justify himself. He had saved Nancy's life. He supposed that should count for something. But then he'd taken his reward and, in doing so, injured the man standing just a foot away. A man to whom he owed loyalty. Someone for whom he'd enjoyed working and who, for the most part, he liked. No amount of sophistry could hide the fact that he'd kissed a woman he shouldn't and kissed her as a lover. Then made it clear he wanted more. Wriggle as he might from the truth, it had nothing to do with shared danger. Okay, he'd wanted to comfort her after the ordeal with March, but it was perfectly possible to comfort a woman without making love to her.

'I'll be off then,' he said, as Leo dithered on the doorstep, seeming about to speak but casting around for the words.

'Sorry, Archie. Not quite awake yet. I've been thinking... I don't like the train. I'd much prefer to drive and I think Nancy would, too. When you've delivered the Cessna and got the conference stuff sorted, get the car out of the garage. It could do with a run.'

'You want me to drive down and collect you?'

'It's a good idea, I think, don't you?' Leo was warming to his theme. 'Yes. A good idea. You'll have a few days in Cavendish Street before you need to come back. My father isn't out of hospital until after the weekend and I wouldn't expect you here until mid-week at the earliest.'

'Fine. I'll be in touch to make a definite day.' Archie gave a small wave and jumped into the driving seat.

He was about to shut the car door, when Leo shuffled over to him. Archie noticed he had a pair of very old slippers on his bare feet. Ned Tremayne's, he reckoned. 'Settle up for the hire car as well as the Cessna,' Leo said. 'You've got a cheque book with you?'

Archie nodded and gave another wave, watching in the mirror as Leo turned to go back into the house. Swinging the car down the Penleven drive and out onto the road, he headed north to St Mawgan.

He drove in silence and by instinct, the familiar fields on either side passing him by without notice. His mind was still busy with Nancy. He could just about bear it when he saw only an occasional glimpse of her, but when she was there, in front of him, his heart did that stupid thing. Like it was on a journey around his body rather than staying where it should. The curtain of dark hair, those soft grey eyes, the slender figure—it did for him. And when they spoke, he could only keep her at bay by mockery. At first, it had been outright hostility, but that was no longer an option, and even mockery was becoming less and less effective.

He had to keep her at a distance, he knew, for both their sakes. But how likely was that? They lived in the same house, for God's sake. This last six months since they'd returned from the Caribbean, he'd been abroad more than he'd been in London. Leo had had a flurry of jobs outside England, but that wasn't going to happen again for months. All he'd have to rely on once she was back in Cavendish Street was her job taking her from home every day. If she were to give up the apprenticeship— she wouldn't do it willingly, he knew—but Leo hated her working and he could see it was a constant source of tension between them. Well, if she gave up work, then they'd be thrown together even more.

It was impossible. He would be a lost man and he'd make her a lost woman. He'd have to move out of Cavendish Street, it was the only way. What could he say to Leo that would be half convincing as an explanation? There was nothing for it. He'd have to change jobs. It had been in his mind a long time and yesterday's kiss had made clear that this was the only thing he could decently do. What work he could get instead, he had no idea. Jobs were getting easier to find than in the years immediately after the war, but an ex-soldier, a failed fisherman, wouldn't have much choice.

It was barely eight o'clock when he swept through the gates of St Mawgan airfield. The journey had been swift, with little traffic on the roads this early in the morning, and once he'd paid the very considerable bill and checked his paperwork with the controller, he was free to locate the Cessna he'd flown earlier and prepare to take off. He should be landing at Croydon within the hour, then it was on to London and Cavendish Street.

He'd have the house to himself for a few days and he'd enjoy that, though most of his time would be spent getting Leo's conference papers into shape. His employer was stringent on the way his lectures were presented. They had to be just so. And why not? The bloke paid him to make sure they were.

Then there was Nancy's request. She was up to something, for sure, but at least she should be safe in Cornwall now the manic stalker was no longer a concern. When he drove them back from Cornwall, he'd find a quiet moment to tell her what he'd discovered. It wouldn't hurt him to find out what she wanted to know.

***

Archie reached Cavendish Street as Mrs Brindley was shutting the front door behind her. She turned abruptly as she heard his footsteps.

'I didn't expect the family back today.' She sounded irritated. Much as usual, Archie thought. 'Nobody telephoned to let me know and there's no food in the house,' she went on.

'That's fine, Mrs B.'

She glared at him. He knew she hated it when he called her Mrs B, but he was tired and irritable himself and didn't enjoy being taken to task the minute he got home. 'It's only me that's here. The professor and Mrs Tremayne won't be back for a few days. I'm sure they'll let you know when they're due.'

'What about *your* food?' Mrs Brindley had softened her tone at this news.

'It's not a problem. I'll get a meal out. There's a pub that sells food in Baker Street.'

Mrs Brindley gave a dismissive sniff. 'Right then. I'll be off. I'll bring some groceries in tomorrow.'

Archie gave her a casual wave and let himself into the house. It was unusual for him to be here alone and the space felt almost ghostly. In the muted light from a cloudy sky, the spiral stairs and high-cased windows seemed to fade into a spectral haze. He looked at his watch. Midday. The pub would be open, but its lunchtime menu was limited: a pork pie or a cheese sandwich, neither of which attracted him. And he was tired. He'd barely slept last night, and the flying had needed all his concentration. A nap first, then he'd go out in the early evening and find himself a decent meal.

He hoisted his haversack over one shoulder and, grasping the attaché case in his hand, climbed the three flights of stairs to his rooms beneath the eaves. It had been two weeks since Leo had woken him in the middle of the night demanding a plane to St Mawgan, but it seemed only days ago.

Throwing haversack and attaché case into one corner, he kicked off his shoes and fell onto the bed. It was good to be back. This modest apartment meant home to him in a way that the cottage in Port Madron didn't. For how much longer, though, would it be his home? The 'problem' once more filled his mind, large and insoluble, and with a sigh he shut his eyes and tried not to think of Nancy.

Chapter Twenty-Seven

Nancy stirred her morning tea in mechanical fashion, unaware of the spoon knocking against the china cup. The shock of Philip's sudden appearance had subsided a little, but the fact that he'd tried to kill her still rendered her numb. Though why? She shouldn't be surprised. She'd always believed that was his ultimate aim. He'd begun stalking her immediately she handed back his ring, his harassment becoming more and more vicious, each encounter worse than the one before, until finally there had come a night when she'd walked into her small bedsitter, tired from a heavy day at work but glad to be home, and found every small item she'd saved for had been smashed to pieces. And a dead crow lay bleeding on her new, white bedspread.

She gave herself an inner shake. It was over. Philip March was over, thanks to Archie. And Archie himself was gone. No wonder she felt flat. And crushed by guilt as much as shock. So full of guilt for that kiss, there should be a different word to describe it.

'It's good to get the conference off my back,' Leo said, coming into the kitchen. There was a broad smile on his face, and he was rubbing his hands together, as though in celebration. 'That lecture was a beast to write. I know the Art Fund stuff backwards, but how best to pitch it has been a real problem. I'm presenting an academic paper—plenty of facts and figures—but it's also a plea for money. Emotions need tapping and that's a tricky combination. I need to get the audience to donate without realising they're being persuaded.'

'It is tricky,' Nancy agreed. 'But you've finished.'

'I am, and I have the day free. Amazing! How are you, darling? You seemed a little low after the party yesterday.'

This was dangerous territory and Nancy said quickly, 'I shouldn't have. It was a lovely party and Susie is a very sweet girl. Perhaps I was tired?'

'You've been rushing around organising the house ready for Dad and it's worn you out. I feel guilty I let you take it on.'

Guilty—that word again. But it wasn't Leo who should be feeling so. He liked to think of her as fragile, a delicate blossom in need of protection, but she was a great deal tougher than that, and really, she'd had little to do for Ned's return. Grace had worked hard at cleaning the house and the men had undertaken the strenuous shifting of furniture.

'Tea?' she asked, walking over to the Aga and putting the kettle to boil on the hot plate.

Leo nodded and sat down at the table. 'The sun is shining and we should go out for the morning. Dad isn't home until the day after tomorrow and we've done everything we can to make him comfortable. Till then, we've a breathing space and we should make the most of it.'

He took the cup Nancy offered and drank his tea with relish. 'Grace is coming later, isn't she? For last minute stuff? But we've got hours in between—what do you say?'

'It's a nice idea.'

'So…where do we go?'

Nancy thought for a moment. 'Archie has taken the hire car. We'd have to stay local, I guess.'

Leo leaned across the table, his expression eager. 'I was thinking of taking you to the Helford River. I'd love you to see it—the countryside is stunning.'

'Isn't that a fair distance?'

'Less than an hour by car. We'd have to hire a taxi.'

She laughed. 'How extravagant, Leo!'

He laughed, too. 'Let's do it. It's our chance for freedom. Dad is still in hospital and Perry's at the mine. One phone call and we can be off.'

He jumped up and walked around the table, putting his hands on her shoulders and rubbing his face against her cheek. 'Look at that sun.' He glanced upwards through the tall window facing them. 'Look at that cloudless blue sky. Can you resist?'

'It's hard to resist, but it will be very expensive,' she repeated.

'*Bof*, as the French say. You're worth every penny. Now go and put on something pretty and I'll make sure the cab is here by the time you're downstairs again.'

The weather was unusually warm today—Nancy could feel the sun on her arms as she opened the bedroom window—and she was encouraged to pull from the wardrobe the one cotton dress she'd brought with her in the hope of just such a day. Decked out in a blue floral tea dress and white sandals, it wasn't long before she joined her husband in the hall. He had been as good as his word. A sleek dark blue saloon, engine ticking, sat waiting for them outside the front door.

Leo was right about the distance, too. Nancy had her first glimpse of the river in less than an hour and thought it magnificent—a wide expanse of undulating water, softly bending itself in and around numerous small tree-sheltered coves, then flowing swiftly to the sea.

'We're not stopping?' she asked in surprise, as first they

passed Gweek village and then Mawgan.

'I'm planning a very special walk by the river.'

'So where are we going?'

Leo put his finger to his lips. 'A secret.'

The road they were following bordered the river as it wound its way around tiny inlets and past scattered houses. When they finally came to a halt, they were at the top of a small hill and Leo helped her out of the car and walked with her to the side of the road.

'Look down there,' he instructed.

A creek lay below, a deep thrust of water, overhung by trees on either bank, their branches trailing in the water and several small boats drawn up on a sandy beach. The tip of a white-washed cottage was just visible through the trees.

'Helford village.' He pointed to several roofs she could see to the left of where they stood. 'The river is no longer tidal this far inland and the ports that used to line the water have gone. Helford, Gweek, Constantine—they're just sleepy villages now. And we mustn't forget Frenchman's Creek.'

'Daphne du Maurier!'

'The very same. I know you love the book.' Romance immortalised in a landscape, Nancy thought. 'It's also great walking country,' Leo added prosaically.

A little further on, the taxi pulled into a car park and, after telling their driver he was free for the next few hours, Leo pointed downhill to the village. 'Let's start there.'

Helford was as idyllic as the water it stood beside: thatched cottages, boat houses, an ancient wooden footbridge and a public house, the Shipwrights Arms, that was picture perfect.

'I thought we might have lunch at the pub,' Leo said.

'It's a truly beautiful place. Thank you for bringing me.' Nancy gave him a quick hug.

She was entranced by the village and most of all by the

river, but the fact that Leo had thought to organise this trip especially for her—du Maurier's book meant little to him— seemed to double, treble, the weight of her betrayal. She tried to push Archie and the kiss out of her mind and concentrate on the beauty all around.

Once past the pub, Leo branched off the main village street, to take a footpath that ran behind one of the white-washed cottages. 'We can do a circular walk. I thought we'd start with Penarvon Cove.'

Nancy was happy to walk anywhere. The village, the river, were entirely magical. And the cove when they reached it was as small and silent and secret as she'd expected, sheltered from the world by close-packed trees growing thick and dense. A flurry of wings broke the quiet and a white-plumed egret came to land a few yards from where they stood, its little yellow feet strikingly bright against the green of the riverbank. They stood and watched for a while as it paddled in the shallows, until Leo said, 'From here, it's uphill, I'm afraid. Is that okay?'

'I need to stretch my legs anyway.'

The climb was steep, but the sun was warm on her back and the air fresh on her face. They walked in single file, Leo in front, and it was when they were breasting the hill, that her husband suddenly stopped. He turned uncertainly towards her, his face paper-white.

Nancy was startled, rushing uphill to his side. 'You're ill, Leo. Hold on to me. No, don't try to talk,' she said, as he struggled to speak. She pulled him tightly against her so that she was supporting him, but it was several minutes before he could stand unaided.

'Sorry about that,' he said in a voice she could barely hear. 'I'm not sure what happened.'

'I'm not sure either,' Nancy said. 'But it's not the first time, is it?' She didn't mean to sound severe, but she was shocked at how ill he'd looked. His face now was regaining its colour and she felt a wave of relief. 'You must see a doctor.'

'I've not felt as bad as that before.' He held up his hands in mock surrender. 'Yes, I know. I'll see the doctor when we get back to London.'

'Is that a promise?'

He bent his head and kissed the top of her head. 'It is. Now let's enjoy this glorious view. We'll cross the cattle grid ahead and carry on along the track to Frenchman's. From this height, you should be able to see back up the river towards Gweek, though you might have to crane your head.'

The track through Frenchman's Creek was all Nancy had hoped. Daffodils still bloomed on either side of the path and vast carpets of wild garlic covered the woodland floor. And always there was the river flowing beside them, dappled in the sunlight, rippling towards the sea.

'I can imagine *La Mouette* tied up here,' she said, looking down at the small, sandy beach. Then in explanation, 'The boat in *Frenchman's Creek*.'

'Ah!' Leo gave her a hug. 'I doubt I'll ever read the book, but I know women like it.'

It was the kind of patronising remark she hated, but Nancy forgave him. She had been seriously worried on that hill and, even though Leo now appeared his usual self, she was still very concerned. It was clear that, if his body were under even a small stress, his breathing was a problem, and the sooner he saw a doctor, the happier she'd be.

At the end of the path, the creek narrowed, and they crossed the road to walk past a large farmyard, then downhill again following a muddy track through the woods and back into Helford Village.

'I reckon after that hike, we deserve a slap-up lunch,' Leo

said. 'Though I'm not too sure the Shipwrights Arms will provide it.'

It might not have been the slap-up meal Leo had spoken of, but to Nancy it tasted superb and she ate every mouthful. Crab salad and a glass of cider, almost the same meal she'd enjoyed with Kitty Anson. It made a good lunch. She should call on Kitty—she hadn't seen her friend since she'd dropped Nancy at Wheal Agnes—and had wondered how she was managing the shop, now she was single-handed.

Leo put down his knife and fork. 'Good?' he asked.

'Need you ask?' She pointed to her empty plate. 'Cornwall does crab salad magnificently.'

'I'm glad we've made a day of it. I thought it important that we got away from Penleven for a while, spend time together. '

Nancy took a sip of cider, and he went on, 'Things haven't gone too well for us lately, have they? Not since we left Malfuego. I've been away too much, and you've been working.'

'We talked about that before.' She felt herself tense. The old argument was rearing its head and about to spoil the nicest day she had spent with Leo for months.

'I'm not going to rant about the job,' he was quick to say. 'I was terribly clumsy when I spoke of it before. It was stupid of me to suggest another baby as some kind of panacea. It was just my way of trying to make a new start, Nancy.' He reached out for her. 'But perhaps we could anyway?'

She cradled his hand between hers. 'I hope so,' she said, and meant it. Anything else didn't bear thinking of. 'I want this marriage to work.'

She had made a solemn vow and she must keep it. She would never feel the way about Leo as she did about Archie, but she owed it to her husband to do all she could to make him happy. Owed him gratitude and loyalty—and love, too.

He was a good man and he deserved a better wife than she had been.

She paused before she spoke again. There was one thing she needed to get clear. 'I need to work, Leo. To enjoy the same freedom as you.'

'I can see that,' he assured her. 'It's taken me time to realise just how important work is for you—too much time. But I do now. You were happy at Abingers and, though my position makes it difficult for you to work at an auction house, it's still important you find your way in the world.'

'A better way, perhaps? At Abingers I was always going to be limited. I was never going to climb the career ladder,' she said ruefully. 'And I'm not sure I found the work as satisfying as I thought at the time. We were selling creativity, but we weren't part of it. We were at a distance. With restoration, it's so different. You're there, close to the artist and the work, helping future viewers appreciate the beauty of what might be a masterpiece. That *is* satisfying.'

Leo sighed. 'I understand you love your job. I'm old-fashioned, that's my problem. I want to look after you. I want us to make a real family like the one I had before my mother died. We were her life, you know—Perry and me. She was always there for us, no matter what.'

Nancy gave him a thoughtful look. 'It's a beautiful sentiment, but when she made the family her entire life, your mother renounced any idea of being a professional artist.'

Leo gave a small shrug. 'It was what she and my father agreed. She was happy to do it.'

'Was she?'

He looked startled at the question. 'Of course she was.'

'You're certain of that?'

He thought for a while. 'She loved Penleven, loved the garden—her creativity there was obvious—and she wanted always to look after us. In the long school holidays she spent every minute with us.' There was another pause before he said, 'But I take your point. Maybe there was a part of her that wasn't entirely happy, but women have to choose, don't they? It may be unfair, but that's the way it is. If you're a mother, a good mother, your children need you at home.'

'Some might disagree,' Nancy said carefully.

'I don't see how it can be any other way. But about the baby—'

'If it happens, it happens.'

If she were ever to become pregnant again, she would have to be brave. Hope against hope that she would not miscarry. If by some miracle the child survived, she would welcome the baby into her life, but if not …

He smiled. 'Pragmatic as always, Nancy. Still, if we make an effort to spend more time together, it might make you eager for a family,' he teased.

Nancy smiled back, but said nothing.

'Do you want to walk more, or should we start back to Penleven?' he asked.

'I think we should go. Grace will be calling at the house very soon and there are several things I need to check with her.'

The taxi driver was waiting for them in the car, having spent his time, it seemed, listening to a football commentary on his new car radio and eating sandwiches—Nancy noticed the screwed-up greaseproof paper.

As the cab swung back onto the road for the return journey to Penleven, she relaxed back into the leather seat cushions. She was tired from the walk and, warmed by Leo's body close beside her, she closed her eyes and drifted into a doze. Leo must have dozed, too, because when the taxi came to an abrupt halt, both of them started forward, looking slightly dazed. Nancy peered through the window. They were not outside Penleven as she'd expected, but on the road leading down the hill to Port Madron, a little way past Wheal Agnes.

Craning his neck to look out of the window, Leo uttered an exclamation, and their driver a low-voiced curse. Then both men burst out of the car. Nancy scrambled from her seat, intent on following them.

'My God, Perry!' she heard Leo shout.

She stopped and looked ahead. The driver was already halfway down the steep hill, and, at the bottom, she could see a car turned on its side. It had ploughed through one of the high hedges bordering the road, the rear of the vehicle ending in a deep ditch. Nancy caught her breath. It was Perry's car. She began to run as fast as she could towards it. Leo and the cab driver had reached the car by now and were dragging Perry's inert body from the driving seat. As she neared the small group, a stitch in her side, Nancy could hear the engine still ticking.

Perry lay on the grass verge, his eyes closed, his face bloodless. There was a red slash across his neck and his hand was twisted at an odd angle.

'Is he… ?' She dared hardly ask.

'He's alive, missus,' the driver said. 'But I've no idea what the damage is.'

'We need to get him to hospital.' Leo was white-faced, his breathing laboured again. 'Can you take us?'

The driver nodded grimly.

'I must go with my brother, but …' Leo looked wildly around. A bright yellow van was coming down the hill towards them. Nancy followed her husband's gaze. It was Kitty Anson.

The van came to an abrupt halt and Kitty leapt out. 'What's going on? Who's car is it?'

'It's Perry's,' Leo said tersely.

She put her hand to her mouth. 'Oh, my goodness.'

'Kitty, we need to get my brother to hospital,' Leo said urgently. 'I'll take him in the taxi. If you could drive Nancy back to Penleven?'

'You don't have to ask, my luvver. But can I help get the poor dear into the cab?'

'No, that's fine. We'll manage between us.'

Leo and the driver bent together to pick up the still unconscious Perry and lay him gently across the back seat of the taxi. 'I'll be in touch, Nancy,' was all Leo had time to say before the cab shot forward, heading towards the Truro road.

'You look awful,' Kitty said, turning to her. 'Why don't you come home with me? There's brandy in the cupboard and you look as though you could do with it.'

Nancy said nothing, but allowed herself to be guided towards the little yellow van.

Chapter Twenty-Eight

She should have gone back to Penleven to wait for Leo's call. Perry had looked dreadful. It wasn't just his hand that was damaged—if there were bones broken, they could be mended—but his ghastly pallor and lifeless body suggested something worse. He'd hardly seemed to breathe. But Kitty had hustled her into the van insisting, as she'd done before, that brandy would help.

A stiff drink was Archie's preferred solution to any calamity and, once Nancy was ensconced in the small, cosy kitchen, and had taken a sip or two from the glass Kitty handed her, she thought they might be right.

'Feeling better?' her friend asked.

'A lot, thanks. Sorry to be so feeble.'

She *had* been feeble, overwhelmed not just by Perry's disaster, but yet another 'accident' in which someone could have died—and still could. Most scary of all, it had come after Jory Pascoe's death. Nancy had felt so certain that Pascoe was the villain but now, unless the man had risen from the dead, it was inconceivable. An unknown person was still out there, still intent on evil. An unknown person who sent anonymous letters, warning of retribution. Two days ago, Perry had received just such a note—until this moment, it had slipped Nancy's mind—and now her brother-in-law was lying unconscious in hospital.

Who was this malefactor? Was it possible it could be Philip March? He had never featured in her list of suspects and, until yesterday, she hadn't known for sure that he was in Port Madron. The messages had been put together by letters cut-out from newspapers, and Philip was, or had been, a journalist. Nancy gave herself an inner shake. That was far too simplistic. Anonymous letters were often fashioned from newsprint: it was a well-known ploy to disguise authorship.

In any case, the torn-out pages from a lined exercise book suggested someone a lot less sophisticated than Philip. And he'd come here specifically to hurt *her*, she must remember. After yesterday's trouncing by Archie, he would surely have scuttled back to London. But what if he hadn't? What if, in his madness, he'd decided weeks, months ago, to widen his canvas? Hurt the family she'd married into, and Perry was simply the latest victim?

'You're not at all feeble,' Kitty said stoutly, topping up their glasses. 'It's your brother-in-law who's in trouble. You're bound to feel a bit desperate.'

'Have you any idea how it could have happened?' Nancy looked across at her companion, though with little hope that Kitty could help.

'I was late on the scene, so I didn't see anything. It's a dangerous hill. You have to keep your wits about you.'

'You think Perry's attention was distracted?'

Kitty gave a small shrug. 'Who knows? But he's probably got a lot on his mind at the moment and it's possible.'

That was true enough. The contract hadn't yet been signed with Francisco Silva; Perry was holding off until he felt his father well enough to hear the news. The future of Wheal Agnes was riding on the next few days.

'He'll be all right, I'm sure,' Kitty said cheerfully, and when her friend made no response, she jumped up from her chair and came round to give Nancy a hug. 'For a while, he'll be the worst for wear, but the hospital will patch him up nicely.'

She wished she could share Kitty's confidence, but tried to put on a bright voice. 'I expect I'm worrying too much. But seeing Leo's face when he realised it was his brother in the car...'

'It must have been awful for him,' Kitty sympathised. 'Do you have a brother, Nancy? Or a sister for that matter?'

'I'm an only child.' Nancy took another sip of the brandy, allowing its warmth to travel easefully around her body. 'How about you?'

'An only child, too. We get to be special!'

'I'm not sure how special. I always wanted a sibling. Growing up on your own can be lonely.'

'You had your parents.'

'Well, yes, but they ...we... I've never been close to them,' Nancy confessed. 'My mother had a series of miscarriages before I arrived. I wasn't expected to live but, somehow, I did. The trouble was that I was a girl and not the boy they longed for. And a girl determined to follow her own path—a cuckoo in the nest, I suppose.'

'A woman after my own heart.' Kitty laughed aloud. 'I knew we'd be friends from the moment we met.'

Nancy was curious. 'Did *your* parents think they knew what was best for you?'

'I only had a mother and the last thing she worried about was my future. She was like yours, she hadn't expected to have a child. But very unlike, too. She never wanted one.'

Nancy didn't like to ask what had happened to Kitty's father. 'That's very sad,' she said quietly. 'Is she still alive?'

'No, thank God.'

She was shocked. Even if she and Ruth Nicholson had

never been close, she had never wished her mother dead.

'Don't look like that, sweetie,' Kitty chided. 'My mother was an out-and-out bitch.' There was real venom in the words. 'She resented me from the time I was born. I was a burden she didn't want, you see. She'd been left to cope alone, and she was angry about it and, since I was the only one around, guess who got the anger?'

'It must have been hard for you. But hard for her, too, being left to raise a child on her own.'

'I guess so. We were the dregs, Nancy. That's how everyone treated us. My mother could only get rubbish jobs, when she could get one at all. Actually—I know I can tell you this and it won't go any further—when I started growing up, got wise to things going on, I was pretty sure that prostitution was one of those jobs.'

'How dreadful for you.'

'It was a wretched childhood, no mistake. We were always on the move, from one rented dump to another, often having to pack our bags at midnight and slip away because my mother couldn't pay the rent. There was no chance of getting a decent education. I learnt to read and write and that was about it. But at least it was enough for me to manage a shop!' Kitty was smiling now.

Nancy's own childhood, dreary and staid though it had been, was looking a paradise in comparison. 'I had no idea you'd had such troubles. How lucky you met Trevor and made your own small family. For a little while at least.'

Kitty looked at her for a moment, then said, 'It was, wasn't it? And he was a good soul. He persuaded me to go back to see my mother. That was when I found her sick. She had lung cancer and there was no hope of her getting better.'

'And you nursed her?' Nancy asked, hoping for at least a smidgen of good feeling.

Kitty smiled again. 'I did. I did my duty and this is my reward. A wonderful home in a wonderful village.'

'I hope it stays wonderful.' Nancy felt her face pucker into a frown. 'But there have been so many bad things happening in Port Madron.'

'You're sounding ominous,' her friend teased.

'Think about it, Kitty. First Treeve dies accidentally, then Ned Tremayne nearly dies in hospital, and now Perry—we don't even know how badly he's injured. Then there's Jory Pascoe. I thought he was behind all the trouble in the village. But he couldn't have been. He couldn't have harmed Perry.'

'Perry's accident was just that—an accident. Human error, they call it, and you shouldn't think badly of Jory. He was a stupid bloke, but what man isn't at some time or other, and too hot-headed for his own good. But he wasn't truly bad.'

'He stole from Treeve.'

'That's true.' Kitty poured another tot of brandy into Nancy's glass. 'Maybe he meant to return the stuff, but died before he could. It could have happened that way. Jory may have quarrelled with Treeve—he was a right quarrelsome man—and decided he'd get his own back by taking things the old chap loved, but then give them back when he thought Treeve had been punished enough.'

For Nancy, the idea was just too far-fetched and she couldn't stop herself saying, 'It sounds very unlikely.'

'So, in the absence of Jory, are you going to put on your investigator hat and find the wicked mastermind stalking Port Madron?'

Nancy had to smile at that description. 'My investigator hat hasn't been too effective so far, has it?'

'Is it ever?'

'Believe it or not, yes. I gained a kind of justice for Marta Moretto in Venice and I discovered the killer on a Caribbean island, though I'd rather not have. It was a sad business.'

'Does Leo join you on these little jaunts?'

Nancy was taken aback. 'Goodness, no. I've been strictly forbidden to tangle in problems that aren't mine.'

'But you still tangle?' Kitty looked amused.

'In this case, my tangling hasn't worked—not so far, at least. Previously, I've been able to talk to people or listen to them talking—you learn a lot that way—but I can't do the same in Port Madron. If I went to Wheal Agnes and started questioning the miners about Pascoe, about Treeve Fenton, I'd embarrass Perry. The hospital would be as difficult. Nobody there would want to talk to me about Ned's seizure. They're desperate to forget the whole incident.'

Nancy let out a soft sigh. 'I'm isolated at Penleven, but even if I come into the village, who can I talk to with any frankness? Everyone here knows the Tremaynes and Leo would be furious if he got to know. Which he would. The anonymous letters are the only clues I have, and he won't allow me to take them to the police. He prefers to think all this mayhem is somehow accidental.'

Nancy had one other clue which she wouldn't mention. Something she'd asked Archie to check on. It was either a loose end that needed tying up or a last grasping at straws. Whatever it was, it was niggling her—the seemingly unimportant could sometimes turn out to be crucial.

'Maybe Leo's right, my love,' Kitty said, emptying her glass. 'Sometimes things can be just as they seem. C'mon. Drink up and I'll run you home.'

***

Archie woke up hours later to a pitch black room. His hand reached out for the bedside lamp, then grasped his watch and saw to his annoyance that he had slept away the afternoon and virtually the entire evening. It was nearly midnight and he was hungry, but had lost any chance of eating.

Struggling to his feet, he looked out of his bedroom window at the lights of London, a glowing carpet stretching into the distance. The capital might be lit up, but he wouldn't find food at this hour, unless he spent a lot of money he didn't have catching a taxi to a posh restaurant.

The kitchen. He'd have to find something edible there. Making his way down the stairs, he drew the curtains as he went. A forage through the cupboards proved a thankless task, his only find a chunk of cheese in the refrigerator, somehow overlooked by Mrs Brindley in her cleaning enthusiasm, and a stale piece of fruit cake still sitting in the old Quality Street tin. How long had that been there? Well, he was a beggar and he couldn't choose. He'd forgo the cheese, but eat the cake with a cup of tea. Then he'd get started on Leo's conference paper. He was wide awake now and might as well use the night to good effect.

By the time the sun pierced the horizon and the first beams of light filtered their way into the study, Archie had typed up the whole paper. It had taken him a lot longer than he'd expected. There had been a constant need to check technical words, both in the paper itself and in the accompanying notes Leo hoped to distribute among the audience. And Archie had made an unusually large number of typing errors, all of which had to be laboriously corrected. His mind was skittering in a way he hated, half of it in Cavendish Street and half back in Cornwall.

He considered tackling the next stage of the presentation — ensuring that the slides Leo wished to use in the bright, new projector he'd recently bought were sharp and clear, and that all the supporting documents were as well organised as the lecture itself and ready for the printers.

Archie considered it, but then decided he needed to wash and change and find food. Half an hour later he was on an early morning bus to the East End. Charlie's caff was where he was bound, a splendid English breakfast waiting for him there. He loved this part of London though he'd no ancestral connection to it. But its old, dilapidated buildings, narrow alleys and cobbled courtyards spoke history at every turn. And the mix of people was like nothing he'd seen in any other city.

He had never been out of Cornwall until the day he'd enlisted as a soldier and begun to understand how varied and exciting the world was. The East End was its microcosm, having provided succour to a string of refugees over the centuries. Though Charlie's was a traditional working man's café, its neighbour on one side was a bagel shop and on the other a restaurant selling curry. Opposite was a pie and mash stall.

A heaped plate of sausage, bacon and egg, with mushrooms and grilled tomatoes, appeared within minutes of his sitting down at the Formica table.

'For you, Archie, one of my best customers,' the proprietor said, with a grand sweep of his hands, wiping them against a none too clean apron. 'Toast and tea when you're ready.'

'Thanks, Charlie. Just what I need.'

Once or twice, Archie had been tempted to bring Leo here to show him what a decent breakfast looked like, but one glance at that apron and his boss would have made for the door.

Two slices of toast and two cups of tea later, Archie set off westwards. His stomach felt at peace, but it would do him good to walk through the City, along the Strand, and into the West End. Bond Street was where he was heading. He'd promised Nancy he'd visit and he had time before he

needed to return to Cavendish Street and finish the work for
Leo. It was a day for walking, the sun glinting off scuffed
paving slabs and the plane trees at last beginning to wear
their summer leaves. He wondered if the sun was shining
in Cornwall. Wondered how Nancy was and what she was
doing today.

He couldn't keep her from his mind, try as he might. But
by the time he saw her again, he'd needed to have worked
out just what he should do. She didn't deserve to have him
messing up her life. She'd had a rough time so far—her
parents sounded like something out of a Dickens novel and
Philip March could have starred in a Hammer Horror.

And the marriage to Leo? She'd married for the right
reasons, Archie supposed, but the wrong man. His boss
was a decent bloke, but apart from losing his mother at a
young age, he was a man who'd travelled through life along
a golden pathway. Leo had known only privilege—private
school, university, an army commission. He was used to
ordering events as he wanted, and when his control slipped,
that's when he got angry. Like that business of the baby. The
miscarriage Nancy had suffered in Malfuego had caused a
major rift between them. Things had been patched up, though
it was more like papered over, but it was difficult to see the
marriage ever working as it should. Certainly not with him
around.

In one insane moment before he'd left Cornwall, he'd asked
her to come with him, a barely disguised entreaty that... what
was that phrase in *Don Quixote*?... that she *throw her cap over
the windmill*. Yet he had no idea of her true feelings, only that
she liked to kiss him. In any case, what could he offer her?
Once the job with Leo had gone, and go it would—running
off with your employer's wife had its downside—he was
virtually penniless. He guessed Nancy was, too, since the

apprenticeship paid very little. The only work he'd get at all easily would be menial and low paid. Even if she were willing to break her marriage vows—and it was a big 'if'—he couldn't do that to her. What he could do, though, was to ask questions. If *he* was asking them, she wasn't, which meant he was keeping her out of trouble.

He'd been so lost in his thoughts that he'd reached Oxford Circus without really noticing. From here to Bond Street was a few minutes' stroll. He'd begin at the top of the street, he decided, and work his way down towards Piccadilly, calling at every high-class jeweller's.

There proved to be plenty of them. Archie must have walked into at least eight shops before he came close to success, garnering very different reactions as he went: from eagerness to hook a likely customer, to open disdain for someone who looked as though Woolworth's jewellery counter might be a better choice. The woman at Lyall & Hart, her dark hair swept upwards in an uncompromising bun, glided towards him the minute she heard the tinkle of the shop bell. A knee-length black dress fitted her slim form to perfection, while highly polished black court shoes tapped their way across the gleaming wood floor.

'May I help you?' Her tone suggested she thought it unlikely, but an unfashionable exterior could occasionally yield results.

'I hope so.'

Archie gazed around him. Every wall of the showroom was fitted with shining glass cabinets, including a large rectangular case behind the discreet leather-topped counter. Only a handful of jewellery was displayed in this acre of glass. Was this all the shop had to sell? Or were these few items arranged in this way to stress their exclusivity? No doubt, the latter.

The woman waved him to an enormous leather armchair and glided noiselessly behind the counter.

'I've a question I hope you might help me answer,' Archie began. 'I'm looking for someone. A Sally Crouch. Do you know her?'

'Should I?' The woman pasted a frown on her face.

'I believe she once worked here.' In truth, Archie had no knowledge of where Miss Crouch had worked or even who she was, but it was as good a bait as any.

The assistant's frown deepened. 'The name is slightly familiar,' she admitted.

'You worked with her?'

'Oh, no!' She was quick to disown the idea, but Archie plodded on.

'Someone else might have known her?'

'Mr Armstrong, I suppose,' she said reluctantly. 'He is our manager.'

'May I speak to him then?'

'I'm afraid not. He's a very busy man.' The woman did her peculiar glide sideways around the counter and went as though to usher Archie from the shop.

'Then I'll stay—until he's less busy.'

The assistant was now bristling, but faced with Archie's doggedness, she appeared to give in. He saw her press a discreet button to one side of the counter and within seconds a black-suited, bespectacled man appeared from the nether regions of the shop.

'I'm sorry, Mr Armstrong.' The woman fell over herself to apologise. 'This gentleman insists on seeing you and I don't—'

The tinkle of the shop bell had both of them look up. 'Leave it to me, Miss Harris,' the manager said, nodding towards the doorway, 'we have customers for you to attend to.'

He turned to Archie. 'Now how can I help, sir?'

Mr Armstrong might be irritated by the intrusion, but a fixed smile on his face told Archie he was likely to get what he needed. The manager wouldn't want him cluttering his premises for long, and the sooner he answered Archie's questions the better. And one never knew, the manager's face seemed to say: even a man like this was a potential customer, and customers were always welcome.

'I'm looking for a Sally Crouch,' Archie said.

The name had the man tense. 'I'm afraid I can't help you. The person in question no longer works here.'

'But she did?' he persisted.

'I'm unsure what your interest in Miss Crouch might be, sir, but that of Lyall & Hart is non-existent.' There was now no disguising the terseness in the manager's voice.

'You don't value your staff?' Archie asked provocatively.

'On the contrary, sir. We value our staff highly—our trusted staff, that is.' He looked towards Miss Harris, who was guiding a middle-aged couple around the glass cases, her soft tones barely audible.

'I take it that Sally Crouch wasn't to be trusted?'

The man adjusted his spectacles and bent his head towards Archie. In a mutter that verged on a hiss, he said, 'Sally Crouch was dismissed for stealing. Is that what you wish to know?'

Archie's eyebrows rose sharply. It wasn't what he had expected to hear. He gazed around the glass cabinets again. Despite their paucity of trinkets, each case must hold goods costing thousands of pounds. 'Not the kind of employee you'd want here,' he said.

'It was most unfortunate,' the manager conceded. 'A chapter the firm wishes to forget.'

'You didn't prosecute, though?'

'We chose not to,' Mr Armstrong said with dignity. 'The

reputation of the firm was at stake. Now if you'll excuse me…'

'But you employed her. Originally, you must have considered her completely trustworthy.'

'Miss Crouch came to us as a trained nurse.' The manager's figure had become alarmingly rigid. 'We would naturally assume trustworthiness from someone in such a position.' He turned away abruptly and walked back through the open doorway to the rear office, leaving Archie to stare at his disappearing form.

Meanwhile the middle-aged couple had left the shop empty-handed. Miss Harris, adjusting her bun with manicured hands, walked back to the counter, a challenge in her eyes. 'Mr Armstrong has answered your question, sir? I think it may be time you left.'

Archie was unperturbed 'The hospital Sally Crouch worked at, before she came here— do you have a note of the name?'

Miss Harris tightened her lips but, after what seemed an inner tussle, disappeared through the office door. She was back very shortly carrying a large ledger, its cover scratched and its pages curling. Flicking quickly through the volume, she found what she was looking for, and turned the ledger so that Archie could see. One manicured fingernail indicated an entry.

'The London Hospital,' Archie read. 'Whitechapel Road. There's another address here—7a Jubilee Street.' It was a road he knew to be in the same neighbourhood. 'Miss Crouch's home?'

'I imagine so,' the assistant said in a bored voice.

'Thank you, Miss Harris. You've been splendid!'

And before he could outstay his welcome further, Archie walked out of the shop and into Bond Street again. Hands dug deep into his pockets, he walked the short way back to

Cavendish Street, thinking hard. Should he go on with this investigation or forget it? There wasn't really any doubt, was there? He knew what Nancy would say if she were here.

Chapter Twenty-Nine

The following morning Leo phoned for a taxi again, this time to take them to Truro in the hope they'd be allowed to see Perry. The hospital had been tight-lipped the previous evening and Leo had come home, after seeing his brother admitted, none the wiser about Perry's injuries. They barely spoke on the journey, Nancy sensing her husband's need for silence. Leo was fearing the worst, she could see.

But when she walked into Perry's ward as the mid-morning refreshments were being delivered, she was relieved to see a big smile on her brother-in-law's face. Leo had lingered behind to speak to the nurse in charge.

'How are you?' she asked, sitting down by his bedside.

'Battered and bruised, but otherwise more or less in one piece. I've a few broken fingers apparently, but they'll mend. They were worried about my concussion, but all the tests show the old brain is still in working order.'

'Thank goodness. Leo has been so worried. I've been so worried.'

Perry took her hand and gave it a small squeeze. 'Sorry to give you both a scare. I've no idea what happened. One minute I was driving down Stannum Hill—I must have driven down it a million times on my way home from Wheal Agnes—and the next minute I woke up and I was in this bed.'

'You were well and truly knocked out.'

'Probably the best thing, but I'm relieved I'm okay in that direction. Francisco Silva phoned—did you know?' Nancy shook her head. 'He actually phoned the hospital, he's so keen to get this thing wrapped up, but I'll need to be a bit more alert than this when I sign the contract. If I sign it.'

'How did Silva know you'd had an accident?' Nancy was puzzled.

'I told him,' Leo said, coming into the ward. He'd been checking on his brother's progress, Nancy thought, still worried despite Perry's brilliant smile. 'Silva phoned Penleven last night after you'd gone to bed early.'

That was the brandy. By the time she'd eaten a solitary supper and then heard Leo's news when he'd returned from the hospital, she'd barely been able to keep her eyes open.

'The nurse says it's just your fingers that need mending,' Leo said. 'And that's a matter of time. If all goes well, you should be able to leave on Monday—along with Dad.'

'Fantastic. It means I won't be away from the mine too long.'

'Whoa! Not so fast, champ.' Leo tussled his brother's hair. 'You need a good rest before you throw yourself into work again. When you do, you might have to hire a car. Or walk to Wheal Agnes.'

'Mine's a write-off, I imagine.'

'Quite possibly. I phoned the garage early this morning and they're willing to try a repair, but it's not looking too hopeful. The chap I spoke to seems unhappy about something and wants to talk to me. I've arranged to meet him first thing on Monday, before I come over to Truro to collect my battered family, doctors willing.'

'Talking of battered family, Dad's ward is just up the corridor. I think we should go and see how the old trooper

244

is doing.'

'The old trooper is doing fine.' Ned Tremayne wheeled himself through the doorway and up to Perry's bedside. 'The nurses told me Leo was here.' He gave Nancy a brief nod, but no other acknowledgement, and for the next fifteen minutes spoke only to his two sons, despite both Leo and Perry trying hard to include Nancy in the conversation. She was thankful when Leo looked at his watch and decided it was time to leave.

Waiting on the forecourt for the taxi to arrive, Leo said, 'I'll come over tomorrow to see them both, but you don't need to. I'm sure there are things at Penleven you want to get on with.'

She was grateful for his understanding, but there was a small part of her that was angry. How many years would it take before Leo's father recognised her existence? She wished her husband would make it clear to Ned Tremayne that he had a wife now and she was here to stay.

'The Helford River seems a long way away, doesn't it?' Leo asked, when they were settled in the cab and driving back to Port Madron. 'What a pity the day had to end as it did.'

'I still have lovely memories of the place.'

'You must hold on to them. I hated to see you look so shaken when you realised it was Perry's car at the bottom of that hill. I'm glad Kitty was there to look after you.'

'You looked pretty shaken yourself.'

'I was. Still am, if truth be told. I've been desperately worried that Perry's injuries were irreparable. All I can say is thank God for broken fingers!'

***

Archie spent several hours of his second morning in Cavendish Street organising the presentation he'd typed earlier. By midday, he had it in good order, packing the numbered documents into separate files and storing them in a sturdy cardboard box. He was on the point of leaving for the printers with the hand-outs Leo had given him, when a mechanic from the local garage turned up to collect the car for a vehicle check. He promised to have it back with a full tank of petrol by late afternoon.

If the bloke did as he said, Archie could leave early the next morning and be back in Port Madron by tea-time. The journey would be an easy one on a Sunday. He'd better telephone Penleven to let them know he was coming, but first he'd make himself a quick sandwich.

It was Grace who answered the call. 'I've been doin' some last minute cleanin',' she told her brother-in-law when Archie expressed surprise at her being at the house, 'in case old man Tremayne comes back on Monday.'

'What do you mean "in case"? I thought it was certain. Where is everybody?' He took a bite of cheese and pickle.

'Mr Leo's at the hospital again. There's been a problem.'

'With Ned Tremayne?'

'No, the old chap's okay. It's Mr Perran. He's in hospital now—he's 'ad an accident. Mr Leo is hoping they can both come home on Monday. Depends on what the doctors say.'

Archie didn't like the sound of it. 'What kind of accident?' he asked. It had to be fairly serious to have landed Perry in hospital.

'His car went off the road. Down Stannum Hill. Landed halfway through the hedge.' Grace's voice took on a gloomy satisfaction.

'Do you know how it happened?'

'They think Mr Perran might have had a kind of blackout,' Grace said. 'He seems okay now but they're keepin' 'im in for observation. I think that's what Nancy said.'

'Is Nancy with you?'

'She's gone to Truro again with Mr Leo. Not to the hospital, though. She fancied doing some shoppin', I think.'

A blackout in an otherwise healthy man seemed unlikely. Archie didn't like the sound of it at all. Yet another accident after all the others. When Nancy had disputed they *were* accidents, insisting they'd been deliberately planned, he'd tried to make light of her concerns. He should have learned by now that she had a nose for trouble and when she started having suspicions, she was usually right.

He brushed the crumbs from his fingers. 'Are the police looking at Perry's car?' he asked. That would establish whether there had been any attempt to tinker with the mechanics.

'I dunno. I think it were towed to the garage. What are you up to in the big city?'

'Working hard. For Leo. This afternoon, though, I'm off on a hunt—for a Sally Crouch.' It sounded ridiculous and he gave a small laugh.

'Who's Sally Crouch?'

'Search me, but looking for her will fill an afternoon. I'll be on my way back tomorrow.'

'I thought we'd seen the last of you.' His sister-in-law gave a loud snort.

'I thought you had, too, but Leo wants to ride back to London in style. He's asked me to bring the car down and collect him. I'll go on to Ma's after I drop it off at Penleven.'

'Right on. I'll tell 'er to have the kettle goin'.'

Archie slowly put down the receiver. How had Nancy taken the news of her brother-in-law's accident, he wondered? If it had fuelled *his* suspicions, it would have made hers even stronger. And encouraged her to act perhaps? He felt a splinter lodge in his heart, icy cold and dangerous. He'd thought her safe, but now...

It might not be anything like that, he told himself. Now

he was guilty of allowing his imagination to run amok. Too much keeping company with Nancy. The car could well have suffered a mechanical fault or Perry a blackout. The bloke was ordinarily fit, but he'd been under a lot of pressure lately and such an attack was perfectly possible. But if it wasn't a mechanical fault, if it wasn't a medical emergency, if it had been deliberate sabotage... then Nancy's theory that Jory Pascoe was her villain went out of the window. Jory was well and truly dead. Someone else was in the frame, someone else was behind the frightening events in Port Madron.

He felt restless and uncertain. How best to help Nancy? He hardly need ask himself the question. He was clueless as to why Sally Crouch was important to her, but it was enough to know it was. Bond Street had provided him with a clue, and he should follow it. He had the afternoon free and he'd do what he'd told Grace. He'd pay a visit to the London Hospital.

Chapter Thirty

Whitechapel Road was its usual dour self, the sky today matching the tall soot-ridden buildings on either side of the wide road. The traffic was light, most of the activity in this poorer neighbourhood conducted on foot or on two wheels. Several shabby lorries trundled towards him and a shining new Bentley was parked incongruously outside a pawn shop. He walked quickly past the Blind Beggar, a second home to many of the East End's ne'er do wells. It wasn't a pub to linger outside and, at this time of the day, was busy turning its patrons out onto the street until it reopened in early evening.

When Archie reached the London Hospital, he found it heaving, ambulance staff urgently wheeling stretchers through the main entrance, dazed patients being admitted or discharged, and inside the main foyer, nurses with clipboards wheeling in and out of closed doors.

He walked up to the uniformed porter standing just inside the main door. 'Afternoon, squire. I wonder, can you tell me where I might find the matron?'

The porter's eyebrows twitched, as though finding the matron was a task no mere mortal could hope to achieve. 'Matron's in 'er office, mate, but you'll need an appointment.' The porter looked him up and down, judging it seemed whether Archie was likely to be granted one.

'Where do I make the appointment?' He had no intention of doing so, but the porter's directions should put him on the right track.

'The sectry's dahn there, the corridor opposite, second door on the right.'

'Thanks, mate.'

Archie crossed to the opposite corridor, walking a fair way down before he reached an office labelled SECRETARY. Ignoring the sign, he walked on to the next office which boasted a much more impressive door and a sign that read MATRON.

He gave a brisk knock.

'Come!'

Archie came as instructed, and immediately took the measure of the woman confronting him. Matron was intimidating, he acknowledged, all stiff apron and collar and an expression to match. But he hadn't travelled halfway across London to be put off by a little starch.

'Good afternoon, Matron.' He beamed at her.

'And you are?'

'Jago. Archie Jago.'

A frown crossed the matron's otherwise unblemished forehead. 'Why are you here, Mr Jago? Do you have an appointment?' The woman began shuffling though the pages of what looked like a large diary.

'Yes,' Archie lied. 'Your secretary must have forgotten to make a note of it.'

Matron glared at him. 'Miss Clements is extremely efficient. I hardly think—'

'We all have our bad days,' Archie put in and smiled again. He'd make this battleaxe crack her face if it was the last thing he did.

'Now you're here, what is it you require?'

Inwardly, he breathed a small sigh of satisfaction. He was in, and the porters hadn't been called to eject him. 'I'd like some information, Matron, and I think you can help.'

'Yes?' The tone was frosty.

'I'm looking for a nurse who worked here a few years ago. Her name was Sally Crouch.'

'The hospital never discloses details of staff, past or present.' The voice had grown even frostier.

'But Miss Crouch worked here?'

'I repeat, I am not in a position to confirm whether or not this woman worked at the hospital.'

'Ordinarily, I'm sure that's true, but this is of the utmost importance. I'm sure I can depend on you to help.' His deep blue eyes gazed at her in what he hoped was a soulful fashion.

Matron rose majestically from her desk and walked towards him. 'I have no idea who you are, Mr Jago, and I doubt you ever had an appointment with me. In fact, I'm sure you did not, since Miss Clements would have immediately made clear to you the hospital's position. Now, I have no more time to waste, so—'

She opened the office door and Archie had no option but to walk through it, feeling deeply disappointed. He had been sure that with a little bravado he'd have discovered whatever it was that Nancy was after, but he hadn't taken account of hospital protocol or the dragon that administered it.

Disconsolately, he sauntered back along the corridor and past the porter. A different man now. They must relieve each other for tea breaks, he thought, and with that idea in mind he doubled back.

'I suppose you wouldn't know a nurse called Crouch,' he asked the man. 'She used to work here.'

'Plenty of Crouches.' The porter gave a snort.

'She left about three years ago,' Archie continued, undaunted. 'Went to work in a jeweller's in the West End. Tall woman, remarkable hair. Tight blonde curls.'

The porter shook his head sadly. 'There wus one girl with 'air like that. Them curls were like a corkscrew. But they wus dark.'

It was possible. Some women changed their hair colour. The kind of women Ma was scathing about. "Racy", that was the word she'd used of them, and it had made him laugh.

'It might be her.' He was tentative. 'When did you last see the girl?'

The porter lifted his cap and scratched his head. 'I ain't seen 'er fer a long time. Years, I reckon.'

'Would you know which ward she nursed on?'

'It wus Wellington, I think. Up the stairs and first left.'

'Thanks. You've been really helpful.'

Archie turned back into the hospital and made for the grand sweep of staircase leading to the first floor. Wellington ward was a door to the left as the porter had indicated, and had been left wide open this afternoon for the constant stream of visitors. A good time to have arrived. With their patients entertained, at least one of the nurses might be free to talk. Archie needed only one. A desk was tucked away to one side of the ward, the nurse behind it busy with paperwork. A captive audience, he thought, and marched up to her.

'Who are you visiting?' she asked, ready to direct him to the right bedside.

'I'm not. It was you I was hoping to talk to.'

'Me?' She looked suspicious.

'A nurse anyway.' He saw her shoulders relax—she was assuming it was a medical matter. 'My name is Jago. Archie Jago,' he went on. 'I wondered if you or one of your colleagues worked with someone I know. A Sally Crouch.'

The nurse's face was wiped clean of expression and suspicion was back in her voice. 'Are you a friend of hers?'

For a moment Archie was unsure how to answer. Was it a good or bad thing to be a friend of Sally Crouch? He temporised. 'Let's say I've met her. Did she work on this ward?'

'There *was* a Sally Crouch who worked here.' The girl's caution was extreme. Something more was going on here, something bigger than simply hospital rules.

'She was a tall girl,' he said encouragingly. 'Dark hair, tight curls.'

The nurse nodded, evidently recognising the description.

'She left to work in a jeweller's shop.'

'I've no idea where she went, and I don't want to know,' the woman said tersely. 'That she left was what was important. The nurses wanted her gone. The hospital wanted her gone.'

'Blotted her copybook, eh?' Archie tried for a light tone, hoping to elicit more.

'If you call attempting to kill a patient blotting your copybook, yes.'

'What!'

He'd been prepared for an accusation of petty theft—some aspirin, perhaps, a few bandages, an experiment at stealing before Sally moved on to the big stuff at Lyall & Hart.

'You didn't know? You should be more careful with whom you make friends, Mr Jago.'

Archie frowned. 'But she was a nurse. How could she do that? Why did she do it?' He was still struggling with the idea that someone charged with saving life should deliberately seek to end it.

'Money,' the nurse said sharply. 'What else? These kind of cases are thankfully rare, but it's either money behind it or some kind of madness. And Sally wasn't mad—she was in debt.'

'And attempting to kill a patient helped in what way?'

'He was an elderly man whom she'd taken time to befriend. To the extent that he changed his will in her favour, or that was the rumour. But she must have got impatient waiting for him to die and decided to help him on his way. She defended herself by saying it was a mercy killing. The hospital called it something else.'

Archie's brain was working overtime. 'Despite what she did, the hospital gave her a reference,' he protested. 'Why would they do that?'

'I doubt they did. Sally probably had other skills,' the nurse said laconically.

So the reference was forged. Miss Crouch was quite an operator, he had to concede. Out of the corner of his eye, he saw a small procession of white-coated men marching along the central aisle and became aware of visitors streaming past. The doctors' ward round was just beginning.

'I'll be off,' he said. 'Thanks for the information.'

He walked down Whitechapel Road in something of a daze. Sally Crouch was a jewel thief and, even worse, a would-be murderer. But who was she? Nancy had said the photograph she'd seen was of Kitty's cousin, but it was Kitty who'd told her that and Nancy had had her doubts. Rightly, it seemed. Except for hair colour, Sally's description appeared to fit Kitty perfectly. Kitty *was* the mythical cousin, almost certainly. But she was also Nancy's friend.

Impelled by sudden fear, Archie jumped onto the platform of a passing trolley bus. He must get back to Cavendish Street. Telephone Penleven again and somehow try to find a way to speak to Nancy alone. Warn her to keep clear of Kitty Anson. Just in case.

***

By the time Archie walked through the front door of the Cavendish Street house, he'd had second thoughts. It was likely that both Leo and Nancy were in Truro still, and even if they were back at Penleven, it would be difficult to speak to Nancy alone. There was a chance she would answer the telephone, but a greater chance that it would be Leo, thinking it was the hospital calling. How could he ask to speak to Nancy without giving a reason, without spilling his fears to her husband? Leo would think he'd gone crazy, dismiss it as fantasy, but be angry, too, that Nancy seemed once more to have courted trouble.

The more Archie's mind turned, the more urgent it felt that he hurry back to Cornwall. While he'd been out, the garage had posted the car keys through the letter box with a note saying the vehicle had been parked around the corner at the nearby mews. It was a sign, Archie decided. He wouldn't wait until tomorrow. He would leave now.

He bounded up the stairs to his bedroom and dragged his old haversack from under the bed, stuffing it quickly with underwear and several clean shirts. They would be sufficient to see him through the next few days. Downstairs again to scribble a brief note to Mrs Brindley, telling her he'd left early and not to worry about stocking the refrigerator until she heard from Penleven. And then he was out of the house and running towards the mews.

Why in heavens name was he running? Nancy had asked him to look for a Sally Crouch. He'd done as she'd asked and uncovered some disquieting facts, but could that explain this wild dash? Hardly. It was a visceral need compelling him, the need to reach Nancy. Some deep instinctual connection that told him she was in danger.

He'd get on the road and find a telephone on the way. If he left it for a few hours, the two of them should be home. Even if it was Leo who answered, Nancy would know something was up when she realised that Archie was already on his way back to Cornwall. He was expected at Penleven tomorrow—Grace would have left a message for them. You didn't change your plans and turn up at midnight unless there was something wrong. It should at least make Nancy wary.

Archie drove at speed, not stopping until he reached the outskirts of Exeter where he pulled into a garage to fill up with petrol and ask if he could use their telephone, saying it was an emergency. Ramming the phone against his ear, he heard its ghostly ring echo through the house. He dialled again and the same disturbing ring filled his head. Where the hell were they? It was nine o'clock on a Saturday evening. Perry was in hospital, Grace was home with her children, but where were Leo and Nancy? Most of all, where was Nancy?

Chapter Thirty-One

Saturday morning and Leo had washed and dressed early, ready for another journey to the hospital. Nancy had felt relieved when he'd said he was happy she stay at Penleven today, but now when she saw him walk out to the taxi alone, she changed her mind. Calling out to Grace, who'd arrived to do a last minute clean, that she'd go with her husband after all and do some shopping, she climbed into the taxi beside him. She had no real desire to explore the Truro shops, but she hadn't wanted Leo to feel abandoned. At the same time, she couldn't endure another hour of his father's stony silence. Travelling to town with her husband, but leaving him to visit his family, seemed a sensible compromise.

Leo was in good spirits; life was looking considerably better than it had only a few hours ago. Perry wasn't seriously injured, and Ned Tremayne was now well enough to go home. Hope stirred in Nancy that she and Leo would soon be free to leave for London, once they'd settled the old man into the new arrangements at Penleven, and Perry had had the difficult conversation with his father about the sale of the mine.

Apparently, Archie was to drive Leo's car to Cornwall and collect them. The news had taken Nancy aback—she'd expected to travel to London by train, and wasn't entirely sure how she felt about it. Seeing Archie again would make her happy, when did it not? And she was eager to learn what, if anything, he'd discovered about the mysterious Sally Crouch. But, when he was around, she worried constantly that one or other of them would betray themselves.

Having seen Leo into the hospital , she wandered desultorily around the main shopping streets of Truro for an hour or so, unenthused by the goods on offer. Coming across a craft market, she spent some time talking to one of the stall holders, eventually buying yet another notebook, this time with a hand-painted floral cover. Philip March had destroyed the last one, but not this, she thought, holding tightly to her package.

Leo was waiting for her outside the hospital, sheltering from the first drops of rain beneath its brick awning. There was an anxious look on his face.

'Am I late?' Nancy hurriedly pulled back the sleeve of her jacket to consult her watch.

'No, darling. You're bang on time.' Leo fidgeted with his own jacket sleeves before saying, 'The thing is, Nancy, Dad's consultant wants to talk to me.' Then seeing her concerned face, he said quickly, 'Nothing to worry about. Both invalids are fine—it's about Dad's routine when he gets home. The rest he'll need, his medication, and simply how best to get him back on his feet. The doc doesn't think Perry should be bothered with any of it at the moment.'

'That sounds sensible,' she said cautiously.

'The trouble is the chap can't see me until late on Monday, and I was hoping the hospital would discharge them both that morning. Before everyone gets tired. He could just about fit me in today though, but not until around five o'clock. I don't think I'll be with him long. I should be home by seven at the latest.'

Nancy's heart sank a little. The prospect of another few hours wandering Truro's shopping streets was not appealing, but it was evidently important that Leo spoke to the consultant. 'I'll wait,' she said, as cheerily as she could.

'You'll do no such thing! The weather looks decidedly uncertain and I'm sure you'd prefer to be back at Penleven. I'll order a taxi to take you home. And don't scold me about the expense. Archie will be back in the next few days and we'll have the use of our own car.'

Nancy didn't fight the suggestion. The small drops of rain had become much larger as they'd talked and the skies heavy and grey. Leo waited with her until the cab pulled up at the hospital entrance, then bundled her inside and waved her goodbye through a curtain of wet mist. The journey was uneventful, the driver whisking her smoothly over the miles to reach Port Madron. Well within the hour they were passing through the village and taking the narrow road up to Penleven.

She found the house gleaming. Grace had done a brilliant job and Nancy thanked heaven she'd thought of asking the young woman to help. Mrs Cheffers' nose had been put out of joint a little, but the care of two invalids was paramount, especially that of an elderly man, and Grace would do a far better job.

Nancy wandered into kitchen to put the kettle on, feeling chilled by the rainstorm. Grace had left a note on the table saying that Archie had phoned at lunchtime and would be back tomorrow. Nancy's heart gave a little flip that she immediately suppressed. She had finished her tea and was washing up her cup when the telephone rang. Archie again? Perhaps he wouldn't be back tomorrow as he'd planned. Or perhaps he had found something out about Sally Crouch. It had been a long shot asking him to investigate the name, but she was glad she had. Since the shock of Perry's accident and the realisation that he might have been another target, Nancy had run out of options. So much for her sleuthing expertise, she thought wryly.

But when she lifted the receiver, it was Kitty Anson at the other end of the line.

'Were you sleeping, my love?'

'Of course not,' Nancy said with mock horror. 'I'm just back from Truro. Leo is still at the hospital.'

'How are the invalids?'

'Both doing well, I'm glad to say.'

'Excellent!' Kitty's voice was warm. 'I've more good news for you. That's why I'm ringing.'

'Really? What is it?' This sounded intriguing.

'You might have been right about Jory Pascoe. He could be your villain after all.'

'That's not possible, Kitty. He was already dead when Perry was attacked.'

'But if Perry wasn't attacked? If his car crash was the accident it seemed? They do happen, you know.'

'Okay,' she said cautiously. 'So what about Jory Pascoe?'

'You might need to put your investigator hat on first.'

'You really have discovered something?' There was a new eagerness in Nancy's voice.

'Don't get too excited. It might be nothing. On the other hand, it might lead you to the man you're looking for. Lead me, too. I don't want to live in a village terrorised by some homicidal maniac.'

'Go on.'

'It's at the mine.'

'What is?'

'The evidence, my luvver.'

'At Wheal Agnes? Surely not.'

'I was surprised, too. It was something I overheard last night in the pub. I was tucked away in a dark corner and one of Jory's old mates—believe it or not, he did have some—was slagging off the Tremaynes, and then boasting that he'd done for them, but no one would ever know. They'd always think it was Pascoe behind the trouble.'

'He doesn't sound much of a friend.' Nancy was dubious.

'It seems as though the chap fell out with Jory a while back. That wouldn't be too difficult. He must have decided to get his own back. When his companion asked what he'd done, this bloke—a weedy little man, I've seen him with Jory once or twice—just tapped his finger against his nose and said that certain events would be blamed on Jory and now he was dead, he couldn't answer back. *I'll never be found out,* he said, *unless*—

Unless what? his mate asked.

Nah. Don't matter. They'll have thrown Jory's tool bag away by now.

'His tool bag?' Nancy couldn't keep the incredulity from her voice.

'I know. It sounded pretty odd to me.'

'More than odd. Why would this man say such a thing, and in a public place?'

'He'd downed an awful lot of pints,' Kitty said. 'But I believed him. He sounded like he wanted to get it off his chest, which would figure, I s'pose.'

Nancy was silent, trying to puzzle out whether she believed this drunken man, whoever he was. It was clear Kitty had no doubts.

'If we could go to the mine,' her friend said, 'we could look for the tool bag. The men all have their own tools, like a hairdresser has his own pair of scissors.'

It seemed an odd comparison, but Nancy let it pass. She

was still trying to make sense of the man's words.

'There's a kind of superstition in mines that a dead comrade's things should stick around,' Kitty went on. 'Even if Jory didn't die in a mining accident, they might not have thrown his tools away.'

Nancy hadn't realised Kitty knew so much about mining. But it was time to be practical. 'The men would keep their tool bags in the lockers and they're in the Dry,' she said. 'Women aren't allowed there.'

'But if the men aren't on site? What's the time? They'll have left by now, but the gates should still be open. How about I pick you up in ten minutes? Worth a shot, isn't it?'

'Well, maybe. But—'

'What happened to the intrepid investigator?' Kitty mocked.

Nancy felt ruffled. It was a small thing Kitty was suggesting. In any case, they probably wouldn't gain access to the site. Kitty seemed to think you could simply breeze through the gates and help yourself. Nancy was sure that you couldn't.

'I'd better leave a note for Leo,' she said. 'In case he gets back before we do.'

'Do you think that's a good idea? He won't mind you trespassing with intent? From what you said the other day, it sounded like he wasn't too happy with your previous efforts.'

Nancy thought quickly. Leo was hostile to anything that might constitute her 'poking and prying', as he called it, and now they were slowly moving towards a better understanding after the difficulties of the past two years, she had no wish to jeopardise it.

'You're right,' she said. 'We'll probably be back before he gets home. And if we're not, I'll say you invited me for tea at the shop!'

Chapter Thirty-Two

By the time Kitty's yellow van drew up outside the front door, Nancy had begun to think she'd been foolish in agreeing to this escapade. The more she turned it over in her mind, the more odd it sounded. Why would any man boast of committing terrible crimes? And they *were* terrible—one person dead and two others badly injured. And that was discounting Jory's own death in the sea.

Kitty had explained that the man in the pub was drunk, but even so his mind would have to be in chaos, first to frame a friend, then to trumpet it to the world. Perhaps that was the answer. She was dealing with someone who wasn't of sound mind, who hated the Tremaynes as much as Pascoe and, in a twisted fashion, had acted out his hatred.

But going to Wheal Agnes to look for a tool bag? Nancy could hear Archie's voice in her head. *What the hell were you thinking, Nancy?* If only he were here today and not far distant in London. She wanted him with her. Wanted to hear him mock her suspicions. Wanted to laugh at his caustic comments—he would have a field day with the tool bag. And she needed to know what he'd found out. Right now would be good time to lay that particular fear to rest.

The toot of a horn forced Nancy to put aside her qualms. She was going to the mine, that's all, a mile or so away, and was unlikely to come to harm. Kitty was her friend and she couldn't let her down. Pride, too, was playing its part, Nancy acknowledged, slightly shamefaced. A niggling irritation was pushing her on. She had been successful in running to ground miscreants in Venice and Malfuego, but in her own country she had so far failed. Was that because Port Madron was her husband's childhood home and she'd felt constrained, unable to pursue her enquiries freely?

Or was it something else? What if every one of those frightening events was indeed a simple accident? It appeared now that Perry's had been. The idea unsettled her deeply. But Pascoe had been in Treeve Fenton's house, she reminded herself. He had stolen from it. Treeve's death, at least, had to be suspicious.

'You look a bit washed out,' Kitty greeted her, as she climbed into the van. 'Not getting cold feet, I hope?'

'Just a bit tired, I suppose. But let's get this done, shall we?' Nancy tried sound brisk and business-like.

Kitty grinned. 'I'm with you, partner!'

***

As her companion had prophesised, the gates were still open, but rather than parking outside the row of offices as she had done before, Kitty eased the vehicle into a small shaded layby a few hundred yards away.

'Don't want to give away our presence, do we? The men might have gone home but there'll be guards somewhere on the site.'

'What if they close the gates before we leave?'

'Then we'll just have to climb over. You must have climbed a tree or two as a kid. A pair of gates shouldn't be a problem!'

Nancy was fairly certain she had never climbed a tree— any kind of childhood hazard had been forbidden—but scaling a locked barrier seemed almost commonplace on an evening that had turned surreal.

They walked through the tall gates to find Wheal Agnes apparently deserted. If there were guards around, they must be at the far end of the property. It was a vast site, Nancy knew. She turned in the direction of where Perry had pointed to an external door that led to the Dry, and beckoned Kitty to follow.

Cautiously, they made their way towards the building, always keeping to the shadows. It was Nancy who pushed open the door to a dimly lit but very large room. She stood on the threshold for an instant, peering into near darkness, then took a few steps forward. The air smelt of coal dust and soap, a strangely attractive mix. Kitty was soon by her side, and for a moment they stood together staring at a large notice pinned high on the wall. *Pilfering from lockers or damaging other employees' property will result in instant dismissal.*

On the far side of the room, an archway had been cut through the wall and Nancy could see a line of open showers beyond. Every one of the remaining walls was filled with rows of lockers, each bearing a man's name.

'It will take some time, but we'll need to read every name,' Kitty said. 'If you take the left-hand side, I'll walk down the right, and we should meet in the middle.'

It did take time, as Kitty had foreseen, and Nancy was halfway along her line of lockers before she heard her companion shout out in triumph. 'It's here! This is Jory's! And believe it or not, it's unlocked.' She sounded excited.

The obstacle of a lock hadn't occurred to Nancy until now, and she scolded herself at how lax she'd become, but still felt delighted to have reached their goal—until walking around to join her companion, her heart sank.

'It's unlocked for a reason,' she said dully. 'The locker's

been cleared.'

Kitty shook her head. 'I didn't expect that. But...' she paused '...perhaps the tools weren't there in the first place?'

'Where else would they be?'

Kitty frowned. 'Let's work this out. Pascoe left the mine in a temper. I remember him telling me how he'd stormed out and wasn't going back. So, once he came up to the surface, would he have bothered to walk into the Dry, just to get to his locker? If he was angry, he'd simply march through the gates, wouldn't he, probably still wearing his miners' overalls? But without the tool bag. He wouldn't want to carry a heavy bag if he was never going to use the tools again.'

'He might have wanted to keep them,' Nancy cautioned. 'Sell them if he was short of money.'

'Possibly, but like I said all the men have their own tools, so they wouldn't be easy to sell, and Jory was in a filthy mood. I reckon he simply dropped the bag, either in the mine or when he came up.'

'If they're in the mine, that's it. We've no chance of getting hold of the bag.' Nancy gazed distractedly around the room. 'We should go, Kitty. It was a clever idea, but I don't think it's going to work.'

'Not so fast,' her friend counselled. 'If Jory chucked those tools to one side when he stepped out of the cage, the bag might still be around.'

'In the Landing House, you mean?'

'If that's what it's called. C'mon. It's worth a look. It must be close by.'

'Okay, but it's the last place we search.'

'Agreed. If it's not there, we make for home.'

Reluctantly, Nancy allowed herself to be ushered through an inner door, this second one leading to a passage that was clearly used by the miners as an area to clean their boots before entering the Dry. The passage ended in double doors, beyond which was the Landing House where the men would wait to take a cage down to the mine workings.

Pushing through the doors, Nancy saw a cage standing ready, its door open. She swallowed hard, remembering how relieved she'd been to see daylight on the one trip she'd made underground.

The light in the Landing House was as dim as in the Dry, but sufficient to see anything that might resemble a tool bag. 'Nothing,' Nancy said, her gaze sweeping the space and her voice tired. 'Let's call it a day.'

'Not just yet, sweetie.' Kitty walked up to her. She was wearing a strange smile. Then without warning, Nancy felt her arms gripped tightly and whisked behind her back. Before she could react, some kind of rough fastening— it felt like twine—was cutting into her bunched wrists.

'What—?' she began, but Kitty had bobbed down, and Nancy felt twine being tightened around her ankles. 'What on earth are you doing?' Her voice was faint with bewilderment. 'Have you gone mad?'

'On the contrary, my love, I'm perfectly sane.' Kitty got to her feet, her smile rigid. 'But I'm afraid your investigating days are numbered.'

'The tool bag …' Nancy stuttered, trying to grapple with the situation and failing.

'Did you really expect to find one?' Kitty asked mockingly.

There was a sick feeling deep in Nancy's stomach. This whole exploit had been a sham! Had she known that all along or at least sensed it? Was that why she'd felt so uneasy, and agreed to it only because she'd thought her friend had been trying to help? A friend, who had deliberately lured her here.

But why had she? She started to form the question when Kitty waved a hand, stopping her from speaking. 'You're going on a little ride,' her companion said. 'Enjoy it while you can.'

She gave Nancy a forceful push backwards, then pushed her again, back and back until, with a final thrust, she had tumbled her through the open door of the cage and clanged the door shut.

Nancy tried to still her mounting panic and keep her voice calm. 'Whatever this is, I'm sure we can work it out.'

'I've already worked it out, my luvver. I must leave you for a moment now—got to pop next door to the winder's cab—but I'll make sure to wave you goodbye.'

'You seem to know a lot about this mine.' Whatever the woman was going to do, Nancy had to stop her, and her only chance lay in talking.

'I've seen the plans. Studied them in great depth.'

'I'm sure they were very interesting, but now you've had your fun, can we go back?'

She tried hard to stop her voice from wobbling, though an image of the labyrinth of tunnels beneath her was playing havoc with her mind.

'It still hasn't dawned on you, has it, my stupid little investigator? Think, Nancy. Who is Kitty Anson and why is she in Port Madron?'

For a long moment, Nancy stared at her, realisation arriving with the spiralling power of a tornado. She'd been right then. Right to get Archie to ask questions, but distraught that the answers had come too late.

'You?' she asked, without really having to.

'Yes, me.'

It seemed she'd fixed on the one clue to prove vital, but it still made no sense. She shook her head, refusing to believe. 'You're the one behind all that's been happening in Port Madron? How can you be? What possible motive could you have?'

Chapter Thirty-Three

In the muted light, Nancy could just make out Kitty's face. Her expression seemed to suggest she was weighing up whether she would talk.

'You really want to know? I think I've time to tell you. It's only fair, I guess, though you're far too nosy. Such a shame, Nancy. We could have been really good friends, but then you spoilt it all, asking questions about Sally Crouch.'

The rope was cutting into Nancy's wrists badly and her legs had gone numb, but her mind was still working. 'You *are* Sally.'

'You suspected it, didn't you, and then you wouldn't leave it alone. When I heard Grace Jago giggle in that stupid way she has and say to a fellow customer that her brother-in-law was off this afternoon to look for a Sally Crouch, I knew you'd never let go.'

'Grace said that?'

'Always beware a gossip, sweetie. Then I saw the taxi bringing you back to Penleven and you were alone. No husband alongside—how perfect.'

Nancy ignored the implied threat, caught up in the drama that was unfolding. 'But why change your name?'

'Anonymity. My father was a Crouch. It's an unusual enough name to be recognised here. I didn't want anyone to know I was a relation of his. Hence Kitty Anson. I like my choice, don't you? It's kind of cuddly. Just like me.'

'You told me you didn't know your father.'

'I told you lots of things, most of them untrue.'

'You were never married?'

Kitty shook her head. 'But if I had been, Trevor would have been my man.'

'So what has been true?' She had temporarily forgotten her predicament in trying to find a way through the morass of lies this woman had told her.

'My mother was a bitch, that was true and she died of cancer—though I wasn't quite the Florence Nightingale I pretended. I turned down the joy of nursing her. But she was useful. I'd lost my job in the hospital, and then the one at that hoity-toity jeweller's. I was desperate for a roof over my head. My dear mother was living in a rough area of London and her flat was pretty disgusting, but it had to do. It provided some kind of shelter.

'One night she was bewailing her misfortune in between the bouts of coughing and I asked her about my father. Of course, I'd done that when I was a kid, but all I'd got then was a slap around the head. This time, though, she told me he wasn't dead like she'd said but living not far away. She was a great liar – I must have inherited the ability. She told me he was an engineer, or had been. A mining engineer, who could have made it rich, but didn't.'

'He had something to do with Wheal Agnes?'

'Not so stupid, then. He had more than something to do with this mine. He'd drawn up plans for an extension that was going to make money. He was certain of it. He'd agreed to work for a low fee on the promise of a percentage of the profit. The extension was constructed, or part of it at least, and the money flowed in. But not to my Dad.'

'So what did he do? Surely he must have pursued it?'

'He tackled the older Tremayne, that would be Ned's father, but the bastard denied any such promise and because my Dad was a soft touch, he had nothing in writing. He'd relied on the Tremaynes' honour, you see. But they didn't do honour and when he took them to court, he lost every penny of his savings. Suddenly Dad was broke, and there was a baby coming—that was me. Things got bad between my parents and he walked out. You think you had a rotten childhood? Try growing up with an embittered mother.'

Listening to Kitty's story, Nancy was mesmerised. 'You found your father?' she asked.

Kitty nodded. 'When my mother died a week or so later, I went to the Institute of Mining Engineers to check. They hold a list of their members and I looked up his name. The wretched woman had told me that at least. According to their records he was still alive and living in north London.'

'You went there?'

'Clever Nancy. Purely for my own selfish ends, you understand. Once my mother died, I was forced to move out of the flat. My dad's place was just as squalid, but it gave me shelter again. He was pretty fazed when I turned up on his doorstep, but he took me in. And do you know? I grew to like him. He was a decent man who'd had some bad breaks. The worst was working for the Tremaynes. Dad talked about them a lot. They ruined his life—and mine. That's when I decided they'd pay for what they'd done.'

'And you've been planning this…this campaign, for how long?'

'A fair time. It had to be properly thought through. My father gave me a copy of the plans he'd drawn up and, as soon as I'd buried him, I came to Cornwall. And lo and behold, there was a job going in the very place I wanted. As soon as I'd settled in here, I went walking around the village and found Penleven. A big house, a family with money. And they'd allowed my father to die in squalor! Allowed a small child to be dragged up in poverty!'

'If what you say is true, your family had a genuine grievance, but this isn't the way to solve it.'

'It's my way, and right now that's all that counts.'

'But it hasn't worked, has it? Your planned revenge? The Tremaynes are alive and well.'

Nancy was being deliberately provoking, eager to keep the conversation going. While Kitty talked, she had been surreptitiously chafing her wrists against the iron railings at the back of the cage. It was a painful business, but she could feel her bonds loosening very slightly and as they loosened, her inner strength grew.

'I haven't killed them—yet. But I've certainly scared them. Really scared them—those anonymous letters were a lot of fun. At one time, I thought I'd send a second letter, asking for money. A kind of gentle blackmail. Pay up or you get what's coming! But then I got bored. I wanted to take some real action and okay, the family have survived for now, but next time I won't make a mistake. I didn't with Treeve Fenton, did I?'

'What did Treeve ever do to you?' Nancy asked, still intent on keeping the woman talking.

'He deserved all he got. He wasn't the dear old man that everyone says. He was a partner in the firm. He stood by and let my father be cheated. And Dad is still being cheated. Perran Tremayne intends to use the plans he drew to extend further beneath the sea. You must have heard about that. But it won't happen. I'll make sure of it.'

'And Jory?' Nancy asked, furiously wriggling her wrists back and forth, hoping Kitty wouldn't spot the movement. 'What did he have to do with it? He was guilty of stealing items from Treeve's house, but nothing more.'

'Poor love. It was a stupid thing to do. And even stupider to blackmail me. The night he decided to steal, he saw me at the Fenton house and put two and two together. My, that night was hard work. Easy enough to knock the old chap out, but so tough getting him into the bath. I thought my back would never be the same again.'

Nancy felt revolted that she could ever have considered this cold, malicious woman a friend. 'Blackmail?' she asked. 'Pascoe tried to blackmail you?'

'Why else would I have employed that useless wife of his? But having Hedra slopping around the shop wasn't enough for him. Nor the weekly payment he demanded. He got greedy.'

'And you killed him.' Nancy bit her lip at how obtuse she'd been. It was so obvious now.

'It was all too easy, my love. Fill Jory up with drink and lead him to the beach.'

'And the attacks on the Tremaynes? Were they easy?'

'They didn't require too much ingenuity. I've been a nurse and injecting a drip with disinfectant was a piece of cake. The tricky thing was to do it unseen. But I managed—the medical staff obligingly went absent for a few minutes, and that's all it took. It was a neat little job, I must say. I was only away from the store for a morning.'

That was when there had been no answer to her knock, Nancy recalled. After her visit to Morwenna, when Archie had stopped at the store before driving her back to Penleven in time for the dinner party. She'd called to offer help to this woman, when all the time Kitty was on her way back from her murderous visit to the Truro hospital.

'As for Perran Tremayne,' Kitty went on, now seemingly unstoppable in her need to boast, 'I haven't kept that old van going for years without learning something about brakes. The trick, Nancy—not that you'll ever need it now— is to cut the brake hose to a precise depth. Not easy to calculate, but if you get it right, the brakes will hold under moderate pressure but rupture when the driver brakes vigorously. Like down Stannum Hill.'

The rope was fraying, Nancy could feel it, and before the cage was sent flying to the depths, she must break free. She shuffled nearer to the cage door. Keep her talking, keep her talking, she told herself.

'Will killing the Tremaynes solve your problems?' she asked. 'Make the life you keep telling me is so happy, even happier?'

'No, Nancy. I'll never be happy. But I'll get revenge for my poor dead father, and you're going to help me. You're only a Tremayne by marriage, but you'll do. And after you, the professor, I think—if he sticks around much longer. Although losing you will probably be punishment enough. I've seen the way he looks at you, lucky girl.'

There was a slight pause, before Kitty said thoughtfully, 'Perhaps not so lucky after all. It's been a stimulating conversation, but really I have to go. And so do you.'

'The miners will find me in the morning,' Nancy said defiantly. She dared not think of the dreadful night ahead.

'They *will* find you,' Kitty assured her. 'And it will be good. Miners are very respectful of the dead. It comes from their facing danger every day.'

'What do you mean?' Nancy felt hollow, nausea beginning to rise in her throat. She had no idea what Kitty Anson was planning, but the woman's crazed actions promised nothing but terror.

Kitty walked towards the door leading to the winder's cab and looked back at Nancy. 'Enjoy your ride,' she said with a cheerful wave of her hand.

Nancy struggled desperately with what was left of the knotted twine. If she could just free her hands, she could wrench the cage door open, untie her ankles and flee. But there was no time. Within seconds, she heard the sound of machinery spluttering into action, then the cage gave a sharp jolt and she was travelling down to the furthest level of the mine, coming to a final halt with a judder.

In the dim night-time lighting, she could see the wide passageway she'd walked with Perry and Leo, tunnels branching in one direction and then another, like a giant anthill. And she was the ant. She breathed in deeply, trying to steady herself. First, she must get free. There was no possibility of operating the cage from underground, but perhaps there were other ways out. The cage ran on electricity and, if that failed, there would have to be an emergency exit. Ladders, perhaps, or a stairway, leading from level to level. If she could rid herself of these bonds and find a ladder, a stairway, she stood a chance of rescuing herself.

In the outside world, night would have fallen and a chill filled the air, but deep in the mine it was hotter than Nancy remembered from her daytime visit. A smell, faintly sour, tickled her nose and drops of perspiration dotted her forehead as she worked on the rope. After minutes of effort, she managed to fit a finger through the final loop and pull the knot apart. Now for her ankles. That took little time but, exhausted, she slumped to the floor of the cage needing to rest.

It was hotter than ever, her whole body sweating profusely. Thinking it might be cooler in the passageway, she summoned up a last surge of energy and stumbled to her feet to pull back the cage door. She took a few tentative paces along the broad tunnel but, if anything, the air was even more stifling.

She had to get out of this place, look for an exit as quickly as possible. With every level above, the temperature should fall a little. But where to start looking? Would an emergency exit be here in the broadest tunnel? Or down one of the narrower passageways?

She was halfway along the broad tunnel, peering left and right down the numerous narrow tracks that led from it, when her ears pricked. What was that? Then suddenly the tunnel was plunged into darkness. And into silence. What was missing apart from the light? What had she been hearing that was no longer there? It was the low thrum of the ventilator fans, the fans that cleared the gas and the dust from explosions earlier in the day.

Nancy stood transfixed, seeing nothing, hearing nothing. Kitty! She was still on the site, still intent on revenge. If there was emergency lighting, she had sabotaged that, too. Kitty had studied the plans of the mine and would know every small detail of its operation. Frantically, Nancy reached out for the wall to guide her back to the cage—if she could return there, then at least she'd be raised to the surface as soon as the men reported for work in the morning. Scrabbling along the tunnel wall, the rock face cut into her hands. She had turned to face where she thought the cage must be, but in the darkness quickly became disorientated. She stopped still, her heart beating so hard it hurt. If she wandered too far, she might not be found for hours.

The faint smell she'd experienced earlier was growing stronger and her nose and eyes had begun to sting. Gas. Poisonous gas! That's what Perry had said. The ventilating fans worked all night to clear noxious fumes and make the mine safe for work the next day. Nancy felt her legs give way, slumping onto the rocky floor. A pain barrelled through her chest and she felt herself scrabbling for breath This was

Kitty's plan. To suffocate her. When the miners arrived for their shift, scratching their heads no doubt as to why the cage was not where it should be, they would lower themselves to the depths and find her. But by then she would be dead.

Chapter Thirty-Four

A rchie reached Port Madron around eleven o'clock that evening. After his abortive telephone call, he'd driven from Exeter at speed. Something was wrong, badly wrong. He drove rapidly through the village, then swung the car right into the narrow road leading to Penleven, through its open gates and up to the house. Light streamed from an open door, intensifying his fears. The entire building appeared lit up and, before he could bring the car to a halt, a figure erupted from the darkness and rushed towards him.

'Have you got her?'

He wound down the window and Leo repeated, 'Have you got her?' He sounded frantic.

Archie clambered from the car. 'Nancy?' he asked, though he knew it had to be.

'Of course, Nancy.' In the beam of light, Leo's expression was wild and his breathing laboured.

Archie took his employer by the shoulders and steered him firmly back into the house. In the hallway, Leo looked at him blankly. 'Why are you here?' He seemed suddenly to have realised that his assistant should still be in London.

'I decided to come early,' was Archie's short response. 'Nancy is missing, I take it?'

'Where is she, Archie?' Leo was still short of breath but

there was desperation in his voice, his hands furrowing through his hair as though he would tug it from its roots.

'Come into the kitchen.' Archie led the way, pushing Leo into a chair. 'Now let me get a grip on this. When did you last see her?'

'Truro. In the taxi. I waved her goodbye.' Leo finished on a half sob.

'She was on her way back to Penleven?'

Leo nodded. 'I had to stay on at the hospital to see Dad's consultant. I expected her to be home, but when I got back, she wasn't here.'

'Then what?'

'I waited an hour. I thought that maybe she'd stopped off somewhere... though I hadn't a clue where. But when she still didn't come back, I knew there was something wrong and I went looking for her.'

'What time would that be?' Archie leaned across the table, his face intent.

Leo shook his head as though trying to clear the haze. 'Around eight o'clock I should think.'

That was when he'd rung from Exeter, Archie thought. 'Okay, so you went looking. Where?'

'The village, naturally,' his boss said dully, seeming to have sunk into an abstraction.

'But where in the village? Did you knock on doors?'

'Yes. Yes. Of course, I did.' He seemed stung by Archie's tone. 'I asked at your mother's, at Grace Jago's cottage.'

'The village stores?' he asked quickly.

'I tried there, but no one was home.'

Archie saw his worst fears coming true. 'Are you sure of that, Leo?' he asked urgently.

'The place was in darkness. I rang the bell several times. Banged on the door. I could have raised the whole village,

I was so desperate.' There was a pause before Leo asked brokenly, 'Where can she be?'

Archie closed his eyes, allowing his mind to roam. If Nancy wasn't in the village, would she have been enticed to go walking? On the headland perhaps? Maybe. Or …

'The mine,' he said, suddenly quite definite.

Leo looked bewildered. 'Wheal Agnes? Why would she go there?'

'I don't know for sure, but this whole business—Treeve's death, the accidents to your father and Perry—they've all been about the Tremaynes. Your family, who own Wheal Agnes. It seems logical.'

'It doesn't seem logical to me,' Leo complained. 'What has Nancy got to do with Treeve or Dad or Perry?'

There was a long silence until Leo burst out, 'Unless she's got herself involved in something bad. Again. I told her to leave it to the police. I couldn't have been clearer, but…' he tailed off. 'It doesn't matter now.'

'No, it doesn't,' Archie said shortly. 'We have to find her. But first, you need to ring the police. Tell them your wife is missing and, as she's a stranger here, you're fearful she's had an accident. Ask them to check Wheal Agnes, then the cliffs.'

When Leo remained slumped in his chair, Archie reached out and shook him. 'Do it quickly! Then get in the car and we'll go and look for her ourselves.'

The suggestion they take action seemed to galvanise Leo and he pushed back his chair and rushed to pick up the telephone. Archie followed him into the hall, hearing clearly the sceptical tone of the policeman on the other end of the line. He didn't blame the bloke. Nancy had been missing only a few hours. But whether it was the desperation in Leo's voice or the fact that the Tremaynes were an important family, the sergeant agreed to send a police car and two officers to the mine immediately, and if they had no luck in finding Nancy there, to scour the adjoining cliffs.

***

When Archie pulled up outside Wheal Agnes, it was to find the gates closed.

'She can't be here,' Leo said. 'The site is locked up. Why didn't I think of that? The guards finish around ten and they'll have gone home.'

'Someone is here.' Archie pointed to the small yellow van parked a few hundred yards up the lane, but clearly visible in the car headlights.

'Kitty Anson?' Leo's forehead knotted. 'What's she doing here?'

'What indeed,' Archie said grimly. 'C'mon. We're climbing in.'

'Over the gates?'

'Over the gates,' he confirmed. 'The police will have bolt cutters, but we can't wait for them to arrive.'

'I don't understand,' his companion said plaintively, as they stood in front of the gates. 'What has Kitty Anson to do with anything?'

'I don't understand either, but you can take it from me that Mrs Anson, or whatever her name is, is a dangerous woman.'

His boss appeared to hesitate, and Archie's patience snapped. 'You either come with me, Leo, or not. Every minute we waste, Nancy faces more danger.'

Without another word Archie jumped, reaching for the top rail of the gate, then heaving himself over and landing lightly down on solid ground. In seconds, Leo had followed him. 'Where do we look?' he asked. 'She could be anywhere.'

'What if you wanted to—' Archie was going to say kill, but then changed it to—'harm someone, where's the most obvious place?'

'Underground, I suppose.'

'Right, let's start at the main shaft.'

'Archie,' Leo gripped his arm, 'something is wrong.'

'Evidently.'

'There are no lights. There should be some light—from the buildings, at least, but there's nothing.'

'Lucky I bought my trusty flashlight then, isn't it?' Archie delved into the deep pocket of his jacket, switching on the torch and directing a beam of light into the distance. 'You lead the way. You know the mine and I don't.'

'I can't believe Nancy would go anywhere near the shaft, but if we want to check, we have to go in there.' He pointed to a building a few hundred yards ahead. 'That's where the Dry is housed and there's a passage from it to the Landing House.'

Once inside the building, torchlight guided them along the lengthy passageway, past the Dry and up to the double doors that led to the Landing House. Leo came to a sudden halt. 'There's no sound either. It's the fans—they're not working.'

'If the electricity supply has been switched off, they won't be.'

'You don't understand, Archie. The fans keep the air in the mine safe. If Nancy is down there, she'll have no fresh air. She'll be breathing gas.'

Archie's felt his face set rigid with fear. He had to get to her, and quickly. Pushing open the double doors, he flashed his torch around the Landing House and came to rest on a gaping hole and a set of cables.

'The cage—,' Leo croaked. He'd come up behind Archie and in the wavering beam of the flashlight, his face was livid.

'Well, we've got our answer,' Archie said grimly. 'Nancy is down there. Do you know how to operate the system? Bring up the cage?'

'Normally, but there's no electricity.'

'There must be some safety mechanism to allow the cage to be raised if there's an electrical breakdown.'

'I suppose.' Leo stumbled his way over to the small adjoining room that was the winder's cab, Archie following him and training their one source of light on the bank of levers and buttons.

Leo peered down at the console. 'Oh, my God!' His breath was coming in short, harsh gasps. 'The ventilation doors have been shut!'

'Can you open them?'

'Yes, yes. I think so.' He bent his head, trying make out the various symbols, while Archie held the flashlight as close as he could. After a mind-numbing few seconds, Leo fumbled with a lever and pulled hard. 'They're open,' he said, wiping a trembling hand across his sweat-covered forehead.

'Now the cage, Leo. Can you see what to push?'

'I think that must be it.' Leo pointed to a red triangle.

'Go on,' Archie urged.

At the press of the button, a dim light filtered into the cab and within seconds, Archie heard the creak and rasp of the iron cage being brought to the surface. Calmly, he pulled a linen handkerchief from his pocket and proceeded to tie it over his nose and mouth. 'I may need this,' he said.

'I've one, too, somewhere.' With shaking hands, Leo began to search his jacket.

'I need you to stay here, Leo.'

'No, no,' his companion said wildly. 'I must find her.'

'I will find her.' Archie's voice was resolute. 'But I need your help. Nancy needs your help. You have to operate the cage for us. Or how else will we get back to the surface?'

He made a dart for one of the benches which lined the

room, jumping onto it to reach high up on the wall. Several miners' helmets were hanging there. 'Lucky, they have spares. You keep the torch, I'll wear a helmet—the emergency lighting isn't great. Is there a signal I need to use?'

'Three bells,' Leo said, deflated. 'Ring three times and wait for me to answer with three rings. You'll know then that I know to bring the cage up.'

Archie clapped a hand on his employer's shoulder. 'Wish me luck!'

The journey down through the various levels seemed endless to Archie, though in reality it could have been no more than a few minutes. It was possible that Nancy had not travelled to the furthest level, but it was a gamble he had to take. The smell of gas mixed with a choking dust became stronger with each level he passed, and he had to steady his nerves for what he might find.

The cage jolted to a standstill and he stepped out into a fog of noxious fumes. Moving his head from side to side, the light from his helmet spanning the passageway, he began to make his way slowly along what appeared to be a main thoroughfare, though where he was headed, Archie had no idea. The passage seemed without end, stretching far into the distance. And, even through smarting eyes, he could see the numerous smaller tunnels that led off from this main track and felt despair. Nancy could be in any one of them.

Dimly, he could see ahead that the long passage was gradually bending towards the left. If, when he rounded that corner, there was still no sign of her, he must retrace his steps, he decided, and begin the hazardous task of investigating each of the smaller tunnels. But when he rounded the bend, the light from his helmet caught something ahead.

Something lying on the rocky floor. A body. Nancy!

Archie rushed forward and almost tripped on the uneven

floor. He knelt down beside her, placing his fingers against the side of her throat. There was a pulse still. Thank God. But it was faint and when he scooped her limp body into his arms and her head lolled against him, he was seized by terror. She was depending on him to save her, to get her out of this poisonous prison, and he could feel himself begin to choke.

Very carefully, he turned to retrace his footsteps to where he hoped he'd left the cage. Progress was painfully slow, the terrain rough and uneven and the light from his head torch wavering. He felt his chest hammer with the effort of carrying his burden as gently as he could, while at the same time trying to breathe. It took twice as long to get back to where he'd started, but at last the cage was there. He lay Nancy gently down on its floor and, gasping for breath, shut the gates and reached with a shaking hand for the bell. Heart pounding, he rang three times. Would Leo hear the bell? The man had gone to pieces with Nancy's disappearance—would he be in any state to operate the machinery?

But then a blessed sound. Three answering rings and the cage was slowly rising to the surface.

***

Leo took his wife in his arms, kissing her forehead, her cheeks, her lips, over and over again.

'We need to get her into the fresh air,' Archie muttered. He was still struggling to breathe. 'Hurry, Leo!'

Spurred into action, Leo shouldered the double doors open and raced down the long corridor. Past the Dry and out into the cool night air. Following him, Archie took several deep breaths, filling his lungs with its fresh goodness. Then, as his eyes gained focus, he realised a car was parked across the open gateway and in its headlights, the silhouettes of two policemen with Kitty Anson held between them. In the beam of bright light, Archie noticed the sheen of handcuffs.

'Professor Tremayne, good evening,' one of the constables called out, as though greeting a newly arrived guest.

The second policeman was more severe, quelling his younger companion. 'Thank you for the tip-off, sir. Breaking and entering is a serious charge.'

'She is guilty of a great deal more than that.' Leo walked into the pool of light surrounding the police vehicle.

'My, my, what have we here?' The older policeman raised his eyebrows as he took in the limp body cradled in Leo's arms.

'What we have here is attempted murder,' Archie said. 'Three attempted murders, in fact, and one for real. That woman needs to be under lock and key.'

Kitty Anson glared at him before turning her head away, a disdainful twist to her mouth.

The younger constable scratched his head. 'Seems like there's going to be a lot of work for the boys back at the station.'

'Then we'll leave you to it,' Archie said, and walked with Leo through the open gates to the car.

Chapter Thirty-Five

Nancy woke at first light, desperate for water. Trying to pull herself upright, her head swam so badly she was forced back against the pillows.

'Here, drink this. But only sips, mind.' It was Leo, bending tenderly over her, a glass of water in his hand.

She sipped from the glass, and tried to focus. 'You're up early,' she said, a little puzzled. Leo appeared to be fully dressed, but the subdued light suggested it was only dawn.

'I haven't been to bed yet,' he confessed. 'Here, have another drink.'

Gratefully, she drank more of the water. 'But why…?' Her voice trailed away.

'Don't try to talk.' Leo stroked her hand. 'You need to save your energy. The doctor will be here later.'

'Wasn't he here before?' Nancy had a vague remembrance of a man with a stethoscope and a kindly face.

'He saw you last night to check your breathing, but he wants to listen again.'

Nancy's brow creased. She was trying hard to remember where she'd been, what she'd done, but there was a veil she couldn't penetrate. She must try harder.

'I was in the mine,' she began. 'Kitty—'

'Hush now. We'll talk later.'

'It was gas, Leo.' The veil was dissolving, the memory flooding back.

'I know, darling, I know.'

'But how…?'

Leo put a finger to her mouth. 'Right now, you must sleep.'

***

She had slept for hours, it seemed to Nancy, only waking when the doctor came into the room and placed his small black bag on the bedside table.

'Now, young lady, let's see how those lungs are doing.'

When he'd heard enough, the doctor packed his stethoscope back into the bag and smiled down at her. 'You had a lucky escape, you know. A little longer and…'

Nancy didn't need him to finish the sentence. Her memory was now sharp. She remembered only too well how she'd been unable to stand, how she'd slumped to the rough floor, struggling to breathe. How she'd felt herself gradually losing consciousness.

The doctor turned at the door to say his goodbyes. 'You'll be fine, Mrs Tremayne, but make sure you rest. Your body has gone through a nasty experience.'

When Leo returned from seeing him out, Nancy was sitting on the edge of the bed. 'I need to get up.'

'What did he just tell you? You have to rest.'

'I can't stay in this bed any longer,' she protested.

'If I let you get up, it's to have a bath and something to eat. Then you come back and rest.'

'You don't understand, Leo. I need to tell someone—about Kitty. I need to speak to the police. She confessed everything.' It had all come flooding back.

'All in good time.'

'But she tried to kill me. And not just me.'

'I know, my darling. I heard it from Archie. Though why he knew about the woman and I didn't—'

'I asked him to find out something when he was in London,' she said quietly. 'Do you know what he discovered?'

'I don't, but I've asked him to call after lunch. I want to know exactly what's been going on.'

By the time Archie arrived, she had eaten a light meal and was feeling a good deal better. The bath had refreshed her, and Leo had cooked scrambled eggs on toast and brewed two cups of strong coffee.

After what had happened, though, she was still unprepared for Archie. When he walked into the kitchen, all she wanted to do was throw her arms around him. Leo had said nothing, but she had a fair idea whom she had to thank for her rescue. It was Archie who would have guessed to search for her at Wheal Agnes. Archie who had braved poisonous air to save her.

***

He greeted her with a laconic smile. 'Well, how's the intrepid miner today?'

'Don't joke,' she said. 'It was terrifying.'

He wanted to take her in his arms and tell her that he knew. But all he said was, 'I imagine so.'

'A drink, Archie?' Leo was hovering by the sink.

'Thanks, boss. Tea would be fine.'

When the tea was made, Leo joined them at the table. He stared hard at his assistant. 'How about you begin by telling us why you knew Nancy was in danger.'

'I didn't know for sure. I suspected.' Archie lifted his cup and drank. 'I found the jeweller's where Kitty Anson worked. She was dismissed for stealing—not a sign in itself of homicidal tendencies, it's true, but she got the job on a false reference, supposedly from the London Hospital.'

'She was a nurse there before becoming a shop assistant,' he explained, when Leo looked puzzled.

'And the reference was false, you say?' Nancy leaned forward. She would be eager to fit the pieces of the puzzle together, Archie thought wryly. 'Why did she forge it?'

'That's the crux. It was at the hospital that killing or attempting to kill seems to have become a motif for her. She persuaded an elderly patient to change his will in her favour, then got impatient and set about hastening his end.'

'Money.' Nancy pursed her lips. 'I should have known. She talked about money a lot, or the lack of it. Kitty had a definite chip on her shoulder—at times, she could sound quite angry.'

'But how does trying to poison Nancy have anything to do with money?' Leo asked.

Archie was about to ask the same question, when Nancy supplied the answer.

'She wanted to hurt the Tremaynes. Kitty's father was a mining engineer. He was the one who drew up the plans for extending Wheal Agnes. The ones Perry intends to use.'

Leo frowned at this. 'I was only a child, but I'm sure Anson wasn't a name my father mentioned, or my grandfather.'

'Her real name is Sally Crouch,' Archie said.

'Anson was the name she assumed to disguise the fact that she'd come to Port Madron to exact revenge,' Nancy put in. 'Her father was promised a share of any profits that came from the extension. His plans were used, or some of them at least, but he was never paid.'

'Does the name Crouch ring a bell, Leo?' Archie asked.

'I'm not sure. Perry would probably know. But revenge? Why didn't the chap simply ask for what he was due?'

At times Leo could be hopelessly naïve, Archie thought.

'He did,' Nancy confirmed. 'He asked both your grandfather and father and they both refused him, so Mr Crouch took them to court. He lost the case and, with it, his life savings.'

Leo shook his head. Archie could see he was trying to absorb this unpleasant revelation. 'You're saying that these accidents—Perry's in the car, the tampering with Dad's drip—are down to Kitty Anson?'

'Treeve Fenton's death, too,' Nancy said quietly. 'She murdered him.'

Leo sprang to his feet, pacing up and down the room. 'Then after that, and what she did to you, I hope she gets what she's due,' he said angrily.

'She will.' Archie finished his tea and put the cup firmly back in its saucer.' She'll swing,' he said, not sounding the least bit sorry.

***

Three days later, Leo arranged a small party at Penleven, ostensibly to celebrate his father's and Perry's return from hospital but also, Nancy was sure, as a small act of thanksgiving for her rescue. Something for which she had yet to thank Archie and thank him truly.

She needed to speak to him alone—she knew it was Archie's arms that had scooped her from the rocky floor, his arms that had cradled her to the surface. But since that moment she'd seen him only once, when he'd visited Penleven the following day and it had been a time for explanations. In any case, pouring out her gratitude wasn't something she could do in front of Leo. Her husband was still smarting from being kept in ignorance and, though he'd not blamed her directly for the trouble she'd found herself in, Nancy knew it was there in her husband's mind. When they argued next—and they would—

it would feature in any quarrel.

As each day passed, though, she was managing to push the memory of her ordeal further and further away. Perry was almost back to his old self, his broken fingers mending well and the shock of the accident, now he knew the truth, gradually fading. As for Ned Tremayne, he had accepted the downstairs bedroom, and Grace as his carer, with surprisingly little fuss. Grace was a gem, Nancy thought, managing the crotchety old man with skill. And today, along with Morwenna, cooking a magnificent party spread that filled every available space in the kitchen.

Peace seemed at last to have come to Penleven. The decision about the mine's future had been made. It turned out that Treeve's last piece of advice to his friend had been to sell and Francisco Silva was flying into London next week with a Brazilian lawyer in tow to oversee the signing of the contract. Perry would stay as manager and Silva's money would be used to extend the mine and hopefully turn the business into profit. Even better, Leo planned to return to London in a few days. The case against Kitty was ongoing, but its seriousness ensured the trial would be held at the Old Bailey and, as a witness, Nancy could give evidence from their London home.

The party this evening would be a gentle affair, lasting only a few hours, but Nancy put up her hair and donned her red silk dress in honour of the occasion. Morwenna was coming, Grace and her husband, Rich, and several other of the villagers whom Leo had known from childhood. And, of course, Archie. Two very different sections of Port Madron society would come together under Penleven's roof, and Nancy enjoyed the thought.

Morwenna greeted her at the front door in Cornish fashion. 'Dearover,' she said. 'What a terrible thing to happen. That Kitty—whatever her real name is—who would have thought it?'

'I told you, Ma,' Grace said smugly, following her mother-in-law into the house. 'That one wasn't to be trusted.'

'But to do something like that to this poor maid.'

'Others suffered, too, Morwenna,' Nancy reminded her. 'Treeve Fenton died. And Jory Pascoe.'

'I know that, my luvver, but Archie told me how he found you. Real upset, he was.'

'I owe him my life,' Nancy said softly.

'Who's for a glass of bubbly?' Perry advanced on the little group with a large bottle and the moment was lost.

It wasn't until halfway through the party that Archie appeared. Nancy felt her heart skip as she caught sight of his stocky figure. He was looking particularly smart in a deep blue shirt. With those eyes, she thought, he should always wear blue.

'You decided to give us a look-in then?' Leo joked.

'Things to do,' Archie murmured vaguely.

Had he deliberately come late, she wondered, to avoid spending too much time with her? Maybe, but she couldn't let him escape without speaking and, as soon as she saw him standing alone, she went up to him, tapping him on the shoulder. 'I've wanted to talk to you. On your own,' she said. 'I've wanted to thank you from the bottom of my heart.'

'For what?'

'You know for what.'

'So, what do you think of my sleuthing skills in tracking Kitty down?'

She could see he was trying to make light of the event. 'Better than mine.' She sounded rueful. 'I was completely taken in by the woman. I feel quite ashamed.'

'Not completely or you wouldn't have asked me to check on her.'

'But to go the mine when she asked me! And even when I felt uneasy about her! I must have been mad.'

'Impulsive, Nancy. That's all.'

'You're good at making excuses for me.' She gave a sad smile. 'I doubt Leo will.'

'If you're wise, you'll not mention Kitty or the mine too often. Here, your glass is empty. Let me get you a refill.'

He went to take her glass, but she shook her head. 'Not for me, thanks. To be honest, I'm uncomfortably warm. Either it's the champagne or I'm sickening for something.'

'It's been hot today and heat lingers, even with the windows open. The party would have been better in the garden.'

'I'm wishing now that we'd done that.' A few strands of her hair had come loose, and she brushed them back from her face.

'Are you okay?' He looked down at her with concern. 'You've lost colour.'

She tried to smile. 'I feel a bit nauseous. It's almost as hot as the mine in here. Perhaps that's the problem.'

'Then come outside for a while. I need a ciggie and Leo hates smoking.'

Chapter Thirty-Six

Once through the front door, Nancy felt herself relax. The air in the garden was fresh, cooling her limbs and clearing her head. Archie lit his cigarette and stood quietly smoking beside her. She felt him close and was content. It was a long while before he said, 'Looking forward to getting back to London?'

'I am. And you?'

'I think so. I can do home, but in small doses.' He chipped at the gravel with his foot.

'I'll miss the evenings here, though. They don't come as beautiful in London. Look at that moon and those stars— they're so bright, it could be daytime.'

'That's Orion.' Archie pointed at a cluster of stars directly overhead. 'And there's the Plough.'

She turned to him in surprise. 'I didn't know you were a stargazer.'

'There's a lot you don't know. Do you fancy a walk?'

She knew she should say no, but to be alone with him for a few minutes, to walk together without the need to speak, seemed exactly right.

Archie threw his cigarette down on the gravel and stubbed it out with his foot. 'I've never shown you my favourite cove, have I? It's where I spent a lot of my time as a boy. Clem

295

Hoskins has been using it for his pots, but apart from that, it's unchanged. Would you like to walk there?'

'If it's not too far.'

'Ten minutes. We'll be back before anyone notices we've gone.'

***

It wasn't something he should have suggested, but the compulsion was too strong—to walk by her side, smelling her scent, feeling her body close. He'd barely seen her since that terrible night and the image of her slumped on the rocky floor, her face ghastly beneath the beam of his head torch, her body limp as a rag doll's, still terrified him. A bad dream that had woken him every night since.

Walking towards the village, he turned off just before they reached the main street and guided her down a high-hedged lane, so steep their feet ran away with them. He watched as Nancy was propelled downhill, limbs flying and laughing out loud. But when they neared the bay, she came to an abrupt stop and stood in silence. The tide was going out and the sand in the small cove gleamed white. Beneath the moonlight, the sea was almost silver. He could see that she was entranced. It was one of things Archie loved in her, her response to beauty, to something deeper than the surface world. He felt it, too, though he'd never been able to articulate his feelings.

'Take your shoes off,' he suggested, as they walked onto the beach.

She did, truffling her bare feet through the sand and making for the quiet swathe of water ahead. He followed her more slowly, but halfway down the beach, she turned to face him.

'Listen, Archie!'

It was the *sssh* of small waves lapping gently at the shore.

A sound he had grown up with. A sound that would echo through his life.

'How peaceful it is,' she said, when he was once more walking beside her. 'And how lucky I am to be alive.'

Something in her voice made him reach out and touch her arm. A tingle, an excitement, stirring deep within. He should know the emotion by now. He'd felt it plenty in the past, though perhaps never so strongly. He was sure that Nancy felt it, too, yet she made no move away.

'Archie,' she began. 'How are we…?'

How are we to cope with this, she wanted to ask. He couldn't answer. He didn't know. All he knew at this moment was that he had to touch her, take her in his arms again, hold her close, close, close. He felt her sink against him, and then he was kissing her in a way she should always be kissed.

Aware only of the moment, they dropped onto the sand. Archie tried to speak, but his voice didn't sound his own. 'Your frock,' he murmured.

She reached up and slipped the dress from her shoulders, pushing the garment to one side. It was madness, Archie thought, but there was no going back. This moment had been coming ever since they'd first met. They had both known that and tried to ignore it. But pretence hadn't worked and now there was nothing left for them but each other.

He made love to her in a way he'd thought impossible for him: deeply, tenderly, wanting every kiss, every touch, to last a lifetime. When, finally, they lay together, breathless and glowing, he stroked her hair, kissed her ear and whispered, 'I love you, Nancy.'

'I know,' she whispered back.

'So…'

'Don't, Archie.' She nestled against him. 'Don't say anything that will spoil tonight.'

***

He had wanted her to tell him what they should do, where they should go from here, and Nancy hadn't been able to. She had no idea. She loved Archie, had loved him, she suspected, from the moment they'd met. His snippiness, his mockery, had counted for nothing against this feeling. It was a feeling she'd never been able to lose. But she owed Leo loyalty. Owed him gratitude. And so did Archie. She couldn't break her husband's heart, she simply couldn't.

They wandered back up the hill, hand in hand, her body still tingling but her mind filled with troubling questions. At the gates of Penleven, Archie stopped.

'I'll leave you here. It's best I get off home.'

She had no chance to respond before the front door opened and Leo's figure appeared, illuminated in the doorway.

'Is that you, Nancy?' She could see him peering into the darkness. 'Archie?'

'Just off, boss,' Archie called out, his voice expressionless. 'Give me a ring if you need the car in the next day or two.'

Nancy heard his footsteps retreating and felt as lost as an abandoned child. With a huge effort, she pulled herself together and walked towards her husband.

'I wondered where you'd got to,' Leo said, as she reached him. He was annoyed, she could tell, but trying hard not to show it.

'I'm sorry.' She stepped past him into the hall. 'I needed some fresh air—the room was just too hot—and Archie was in the garden smoking. He came for a walk with me.'

Leo looked down at her and she forced herself to meet his gaze, aware of his eyes searching her face. 'You could have asked me to go with you.'

'I should have done,' she lied, 'but you were busy with your guests.'

Leo continued to gaze at her, a hard, probing stare, until she felt her face scorched. He said nothing, but—

He knows, she thought, he knows.

How were they to get through this once they were back in London? Could they ever get through it?

If you've enjoyed this novel, do please leave a review—a few lines is all it takes. It's helpful to readers and makes authors very happy! I'll be sure to read every review!

**

Where next for Nancy? *Rio Revenge* takes her to South America and Carnival —hot, dangerous and steamy in all kinds of ways!

And follow me at **https://www.bookbub.com/authors/ merryn-allingham** to be the first to know whenever there's a new release, pre-order or new discount!

FREE COPY OF THE DANGEROUS PROMISE

Sign up to Merryn's newsletter and, as a special thank you, claim your FREE book.

The Dangerous Promise introduces Nancy Nicholson, the feisty heroine of the Tremayne Mysteries Series, setting her on a journey that sees her become an amateur detective and find the love of her life.

Merryn's newsletter is sent only when there is something special to communicate—such as new book releases, special promotions, and price reductions.

Click on the link below to be taken to the sign-up page. Your details will not be shared and you can unsubscribe at any time.

https://merrynallingham.com/free-book/

Other Books by Merryn Allingham

A Tale of Two Sisters (2019)

House of Lies (2018)
House of Glass (2018)

The Buttonmaker's Daughter (2017)
The Secret of Summerhayes (2017)

The Girl from Cobb Street (2015)
The Nurse's War (2015)
Daisy's Long Road Home (2015)

Made in United States
North Haven, CT
07 August 2023

40073224R00183